The Polaris Effect

This book is a work of fiction. Names, characters, places, and incidents are either the product of the author's imagination or are used fictitiously. Any resemblance to actual events or locales or persons, living or dead, is entirely coincidental.

Tribeca Press
New York, New York

For my parents

1

Thorpe Residence
Central Park West, New York

Red embers from the Arturo Fuente Opus X glowed ominously in the dark library. The cigar was an old standby for Edward Thorpe, an indulgence he allowed himself on particularly remarkable occasions. Yet tonight, the ashes burned and fell away without him noticing, and the dying cigar was hardly puffed on. Despite decades of unblemished business and personal success, the soft spoken entrepreneur rarely reflected on the good he'd done around the globe. Now, a profound despair rendered him nearly catatonic as the knowledge that his empire, his dream-become-reality, would ultimately be destroyed by forces far greater than himself.

His personal legacy concerned him less. He'd accepted that should certain atrocities come to light, he would be scape-goated and villainized, unable to defend his innocence from the grave. The knowledge that his company – a source of so much scientific and medical advancement – would inevitably be scandalized, caused a torment rivaled only by the pain he'd felt at his wife's burial a decade ago.

"Mr. Thorpe, your appointment is here."

The raspy, accented voice of his housemaid startled him into the present moment, cigar ash falling to the ivory chess set where his Vacheron-wrapped wrist rested.

"Thank you, Rosemary. Please, go home now; there's no need for you to show the gentleman out."

"Your evening tea is steeping."

"Good night, Rosemary."

She nodded and quietly departed.

His long, arthritic fingers, invited the visitor to enter the plush library. Thorpe suspected the man's purpose, but not his identity. The tall figure stepped into the shadows, his shapeless face becoming more recognizable as he emerged from the dark hallway. Ignoring the rich chocolate leather chair facing Thorpe, the guest approached the window facing the dark expanse of Central Park. Thorpe sat in silence, willing the moment to come. His first feeling of inadequacy in many years had occurred just hours before as he raised his antique Colt revolver to his temple. The cold steel pressed into his weathered skin had rendered him helpless, unable to control his destiny. Slowly he swept the ash from the chessboard with his aged but steady hand.

"It truly is a spectacular view you have here. Gives a man the sense he's taking in the whole world."

Thorpe did not register the words, only the voice that spoke them. His eyes welled and he focused on the final red embers of the cigar.

"Breathe deep, Mr. Thorpe. Accept responsibility. It's your fault I'm here."

The visitor stood over Thorpe now, behind the old man's wing-backed chair, shadows mingling over the chessboard as the fireplace played tricks with the light. The sudden prick in his neck surprised Thorpe; he'd expected something more drastic, more painful. Then the convulsions began.

2

FBI Headquarters
Midtown Manhattan

Kate Capelli crossed the spartan classroom and quietly seated herself among the agents taking notes. She tossed a folded receipt across the table to her partner, the paunchy Danny Ford.

"Why do I care that you bought milk and Chobani yogurt at Jimmy's Deli?" he whispered.

The humorless PhD at the head of the room raised an eyebrow in their direction, leaving little to the imagination regarding his feelings about classroom chatter.

Capelli looked down at her desk, playing the good pupil, and flipped over the receipt. Ford took it in: "We're here because of you, asshole."

His recent choice of words had landed them in the painful and useless FBI sensitivity training course. He could name a guy in the agency for each finger and toe that *actually was* a racist but, somehow, it was his unfortunate fate to throw out the term "rag-head" while cracking a joke – and here they were. The higher-ups didn't seem to care that it was a one-time offense with no bearing on his personal beliefs; and – in the bureau – where you went, your partner went. He'd brought a Bavarian cream donut as peace offering but Capelli was back on her health kick. That usually only occurred when yogurt went on sale at Jimmy's.

After an hour of mind-numbing PowerPoint presentations, Capelli's ancient Blackberry buzzed.

"All right partner. We gotta go."

Ford – assuming he'd get a work-related text, too – was grateful for his partner's escape efforts.

"Agents Capelli and Ford!" The stern instructor boomed. "You will have to complete a full training course at a later date should you choose to leave now. Even if your absence is agency related."

"Talk about a sensitive guy," Ford grumbled, exiting the room.

"When he's done with you, you'll be a regular cupcake." Capelli smirked. "And next time around, forget the donut. Make it an omelet at Pastis.

"There's an awful lot of marble in this joint. Feel like I'm at the Met or something." Ford tugged at his collar; extreme wealth always intimidated him. Despite his razor-sharp mind and successes at the FBI, he still felt like a Brooklyn beat cop and was just fine with that.

"Vic was head of Polaris pharmaceuticals," Capelli explained. "Guess he could afford half the world's marble."

"File said this guy was in his eighties and smoked cigars regularly. Medical examiner sure it's not a natural death?"

"We'll see what the autopsy says. But according to the officer in charge, the ME thinks she spotted a needle mark on the victim's neck."

Entering the study, Capelli noted the last of the local PD packing up to leave.

"You Officer Stevens?" Capelli approached the unremarkable NYPD officer who'd been taking in the park views from the library.

"Yeah. First on the scene. M.E.'s ready to take the body but we wanted you all to get a look at the crime scene first."

"That's much appreciated, Officer Stevens. Care to give us a run-down?"

"Dog walker came in around 7:00 this morning and found the body. Apparently there's a housekeeper,

Rosemary Valdez – she typically arrives at the same time but hasn't made an appearance yet. My partner's trying to locate her whereabouts but hasn't had any luck. No sign of forced entry, no bruising or scrapes on the vic that would suggest a struggle. Not to mention all the valuables appear to be left untouched."

Capelli crouched next to the body. Looking into the still-open eyes of Edward Thorpe she couldn't help but feel a twinge of sadness for the old man. His mouth was twisted awkwardly in pain, creating the illusion he was wearing a death-mask – while his hands were clenched in fists that grew increasingly tighter as the rigor mortis fully set-in. There was dried vomit running from his mouth to the floor but no sign of blood or any obvious wounds. The only indications of a disturbance were some scattered chess-pieces and the stub of a cigar, presumably knocked over as the victim fell to the ground.

"So what do you think, Capelli? Foul play?" Ford was taking in the perfect rows of first edition novels, impressionist paintings, and a timeline of family photographs on the fireplace mantle. It was hard to figure this for a murder scene.

"I don't know. I can't tell if this really is a needle prick on his neck or not. Maybe my eyes are finally going. Call the M.E. first thing tomorrow and get the analysis."

"What's the problem? Your phone doesn't work?"

"She likes you – the Puerto Rican hottie – the one with the tattoo on her wrist that says 'lover'."

"I never said she likes me. I said she always smiles when I walk in the room."

"Either way, Romeo, you make the call. Meanwhile, I'll get in touch with his family, locate the maid, and see where we stand."

3

Doctors Without Borders Camp
Jowhar, Somalia

The boxy dark-green medical truck rumbled over an uneven dirt road leading from Mogadishu to Jowhar. Somalia wasn't known for its infrastructure and this road was no exception. The jackhammer ride was made worse by non-existent shocks on the ancient military-turned-medical transport Humvee.

These first five miles departing battle-torn Mogadishu were the reason Dr. Luc Turner's otherwise black hair was spotting gray. The rough ride was merely unpleasant. It was the risk of a rebel ambush that had Turner breaking a nervous sweat. The fighting had become severe enough to temporarily close the medical camp in Mogadishu and there were no signs of any truce. But since runways near the Jowhar camp were inadequate, cargo planes were still flying medical supplies into Mogadishu. Turner had drawn the short straw this Tuesday to make the pick-up.

"I don't know, Jean-Pierre," Turner addressed the immense Nigerian sitting shotgun. "Being a doctor, you get used to death. But this stretch of road gets me praying."

"Don't worry; they don't kill movie-stars even if they kidnap them." Jean-Pierre replied with a vague smile.

Turner's nickname at the camp was Dr. Hollywood. He wasn't naturally vain – initially he'd hated the moniker – but now it helped offset the salt-and-pepper reminder that he was aging.

Turner had hoped for a bit of reassurance, but JP just placed the much used AK-47 he'd had at the ready back on his lap; they were out of the woods for now.

After 45 additional miles of uncomfortable driving conditions the men finally arrived at home base. The healthier youngsters, seeing the familiar vehicle, began running alongside, banging on the flanks, hoping there may be a candy bar or soda among the vitamin packs and antibiotics. Turner always marveled at the drastic health improvements a few weeks of nutrition and vitamins had on the children. After watching so many succumb to illnesses easily treated in other parts of the globe, it heartened him to know that a few innocent victims of circumstance would have a chance to see another day. His only wish was they'd stay at the camp forever, rather than risk recruitment into one of the many pirate gangs that had innocent young boys transforming into violent savages in the blink of an eye.

"It's your lucky day! I'd say you need your vitamin shots first but I fear there'd be a mutiny!" He passed out Hershey bars to the many grubby fingers and did his best to ration fairly, though the onslaught of chocolate-crazed children made the task impossible.

4

Polaris Pharmaceuticals Headquarters
New York, New York

"**M**y sincerest apologies for keeping you," said the suave, Brioni-styled man as he crossed the Polaris sky lobby. "I've been trying to calm the concerns of many investors. They get a bit panicky when the CEO passes unexpectedly. Agents Capelli and Ford, is it?"

Capelli had seen enough Page-Six gossip to know that for most, Vance Thorpe, son of the late Edward Thorpe, was a much sought-after bachelor. Her definition of handsome didn't quite jive with the slicked-back hair and overly-pressed look of the man who stood before her – though something in his confident gaze did give the man a subtle alluring quality, she admitted.

"I'm Agent Capelli, this is Agent Ford. Would it be possible to speak somewhere?"

"Of course. My father's office is right here."

They left the plush lobby for an even more lavish corner office that overlooked Bryant Park. It was a far cry from the borderline space-age décor used in the building's public spaces – a style one would expect from a cutting-edge pharmaceutical company. This particular office was decorated in rich mahoganies, elegant tapestries, and held row upon row of medical, history, and biochemistry texts.

"First off, Mr. Thorpe, we'd like to offer our condolences for the death of your father. This must be a difficult time."

"Thank you, agent Ford, it's appreciated. You're right, it's a hard reality. Just when I've finally accepted the passing of my mother a decade ago, this. I'd love to have a few days to process everything but the business community requires reassurance in such moments. These 24 hour news cycles are brutal when there's any kind of shake-up."

"I'm sure," Capelli nodded. "Don't worry, we won't keep you long. Anyhow, there's not much to report on your father just yet – we'll have more conclusive information after the autopsy results come in. By the way – do you know a woman named Rosemary Valdez?"

"Sure. Rosemary is my father's housemaid. Does everything for him. Cooks, cleans, anticipates his every need, basically."

"Well, we found Ms. Valdez dead in her apartment this morning." Capelli watched as Ford's words sunk in. "Again, no official cause of death but she appears to have bled to death. Did she have any family troubles? Anyone who might like to see her dead?"

Thorpe began fiddling with a small globe near the desk lamp, spinning it with a blank stare until he seemed to snap into reality.

"Rosemary was a kind woman; she always spent Thanksgiving with us. As a guest, not as a maid. I can't imagine someone would want to hurt her. I don't know much about her personal life. I've never met her relatives. I believe most are back in Guatemala."

"What about your father?" Capelli chimed in. "Did he have any enemies?"

"I was under the impression my father's death was natural. Are you suggesting it's not?"

"We aren't sure. The death of Ms. Valdez raises some concerns. We'll keep you apprised of any new information – please call us if you think of any relevant details."

5

Gstaad, Switzerland

With long, deliberate strides, the tall, gaunt man slowly crossed the dark expansive living room. Unmoved by the stunning Alpine views he paced along the cabin windows, awaiting a call that should have come hours ago. If problems arose, anticipated or not, he could handle them. Delay in crisis management, however, was the one factor that could hinder the operation.

Cursing his usually stoic nerves, he sat at the sterile-looking kitchen table. The home was not a typical, cozy mountain cabin. All furniture was either white or glass, in a variety of overly-modern geometric shapes, and kept impeccably clean – never so much as a fiber out of place. After a moment of stillness, his long, perfectly manicured fingers began drumming the tabletop. Immediately, upon noticing what he was doing, he retrieved glass cleaner and removed the fingerprints. At least his obsessive-compulsive behavior provided a moment of distraction during the wait.

The ping of his secure video conferencing line alerted him to an incoming caller. Finally, he would have a status report. He confirmed the secured connection and powered up the screen.

"Mr. B. You've kept me waiting."

"My apologies, Mr. A. It won't happen again," replied the face on the monitor.

"That was assumed. Now where do we stand?"

"The operation proceeded as planned, Thorpe is dead – though it appears they will conduct an autopsy. Also, there was an unexpected houseguest who had to be eliminated."

Mr. A was not pleased. They'd painstakingly observed every detail in the target's daily habits, including the comings and goings of visitors and home-workers.

"We have contingencies for the autopsy," Mr. A tried to sound nonplussed. "How was the maid eliminated?"

"My congratulations to your sources. She was outsourced."

This was the answer Mr. A was afraid of.

"The authorities will find him."

"The contractor has no connection to the victim."

"The authorities *will* find him. Be sure they don't."

"Understood. I'll update you tomorrow."

"Do not keep me waiting."

Mr. A was boiling inside – though to look at him you'd never know it. His nearly albino face remained rigid and pale. He'd known better than to let his colleague take the lead on such a task. And now, with rumblings of hesitation in Prague, an additional elimination seemed necessary. It was time to begin preparations.

6

Ford Residence
Brooklyn, New York

The unseasonably warm fall day came as a great relief to Agent Ford. Recent monsoon-like rains, followed by a brief but unpleasant cold snap, had put a stop to father-son time in the small backyard of the Ford family's modest Greenpoint townhome.

"Okay, Brian, let's try it one more time. I think we're almost there."

Danny was convinced he could raise the greatest football player that ever stepped on Astroturf. He believed strongly in teaching the game at a young age to develop muscle memory and Pop Warner fundamentals. But, despite his best efforts, Ford's five-year-old had yet to play a successful game of catch with a Nerf ball. What worried Danny more was the kid's infatuation with the baby grand that Ford saw as nothing but living room furniture. Despite a lack of progress, and interest, he continued the Saturday morning rituals and hoped that the little guy would catch on. He'd also need to overcome his parents less-than-athletic genes which put them at 5'3 and 5'10, respectively.

"Hey, Danny! Give the kid a break and get in here. Kate's on the line for you."

Caroline Ford took great pleasure in her son's reluctance to play catch, and her husband's frustration because of it. She'd read one-too-many articles in *Parenting* about football's long-term impact on the young brain – no child of hers was going to end up clobbered on the 50 yard line. Instead, she hoped he'd be the next Jean-Georges – but culinary school was a long way off.

"Kate says it's something about the Thorpe case. I'll watch Brian."

"Okay, but keep him away from the piano. We don't need him turning out like that crazy aunt of yours, singing show tunes in some village dive." Ford grabbed the phone from his wife.

"Geez, Capelli, you live at the office? It's Saturday, you know."

"Yeah, yeah. I got a call during my wax if you must know. What are you doing? Still trying to make that kid an athlete?"

She took his silence to be a sign of discomfort. Only two things muted Ford – talk of "women's things," as he'd say, or the possibility his son wouldn't be the next Eli Manning.

"Get to the point."

"We've got ourselves a case. The lab did an initial tox panel on Thorpe. Looks like he was killed by a Taipan."

"Eh?"

"It's a snake."

"Snake? I didn't see any snakes in his place."

"He wasn't bitten. M.E. says it was injected. I've located a venom specialist in Miami who studies Taipans. Sent him the toxicology reports. We've got a conference call in two hours."

"Christ, you've got to find a man." Ford hung up and looked over to see his son humming away at the piano.

"I'll watch him, honey," Caroline Ford smiled. "You go do what you have to do."

7

FBI Headquarters
Midtown Manhattan

Walking down the drab corridor to her office, Kate felt grateful she'd found an excuse to work on Saturday. FBI business was all that kept her from a deep state of personal loathing. 'Divorced at 33' was not something she'd thought would be on her romantic resume. Coupled with an ill-advised fling with Eduardo, her barely English-speaking ex-boxing instructor, she was batting about a hundred. She pushed open the bullpen door with a steaming plastic bag.

"Hey, Danny boy, I happened to pass by Grand Szechuan. We've got General Tso's chicken and Mongolian Beef."

"Guilt food for dragging me in, huh? You know, if you need an activity you could help teach my kid to play football."

"Seriously? Your kid is five. Teach him to spell his name first and take it from there."

Just as Ford was formulating his quippy response, the conference room phone rang so loudly he dropped a piece of General Tso's on the speaker. Capelli swiped it away, rolling her eyes at his perpetual sloppiness.

"Hello, Dr. Yamaguchi. This is Agent Capelli and my partner, Agent Ford, is here as well. I really appreciate your getting back to us so quickly."

"Not to mention it's Saturday," Ford emphasized, glaring at Capelli.

"Not a problem. It's not every day the FBI comes calling. Happy to help out where I can."

"It's appreciated," Capelli answered. "So, looking over the toxicology reports, what can you tell us?"

Capelli had yet to adopt the high-tech ways of her colleagues. She had her Bic pen and yellow legal pad at the ready. As usual, Ford didn't bother with notes. He looked like a mess but the guy had a mind like a steel trap. He'd remember this conversation verbatim.

"Well, this particular venom was from the Oxyuranus microlepidotus, commonly known as the Inland Taipan, indigenous to Australia."

Ford silently "oohed" hearing the scientific name Yamaguchi used. He couldn't help but think most PhD's had to prove how much they knew about their chosen field. Fair or not, Ford decided this Yamaguchi was a brilliant virgin.

"Its venom is the most deadly in the world, though it tends to be a non-combative snake so the number of Taipan fatalities are low, due to infrequent attacks. The poison contains a pre-synaptic and post-synaptic neurotoxin which can cause paralysis as well as a procoagulant. The procoagulant interferes with clotting and can cause major bleeding in a bite victim. There is also a myotoxin in this particular venom, though the other toxins would be the cause of death or the most severe symptoms."

"So in plain English, you're telling us it's not just a bee sting." Ford grunted.

"You agree with the M.E.'s assessment that this venom was our cause of death?" Capelli jumped in, her Bic at the ready.

"Oh, most certainly. According to the toxicology there was nothing else present in the blood to suggest otherwise. Since no bite marks were found, and the snake would be unlikely to attack unless severely provoked, I'd propose that the venom was injected directly into the victim via syringe."

"That's what the M.E. thought, too," Capelli countered, "Glad to hear you agree doctor."

Ford leaned in toward the speaker, "Dr. Yamaguchi, what would our victim have experienced after being injected?"

"Well, first there'd be muscle weakness and likely flaccid paralysis. This would result in respiratory failure and then kidney failure. Normally death from such a bite would take anywhere from 45 minutes to a few hours, but this was likely much quicker if injected directly and at a high dosage."

"How much venom would kill an adult male?" Capelli asked, before Ford could make a sarcastic comment about flaccid paralysis.

"Oh, not much at all. Just a few milligrams of venom could kill up to 100 people."

8

Doctors Without Borders Camp
Jowhar, Somalia

Dry African winds thrashed the quarantine tents with ferocity, the sand whipping Dr. Turner as he ran between the patients' various housing quarters. After the casualties he'd witnessed since joining Doctors Without Borders he'd grown increasingly convinced that there was no mercy, no God. Still, on the off chance there was someone listening, he'd considered praying for rain. The drought conditions had become unbearable. This, coupled with a recent outbreak of a yet undetermined illness, had him feeling overwhelmed – something which rarely happened to Luc Turner.

"How are you feeling, Amaka?" Turner tried his best to remain non-biased with his patients, but little 6 year-old Amaka had a special place in his heart from day one.

Skeletal, filled with parasites, and covered in disease-bearing bites, the malnourished girl had been near death when she arrived for treatment a year ago. Proper hydration and nourishment had made her one of the healthiest, most vibrant children in the camp. She'd been learning English at a rapid pace and was getting stronger with each passing day. Her eyes went from dull and crusty, filled with pain, to clear, bright, and joyful. So, as Turner watched her deteriorate over the past several days along with dozens of other patients, he grew increasingly concerned. Amaka was so weak that a verbal reply required too much trouble; she simply shook her head and curled in a ball on the small cot.

This setback had affected Turner with a novel sense of despair. There'd not been a major illness in the camp for months due to their rigorous quarantine procedures. The new sickness would likely mean death for those already malnourished and ill. He wasn't sure how many more burials he could bear – he searched the camp for someone who could give him a useful update.

"Jean-Pierre, how are the others doing?"

"I did what you said, we've quarantined those showing symptoms in a temporary tent, but it's spreading like wildfire. I fear that soon all the camp will be infected."

Turner rubbed his forehead, trying not to appear out of answers.

"Okay. Let's get water samples, food samples, and blood samples. We can send them to the lab in Kenya.

They aren't the best but we'll have a quicker turnaround time than anywhere else. We've got to diagnose this."

"Fever, sweats, cough, and general weakness. Those symptoms could be the flu or the start of a new plague – anything really."

"We'll just have to keep a close eye and see what else develops – because what little medicine we have isn't working."

"Yes, hopefully it's nothing too severe. I'll begin collecting samples."

"Thanks Jean-Pierre. And be sure to wear a mask."

9

FBI Headquarters
Midtown Manhattan

Rain was beating on the windows, adding to the already depressed mood in Capelli's office. Aside from the snake venom, there were no leads in the case of Edward Thorpe. It was as if a ghost had floated in, touched nothing, injected Thorpe, and floated back out with no eyewitnesses. Rumors were swirling that local P.D. had a lead in the Valdez case, but they were holding details close to the vest to protest the feds taking over the high-profile Thorpe murder.

Ford walked in with a tray of skim lattes and two donuts.

"So – the maid saw our perp and he felt the need to shut her up." Ford reclined in his chair, pushing it to the brink of an embarrassing capitulation, and took a satisfying sip of coffee.

"Wow, that's great detective work, Ace. I'm waiting on a call back from the NYPD. Some loose ends I need clarified."

"Fat chance they reply anytime soon. Calling them is like cold-calling a mute – unless you still have your contact at the NYPD."

"My ex? Not happening. He's probably the one delaying the process in the first place."

Capelli's marriage began crumbling when she left the NYPD for the FBI. The switch gave her husband a not-so-small inferiority complex that he'd decided to remedy by sleeping with a vast array of large-breasted women. Amazingly, he felt no guilt for the indiscretions and was still bitter about her move to the Bureau.

"Besides, if they find anything that links back to our vic they're obligated to report it."

"Obligated – like I'm obligated to take sensitivity training?"

"They won't let you welch. You're going – and so am I."

Ford replied with a "like-that'll-happen" eye-roll and decided to follow a more productive trail.

"So, on the way over, I rang our friend Dr. Yamaguchi...

"Oh – tell me you were nice this time." Capelli cringed the thought of an unmonitored Ford calling anyone, let alone someone he considered pompous.

"I was a teddy bear. So friendly, in fact, that after I told him our database turned up zilch, he agreed to help us locate registered Inland Taipan handlers and owners. Thing is, he thinks it's more likely our killer purchased the venom on the black-market on-line from a foreign seller. I've already got Jimmy's IT guys running a search."

"What kind of donut is this?" Capelli asked, her chewing becoming a grimace.

"Bacon-maple-sausage. It's from that artsy-fartsy donut shop on Hudson."

"Listen, next time – don't be afraid of chocolate frosted. It's a donut. This – this is a blue plate special at IHOP." Saying this, Capelli tossed the remains on the table. "I want to head back to Thorpe's, take one more look without all the CSIs and locals."

10

Thorpe Residence
Central Park West

Capelli had her Glock 22 at the ready. She'd expected the townhome to be empty but was surprised to see the crime scene tape had been cut and the front door unlocked. While she was in no mood for a shoot-out, part of her hoped the perp was inside. A quick collar was always good for the resume. Her work performance had been lackluster as of late and a quick close to this case would be a welcome success.

In an effort to boost her self-esteem and spark some semblance of a love life, she'd started dressing in more form-fitting suits to accentuate her long, lean frame. Conservative high heels had also become a staple, a wardrobe change she was regretting as she entered the marble echo-chamber foyer. Glancing around the first floor, she suddenly heard something creak upstairs – a drawer or a cabinet – the intruder likely rifling around the library where the body had been found. She pressed against the wall, slowly making her way up the curved staircase, heels hanging off the back of each step to avoid a loud clacking sound. Her forehead was beginning to sweat and she willed herself to regulate her breathing. Surprise was on her side, she told herself. Standing outside the library door, she assessed the situation. The careful footsteps seemed that of a single intruder. She led with the Glock, sliding around the corner, and entered the library. "FBI! Raise your hands!"

"Whoa, there, Agent Capelli. Don't shoot." Vance Thorpe flashed a bleached grin. "Didn't expect you."

"That makes two of us. What are you doing here? This residence is a crime scene. You need FBI permission to enter."

"My apologies, Agent Capelli. I just assumed since I was family, it would be alright."

"Smart money says you know better than that. What has you stomping all over my crime scene?" She holstered her weapon, finally calming down as the adrenaline subsided.

"The other day you asked me if there was anyone interested in harming my father. I'd completely forgotten an incident that occurred around six months ago. A middle-aged man, clearly disturbed, managed to elude security and disrupt our annual board meeting with our overseas partners. I thought I'd look through some of father's files to see if there was any documentation of what happened."

Capelli arched her eyebrow, not firmly convinced by the greasy exec's story.

"Well – find anything?"

"Nothing here. Not yet, anyway." Vance Thorpe rose from the desk in an obvious attempt to end the impromptu meeting. "If you'd like to stay and help me search…"

"Any other witnesses to the event that may have a clearer recollection of what happened?" Capelli cut him off. She wasn't sure if he was scrambling or coming on to her.

"Well, all the heads of our foreign offices, of course. Father's secretary, Janet Williams – she'd remember the event best The fellow shoved past her to enter the meeting. She asked him to wait in the lobby, but there was no talking him down." Thorpe adjusted his tie and pocket square, apparently finished with this inquiry.

"Well, Miss Capelli? Do I have to search alone – or will you help me?"

"*Agent* Capelli is going to have another look around. You're going to leave – until I see a permission slip from my director."

"You're all business, aren't you?" Thorpe paused just before exiting. "Very well. A pleasure, as always."

Capelli watched from the second floor as Thorpe descended the curving staircase and strode out of the townhome. He looked a perplexing combination of haughty and concerned, but about what Kate couldn't be sure. As the hallway went silent, she considered whether she was all business – then reprimanded herself for letting some silver-spoon playboy get in her head.

11

Doctors Without Borders Camp
Jowhar, Somalia

"Luc!" Jean-Pierre urgently whispered into one of the three quarantine tents where the doctor was helplessly tending to the infirmed. The disease had spread so rapidly that nearly half of all the camp's patients had been relegated to the make-shift housing. Turner held up his hand, suggesting he'd be out in a minute. Looking down the row of ill children he felt a knot in the pit of his stomach. They'd been through so much simply making the journey here; now it was beginning to look like they were pilgrims who'd made an exodus toward death.

Turner pushed out of the tent into the relentless desert gusts that'd been blowing for over week now. Beyond the pelting sandy dirt, what greeted him was a welcome sight. A tall female figure, lean but curvaceous, stood conferring with Jean-Pierre, using her medical van as a shelter from the weather. Dr. Eva Abrams was a colleague currently assigned to the camp in Dadaab, Kenya, where Turner had spent a six-month stint two years earlier. She was equal, if not better than, the most talented surgeons he'd studied under at Harvard Medical School. He'd once seen her simultaneously save a victim with a gunshot wound to the chest while stopping briefly to re-set the dislocated shoulder of a man whose screams were a distraction. Most with her considerable skills would opt to make a fortune at a posh private hospital in New York or LA, but Dr. Abrams chose to rough it in Africa. That quality, along with long chocolate-colored hair and captivating green eyes, had made it impossible for Dr. Turner not to take notice of her. He was both surprised and pleased that she had been the one to pursue him. Before long they had developed a passionate affair, now only occasionally re-kindled when he traveled to Kenya or she to Somalia to assist on a case. Turner had always questioned whether she had actual feelings for him or was simply looking for companionship and release in the miserable Dadaab camp. Truthfully, he didn't care. The same tough spirit that molded her into a top field surgeon made it difficult to connect emotionally.

"Hello, Dr. Turner," Eva greeted him playfully in a seductive tone, causing the shy Jean-Pierre to look away, but not before winking at Turner.

"Hey, Abrams." They shared a warm embrace but nothing more; the current state of the camp didn't exactly stoke the flames of romance.

"Have you made any progress on the disease?" Eva sensed the depth of his concerns and shelved the playful banter for later.

"Until your guys analyze these samples back in Kenya there's not much I can do. We have no antibiotics left and the spread is rampant. Four days ago the symptoms presented in a few patients, now hundreds are symptomatic. It's almost certainly airborne; we've done our best to contain the sick and take excessive precaution, but you know how it is out here."

"I'll have Eddie rush his analysis of these samples. In the meantime I brought some IV's and basic supplies. I wish I could do more but we're low in Dadaab until next week's delivery. Oh, and I brought the Mantoux test but there's no way this is TB. It's spreading much too fast."

"I know. When I asked for the tests there were only a few cases which seemed to fit tuberculosis, but now that's obviously out. Jean-Pierre, check on tent three will you? I want to catch Dr. Abrams up to speed."

Abrams and Turner jogged to the dilapidated old living quarters, shielding their eyes from the swirling dust. As they stepped inside Turner's living room, he secured the door against the wind – realizing too late he hadn't had time to spruce up the place.

"Not much has changed." Eva muttered, brushing dust off her arms. "That's the problem with having all male docs here. It's like a college frat house swallowed an African shanty town."

"Sounds like someone wants to sleep outside tonight."

"Maybe I will. But give a lady some dinner first."

"All we've got is the standard chicken and rice – but I've managed to acquire some spices courtesy of Jean-Pierre's lovely wife. I could use a little sustenance before getting back to work."

"Of course, you'll sterilize the table before we eat."

"I forgot how much I missed you, Eva." Turner grinned.

12

Prague, Czech Republic

The pale-skinned man walked with slow, deliberate strides up Nerudova Street; taking in an array of tourists, whores, and locals, all of whom seemed to have consumed one-too-many pints of *pivo* this chilly fall evening. The cobblestone road was named for the Republic's famed novelist, Jan Neruda, and – with its steep incline – was the source of many sore leg muscles for unsuspecting sightseers. But for this particular individual, the steep grade caused little strain. A rigorous dedication in martial arts, primarily Sambo and Krav Maga, maintained his impeccable shape despite his increasing years. He was first introduced to Sambo during his youth. The combination of judo and Eastern European wrestling had turned his body into a deadly weapon from a young age. He'd learned Krav Maga, a form of hand-to-hand combat, from an Israeli ex-Mossad agent during his days as a mercenary. Though a recluse, the man preferred this tourist-trap neighborhood — where amidst the smell of beer and cackles of jokes in foreign tongues, he was never given a second a look.

Opening the heavy wooden door to his aparthotel lobby always proved to be unpleasant; the stench of fatty sausages and rancid sauerkraut accosted his senses from the first-floor beer hall. Without wasting steps, he bypassed the restaurant and climbed the old, stone stairway to his third floor bedroom. One would never suspect the sterile, modern studio that he'd created to mimic his home in Gstaad. The room was small, with stainless steel appliances lining the wall in a perfectly symmetrical design. There was a small twin bed with crisp, perfectly applied white sheets, a modest sitting area that housed his computer, state-of-the-art video-conferencing screen, and scrambled phone line. Most guests of the hotel were tourists on a tight budget, unlikely to ever return to the less-than-glamorous accommodations. This particular man had made — with the help of a large bribe — an agreement with the hotels owner, Jaroslav, to purchase a room under complete anonymity. Jaroslav was happy to turn a blind eye to the man's coming and going — each visit meant another generous cash delivery slipped under his door. He never took issue over the fact he could not enter the room as a result of the specialized security system that only the elusive guest could access — it was one less room for Petra to clean.

After lighting several candles and cracking a window to the cold air, the man, Mr. A, completed his evening ritual of push-ups followed by a near-boiling shower in which he meticulously scrubbed his alabaster skin and closely-buzzed white hair three successive times. Once finished, the nighttime hours would be spent reviewing every detail of the upcoming assassination.

13

FBI Headquarters
Midtown Manhattan

Capelli swiped past the security doors of the unmanned south entrance – noting the empty coffee cup on the guard's desk then walked past the vacated cubicles on the D-2 floor. Non-essential personnel rarely stayed past five and it was nearly five-fifteen.

"How did it go at la casa Thorpe?" Ford mumbled through an enormous bite of a loaded burrito.

"Interesting. I found Vance Thorpe rifling through some papers in the library. He claimed to be looking for documents of a threat against his father that occurred awhile back... he seemed a little squirmy though."

"That's what happens when you've got a gold-plated stick up your ass. He's probably just worried about Polaris' stock values." Ford washed down another bite with a gulp of Pepto-Bismol. He always took precautionary measures when it came to Mexican fare. "What was the threat about?"

"Apparently some guy came storming into a board meeting they were holding at Polaris. Little Thorpe couldn't remember what the gripe was but claims the guy was visibly troubled by something. Says security removed him quickly and that was the last of it. I've got Old Man Thorpe's secretary coming in for a chat. Maybe she can shed some light on the case."

"Secretaries know more about their bosses' lives than the families do." Ford chimed in, his words muffled by sour cream and jalapeño.

Kate grabbed a few fried something-or-others before Ford could clog another artery.

"Hey!"

"I'm saving your life. By the way, I thought Caroline was cooking that pot-roast you like."

"Yeah, well, I got hungry ahead of schedule. And what she doesn't know won't hurt her." Ford wiped the remnants of dinner from his lips. "Hopefully this secretary has a penchant for exotic snakes. Jimmy and I have gotten nowhere there. We've tracked a shitload of black-market venom sales but everything's a dead end. Amazing how many nutbags spend thousands on a little snake spit."

"Stop worrying about the nutbags and clean up. She's coming in."

"Who?"

"Old Thorpe's secretary."

"Now?"

"She didn't want to have people see her come in for a chat. Thought it might get back to young Thorpe – hurt the company image."

"But I told Caroline I'd be home for dinner."

"Yeah, well, you'll be late. And you still got some of your first dinner on your face – clean up."

Janet Williams anxiously tugged the hem of her wool pencil skirt. Normally a calm, collected woman, she'd been uncharacteristically nervous since the passing of her boss. Forty of her sixty-five years had been spent working at Polaris – she'd been along for the ride as the company's ground-breaking discoveries had developed medication that saved millions of lives. Now she was a witness, called in to see the federal agents investigating the death of her beloved boss. Never in a million years did she think she'd be walking toward an FBI meeting room. The space was pleasant enough, with slightly worn chairs and a classic white coffee service on the small mahogany conference table. It was nothing like the poorly lit, sparse, interrogation rooms on television – she imagined they saved those for actual suspects. Her heart jumped a beat as the door swung open.

"Good afternoon, Ms. Williams. I'm agent Kate Capelli, this is Danny Ford. We really appreciate you coming in."

The older woman's elegance took Capelli by surprise. Long, silver hair was pulled into a classic French-twist, her face nearly wrinkle-free, and she maintained a knock-out figure in her fitted wool suit. Kate couldn't help but wonder if she and Thorpe had ever been more than colleagues.

"I must say, this is a bit surreal. But I'll help in any way I can."

"I appreciate that. Please," Capelli motioned to a stiff faux-leather chair and waited until everyone was seated, then poured coffee into three white cups. "Now, can you tell us a little about your relationship with Mr. Thorpe?"

Janet assumed this was a loaded question. Everyone from co-workers to the society pages had long suspected an affair between the successful business mogul and his lovely secretary. It was cliché, and in this case, untrue. He'd been deeply devoted to his late wife, Audrey, and that loyalty carried on even after her death. Admittedly, in the early days, Janet had more-than-a-little crush on her boss, but that had a developed into deep respect for the man he was rather than a romantic relationship.

"I worked with Edward for the past forty years. Initially it was mundane secretarial work, but over time I became more of a trusted assistant. He'd ask my advice on various things, from new research practices to hiring decisions. His wife and I became the closest of friends. She was a wonderfully warm and philanthropic person; it was heartbreaking when she passed. The Thorpes were like a family to me."

Janet looked over at Ford. She couldn't help but smile watching the chubby agent sip from a dainty china cup. He seemed more a big-gulp type.

Capelli retrieved her Bic and rifled through her notes.

"Ms. Williams, Vance Thorpe mentioned an incident that occurred during a Polaris board meeting about six months ago. Apparently, a man disrupted the meeting in a rage, directing his anger at Edward. Do you have any recollection of that event?"

"You must be referring to John Kraft."

Capelli and Ford both edged forward on their chairs, interest piqued. Neither had expected much from this interview, let alone the name of the intruder.

"So you remember the incident?" The Bic was poised over a yellow legal pad.

"Oh, yes. It's very sad actually. Turns out, Mr. Kraft had been calling and writing Edward on a daily basis, asking for help. Not surprisingly, in a company the size of Polaris's headquarters, the calls never got through nor did the letters arrive at Edward's office. You see, there are hundreds of employees, about twenty of whom answer the phones and screen calls before they get patched through to the boss. This may sound cold but it's necessary. Too many quacks call in, conspiracy theorists raging on about big pharma and what have you." She sighed, collecting her thoughts.

"Anyway, Mr. Kraft never got through. Kraft's young son, only eight years old, was participating in a leukemia trial at Polaris. A nurse who administered the treatment took a liking to the father and son, eventually letting it slip the son was only receiving a placebo treatment – divulging information like that is a big no-no when it comes to running a passable trial. Mr. Kraft was outraged, as any father would be, and began writing to beg that Edward give his son the experimental drug. His boy, Timothy, passed before he ever reached Mr. Thorpe."

Ford and Capelli listened intently, both sensing they finally had a lead.

"Well, as you can imagine, the death of his son put Mr. Kraft over the edge. He'd assumed Mr. Thorpe had received his pleas and was simply ignoring him. Kraft managed to bypass the building security and disrupt the board meeting, screaming about how Mr. Thorpe had killed his boy. Security removed him, a sobbing mess. That's when Edward requested I look into the situation and we learned about the boy and the trial."

"Were there any other incidents with this man?" Ford chimed in.

"Well, not incidents per se. Mr. Thorpe felt horrible about everything that had transpired. He'd always hated that placebos were used in trials and felt for the man. At one point, he reached out to Mr. Kraft, offering to help with funeral expenses and start a scholarship in the boy's name. This was probably a conflict of interest but Mr. Thorpe was an incredibly soft-hearted man and wanted to honor the boy in some fashion. Kraft would have none of it though, accusing Edward of trying to buy his silence."

"Were there any other incidents with this Kraft?"

"Not that I'm aware of. But Mr. Thorpe became very withdrawn the past few months. I'm not sure if the Kraft affair had something to do with it, or if he was missing Audrey, but there was sadness about him."

Capelli had jitters in her stomach, eager to pursue the lead on John Kraft.

"Just one more question, Ms. Williams. Vance Thorpe didn't recall any details of the incident. One would think, if the situation bothered Edward the way you say, he'd have opened up to his son. What was their relationship like?"

Janet Williams fumbled with her coffee mug, the muddy liquid having turned cold long ago. She seemed lost in thought, staring at nothing in particular as she considered how best to answer this inquiry.

"Ms. Williams?" Capelli gently placed her hand on the woman's forearm in a comforting gesture.

"Sorry, I just... well... their relationship was interesting. As father and son they were opposites in many ways. The last few years they behaved more as business partners than family. Unlike his parents, there's hardness in Vance, he's a very calculating man. When it came to Polaris, Ed was happiest when life-changing research breakthroughs were made. Vance was more driven by stock prices and dollar signs, not the human element."

"Was there increased friction between them over the past months?"

"I'm not sure. Like I said, Edward had become very withdrawn. Vance was due to take over when his father retired and he was aggressively trying to increase his input in the company's decisions. That seemed to annoy Edward but he never mentioned it directly."

Ford stood, loosening his paisley tie, a wardrobe staple better suited to Barney Miller. The gesture was an agreed upon signal for Capelli to end it. Her questioning tended to become a rigorous barrage of questions, exhausting witnesses. Ford liked Janet Williams and thought the older lady could use a break. Besides, he was almost certain they'd need her insights in the future and wanted to remain in her good graces.

14

Ford Residence
Brooklyn, New York

"Sorry to crash dinner like this, Caroline."

"Hey, if Danny's going to be working late I'd rather have him here than at that drab office of yours."

"Well, I've spruced it up some. I've got an IKEA rug now–"

"And I've seen the bureau fridge. You could do with something other than Swanson dinners. How you maintain that figure with your lousy diet I'll never understand."

"Well, I'm not burning any calories in the sack, that's for sure."

"I've told you before, I know a great single guy for you. Give me the green light and you'll have a date by Saturday."

Kate glowered good-naturedly at Caroline. In her mind, a blind date would be acknowledging she'd officially hit rock-bottom in her personal life. Perhaps she was prolonging the inevitable, but for now she'd stick with denial.

"All right, all right. No blind dates. The lasagna is about ready. If you can find my husband – he's probably torturing Brian with than Nerf ball again."

After consuming ungodly amounts of lasagna bolognese, Capelli and Ford descended into the basement – also known as his man-cave – each with a glass of Knob Creek. They settled into a pair of hideous leather recliners that were holdovers from his college days, much to the chagrin of his interior-decorator wife.

"Brian's quite the natural musician." Capelli couldn't help herself; something about Ford's sarcastic demeanor gave her the urge to get under his skin.

"Yeah, he's got Hot Cross Buns down."

"So. I'm liking John Kraft for this. I'd like to bring him in first thing tomorrow and check his alibis."

"He certainly has motive. If somebody screwed my kid out of a cancer treatment, I'd kill him without hesitation. Only thing I don't get is why would a guy who's strapped for cash use venom selling for over a grand a pop as his murder weapon? His records show he manages a mechanics shop; I mean, he's probably got an ex-con working under him that could provide an untraceable handgun for a fraction of the cost."

"Stereotyping much? If I recall, this is how we ended up in sensitivity training."

"That comment was in no way racist. And it's based on hard evidence."

Ford downed the remaining Knob Creek, his cheeks becoming a shade of the latest Maybelline blush.

"I think it's time I head out." Capelli said, placing her tumbler on the old card table. "Let's pay a visit to Kraft in the morning; we don't have enough to justify formal questioning but I'd like to get a feel for the guy. See if he's got a snake locked-up near the pressure hoses.

15

K&R Mechanics
Queens, New York

The unmistakable stench of oil and rubber accosted Capelli's senses as she approached the automotive shop, sparking a moment of déjà vu. Her father had been a street cop with a proclivity for classic cars priced far beyond his means. When Kate was ten he came home with a beat-up 1955 DeVille that had been acquired for a measly $500 at the policeman's auction. Apparently, the car had been involved in an unsolved drug bust and the perps were smart enough to cut their losses rather than reclaim it from the impound. They'd spent the following summer fixing the hunk of twisted metal until it was in near perfect condition. She wasn't too much help in the process, but learned her tools. When her father needed a monkey wrench there was always one waiting in her little hand. A year later her father was killed in the line of duty. Two months after that her mother sold everything, including the car – Kate still resented her for it.

"I hope this guy doesn't run – I'm in no mood for a chase."

"What's your problem today, Danny? You're cranky. Caroline hold out on you last night?"

He rubbed his eyes and shook his head, trying to get the cobwebs out.

"She's been holding out on me since Lucy was born last year. Only on special occasions does she put herself at risk for having to go through childbirth again. I've grown used to it. My problem is the two additional Knob Creeks I sucked down after you left."

"I guess I'll do the talking today."

Capelli opened the squeaky glass door to the customer service area, the rubber stench becoming increasingly pungent. Ford entered behind her, tripping over the slightly raised floor in the shop's waiting area.

"Jesus Christ man, pull it together."

He flashed a thumbs-up in reply.

"What can I do for you today?" The slightly overweight receptionist asked, flashing a gap-toothed grin.

His nametag read "Ronnie" and he had unfortunate case of early balding and a lazy eye.

"We'd like to see Mr. Kraft. Is he around?" Capelli had anonymously called in earlier to confirm Kraft would be at the shop today, but she asked anyway so as not to raise suspicions.

"Yes ma'am, he is. Are you friends of his?"

"Yes, we are."

John Kraft entered the waiting area ten minutes later, wiping his hands of grease and oil with a well-worn rag. He was average in many ways, stood about 5'11, wasn't overweight but certainly hadn't been doing two-a-day work-outs with a personal trainer, and had closely-cropped brown hair with a few stray grays. His face bore a sadness that aged him far beyond his 34 years – not surprising considering the death of his son. He shot Ronnie a "what do you want from me" look, annoyed at this disruption from his carburetor repair work. The clueless desk clerk nodded towards Capelli and Ford, assuming Kraft would recognize his "friends."

"Help you?" Kraft asked in a tone that was neither friendly nor rude.

"Mr. Kraft, is there somewhere private we can speak?" Ford stealthily flashed his badge, away from the curious receptionist's line of sight.

"Here is fine. Ronnie, can you give us some privacy?" His voice caught as he replied. Guilty or not, badges tend to cause anxiety.

Ronnie shuffled out of the waiting area, allowing the door to slam in protest to his exile. Kraft watched him exit, then retrieved a dilapidated old office chair from behind the counter and sat facing the agents. Any anxieties he'd felt had already dissipated. He now wore the blank stare of a man who had nothing left to lose.

"Mr. Kraft, we'll try to keep this brief so you can get back to work. Do you know a man named Edward Thorpe?" Capelli leaned in slightly as she asked the question, causing Kraft to lean back in retreat.

"I know of him. That son of a bitch killed my son."

"Mr. Kraft, that son of a bitch – as you so eloquently call him – was murdered recently."

"Yeah, I read about his death in the Post. Karma's what I'd call it, that man giving fake treatments to my son. He deserved the same fate as Timothy."

His eyes welled with tears but his jaw remained set and defiant.

"We know about your loss, Mr. Kraft, and we're terribly sorry. I can only imagine how difficult the past few months have been. We heard that you threatened Mr. Thorpe at his annual board meeting and wanted to speak with him in person. Is that true?"

"Hell yeah. Because of him, my son died. Timothy didn't deserve to be tossed aside that way – he needed a cure! If I was a rich man, there's no chance my son would have been given those fake meds."

"Mr. Kraft, we read through the agreement you signed prior to Timothy's participation in the leukemia trial. It specifically stated in section 2C there would be a placebo treatment used for 25% of the patients, a sampling that would be chosen completely at random. Were you aware of this?"

Kraft shifted in his chair. The truth was, he'd been so desperate for his son to receive medical care that he'd never carefully read the agreement – he signed on the spot. It wasn't until he'd visited a lawyer to bring a lawsuit against Polaris that the placebo treatment had been brought to his attention. Even that hack lawyer Finkelstein had known the lawsuit would be a non-starter.

"At the time, no. I was angry and my son had just died – that man needed to know what his company was doing to people, to their families."

"So you threatened to kill him?"

"I don't know what I said. I had a speech prepared but by the time I found the boardroom, security was right behind me and I just started yelling. I wanted him to know about Timothy."

Kraft's fists curled into a tight ball, his jaw tensed, and the sad, brown eyes were starting to glaze. Ford chimed in, hoping to bring the subject's defenses back down.

"I have a boy, Mr. Kraft, and if anything happened to him I'd want someone to pay, too."

Kraft warily eyed Ford, but began to calm slightly.

"So, you see, I understand where you're coming from. But you can't take justice into your own hands. We have witnesses from that meeting who will go on record that you threatened to kill Mr. Thorpe. So, I need to know where you were on Monday night. If you have a strong alibi then we'll say our goodbyes and let you get back to work."

"I was home."

"Was your wife there with you?"

"My wife hasn't been home for a month. I reminded her too much of Timothy. Said every time she looked in my eyes she saw her son and couldn't take it anymore. Divorce papers were sent to the house last week."

Ford felt for the man. If the situation were reversed, he'd want to off someone too.

"So…" Capelli broke in. "Nobody can back-up your whereabouts on Monday?"

"From 6 o'clock on I was alone at home. Had a couple Buds, warmed-up a frozen DiGiorno, and watched *Ice Road Truckers*. That's the one perk of being separated; I'm king of the remote."

As Kraft spoke, he pressed his index fingernail into his thumb with such pressure it had drawn blood. The pain distracted him, keeping tears at bay.

"There's no one that can corroborate that?"

"I guess I should've gone with delivery, not DiGiorno."

"That's a good one, Mr. Kraft." Capelli took pity and offered a few forced chuckles.

"Actually, my neighbor Bill Hayes popped by for a few minutes. Didn't stay long enough for a cold one, but came to check in. He's the ambulance chaser of realtors; buys up properties cheap from old ladies who are moving into assisted care and don't know better. Flips 'em and makes a killing. Pretty sure he was trying to get a read on my mental state; guy's been waitin' for me to off myself and scoop up the property. Damn vulture. I've thought about doing the deed once or twice but don't want him to have the satisfaction."

"What time was this?"

"Oh, let me think... I'm not sure what time exactly but it was between *Deadliest Catch* and *Ice Road Truckers*. His visit made me miss the last few minutes of *Catch* and first few of *Road Truckers*. I hate that; it's not the same when you miss the beginning."

Capelli made a note of Bill Hayes' name and a reminder to find an old TV Guide for the night of the murder. She gave a nod to her partner and they stood simultaneously, Ford readjusting his paisley tie.

"Mr. Kraft, we appreciate your time today. I need to ask you to remain in town, until we check your alibi."

"You really think I did this? I mean, I'm glad the guy got his due but I'm no killer."

"We're pursuing every lead. If you're innocent, you have nothing to worry about."

Ten minutes later, Ford was guiding the unmarked car back on Queens Boulevard, licking his chops.

"What's your take on this guy?" Capelli asked between bites of the turkey and rye she'd packed. Ford hadn't planned ahead and was driving in search for the nearest McDonald's to no avail.

"Call me crazy but I kinda like him. Though he certainly has motive if he really believes Thorpe was at fault for his son's lack of treatment."

"Yeah, and the divorce papers arriving days before the murder could certainly be a trigger."

Ford gave up on finding a drive-through and grabbed the second half of Capelli's sandwich.

"Alright, asshole. Because of that you get to track down Bill Hayes, our dodgy realtor."

16

Doctors Without Borders Camp
Jowhar, Somalia

Luc Turner was beside himself with frustration. He paced back and forth with such ferocity the walls shook, as if mimicking his anger. The shattered glass from an empty pilsner was scattered about the entryway floor, a victim of his irritation with the pitfalls of third-world communications. Today of all days, his cell phone and internet capabilities were nil. He'd spent the previous hour searching for the backup satellite phone they kept hidden in a safe place – such devices were a hot commodity for local rebels. Turner learned that the hard way after having phones confiscated on two consecutive trips to Mogadishu – at gunpoint, no less. Of course, now he'd forgotten where this 'safe place' was.

Finally, his memory recalled a clue – Turner flipped open a dilapidated cigar box, dug through Jean-Pierre's stash of Lion bars, a European chocolate-wafer that the hefty African seemed to consume in bulk – and pulled out the phone. He quickly dialed the Kenya camp and wolfed down a Lion as he waited for a connection. As he wiped his chocolaty fingers, a female voice with an indeterminate accent answered. Turner didn't bother with pleasantries.

"I need to speak with Dr. Abrams immediately."

"Who is –"

"IMMEDIATELY!"

"I'm sorry, sir, that's not possible. Dr. Abrams is in the field for the next three days."

Her terse tone suggested she was none-too-pleased with Turner's abruptness.

"Is there anyone else who can give me a status on the samples from Jowhar?"

"Samples from Jowhar... are you sure we ha... "

"Yes, you have samples from Jowhar. They should've reached the lab two days ago!"

Any other day, Turner would have used his gravelly voice and a few witty lines to win the woman over, but he was in no mood for banter at this particular moment.

"Hold on a minute."

He heard a static-y clunk that suggested she'd put the phone down. *Oh Christ, make it quick,* Turner thought to himself as he resumed his pacing ritual across the miniscule trailer.

"Sir, I'm sorry, you never gave me your name. Where are you calling from?"

"Dr. Luc Turner in Jowhar, Somalia. I've got a disease outbreak on my hands and no medication to stop it. Dr. Abrams retrieved blood and sputum samples from my lab three days ago for analysis. Analysis that I desperately need in order to get the proper antibiotics here as soon as possible. Two people have died in the last twenty-four hours and this conversation is becoming a waste of time. I'm sorry to sound like an asshole but I'm in a bit of a desperate situation here."

"Okay, Dr. Turner. I paged the lab and they received the samples only yesterday. They began analysis on them this morning and I will personally keep an eye on their progress for you. Okay?"

"Okay, thank you Ms…"

"Katrine Johansson."

"Thank you, Katrine. Please inform me the moment you have results."

Turner exited his shack-like residence feeling completely helpless. Together, with Jean-Pierre and his wife – Noelle – he'd buried two elderly women this morning in sandy, wretched graves who'd succumbed to the illness. Jean-Pierre recited a prayer for the departed, his deep accented voice a haunting reminder of life's frailty in the cool early stillness.

The progression of the disease was fast and inconsistent. Initially, the patients had presented with similar symptoms that were now inexplicably growing increasingly varied. What began as a respiratory illness was mutating into something irreducible to a category in a medical encyclopedia. Some patients complained of joint pains so severe they could no longer walk. Others had blood in their urine and a few had begun developing measles-type rashes.

Pulling a doctor's mask over his thick, now matted hair, he entered quarantine tent A, dreading what he'd find. Cots and sleeping bags had been on short supply when the camp was relatively healthy. Now, about a third of the patients were forced to lie directly on the dirt floor, a few lucky enough to receive a light blanket. He cursed the violent rebels who raided the camps, trucks, and airplanes – they were the reason Jowhar had received only an eighth of their normal supply levels during the previous three months.

Turner spotted Jean-Pierre sitting alongside Amaka's cot, immediately fearing the worst as a jolt of panic shot through his body. Peering over his friend's shoulder, he saw Amaka was sleeping – not peacefully – but she was alive.

"Her fever is nearing 102. It's bad Luc; I don't know if she'll make it through the night."

17

Memorial Cemetery of St. John's Episcopal Church
Laurel Hollow, New York

"**I** hate the burial beat. It seems so invasive," Capelli muttered, her eyes fixed beyond the steady whoosh of the windshield wipers.

"So is a colonoscopy. But you gotta do it now and then."

Ford was washing down his fried egg and cheese wrap with lukewarm deli coffee. He was pissed at Capelli. She'd insisted that he order a wrap — swore up and down that it'd be just as good as his usual butter croissant. Of course, she'd been wrong and now he was sitting in a car waiting for Old Man Thorpe to go six feet under with a shitty breakfast as consolation. When he wanted to measure 34-24-34, he'd listen to her. Till then, he'd do breakfast his way.

"How's the wrap?" Capelli regretted asking immediately. She dug for something to say before Ford exploded. "Who knows, maybe our killer will walk over and confess – help us get this thing wrapped up." She nearly smacked herself for using "wrap" again.

"So far I see a bunch of guys who eat too much red meat and waste a lot of money on tailored Italian suits."

"How do you know they're Italian? Mr. buy-one-get-the-second-half-off at Joseph A. Bank."

Capelli polished off her lemon yogurt and disposed of it in a plastic deli bag. She hadn't been laid in months and was attending a stranger's burial – Ford had no right to monopolize the bitching.

"It's not bad here – all things considered. Those oaks gotta be pre-revolutionary war. I think I'll tell Caroline I'd like to be buried here."

"You want to be buried? How can you not prefer cremation after the exhumations you've seen? The last thing I want is to slowly decay into something suited for a horror flick."

"That's not for me. Heard a lot of those ovens get filled with three guys at a time to speed things up. Knowing my luck I'd be mixed-in with some gang banger."

"Yeah, well, when you're dead, you're dead." Capelli grumbled.

"If that's so, why do you care if you decay in the grave?"

Capelli sipped her coffee – Ford had a point.

"If this is really all there is –"

"– then why are we staking out another man's funeral?" Ford finished her thought.

"Yeah."

"Cause I can't be quarterback for the New York Giants. I figured that out when I got cut during JV tryouts in high school. That day all my life was ever gonna be was Plan B."

Capelli took Ford in, all seriousness.

"Are you for real?"

"No," Ford grinned, but it was the kind of grin a child gives his mother when she asks if someone got in trouble at school.

"Hey, is Vance texting at his father's burial?"

Capelli dug around the back seat, relocating the Sports Authority bags belonging to Ford. He'd determined Brian didn't like the type of ball they were using, so he bought out the sporting goods store of child-friendly balls – determined to find one his son would try to catch. She finally located the binoculars she was looking for.

"Here. Let me know what you see. And you should return those balls for a violin."

Ford scanned the burial attendees, looking for any suspicious behavior. They'd parked at a safe enough distance so as not to disrupt the proceedings, but close enough to keep an eye out for anything out of the ordinary. They'd also come as protection. If John Kraft was the killer it wasn't beyond the realm of possibility that he'd come after the Polaris execs that were in attendance. Ford let out an impressed whistle.

"This guy must think he's Jay-Z."

"I doubt that."

"Take a look at his phone. Looks like a Vertu. Those puppies start around eight grand a pop – come with a concierge and everything. I guess Polaris stocks are on the upswing."

"That's ridiculous. Eight grand?"

"Minimum."

Capelli grabbed the binoculars; this pompous heir-to-Polaris was getting under her skin. She watched the Polaris scion manipulate a gold-plated cell phone while his other hand balanced an ivory-tusked umbrella handle.

"Doesn't look much better than my Blackberry. Hang on... he's got two phones. He put the Virtue

75

whatchamacallit away and is now on some cheap Nokia. Looks like a GoPhone."

"Maybe he's got a mistress? Using it for privacy purposes?"

"Yeah, well, he's not married and I doubt he's cheating on that leggy blonde who's been pawing all over him."

"I certainly wouldn't."

"Use your other brain and start identifying some of these attendees. I printed photos of the overseas Polaris executives. Start with them."

The remaining twenty minutes of burial proceedings allowed Capelli and Ford ample time to identify the executives from Polaris offices in Prague, London, and Buenos Aires. Those from Cape Town, Hong Kong, and Sydney had not made the trip. The remaining guests were close family and friends passing Kleenex amongst one another, mourning the loss of a great entrepreneur, philanthropist, and friend. Capelli kept her peripheral awareness on high-alert, expecting John Kraft to appear – but so far, he had stayed away.

It wasn't until the coffin made its descent into earth – and Capelli was taking pleasure watching the willowy blonde's four-inch Laboutin heels sink into the still-damp grass – that Ford noticed something awry. As the majority of mourners departed for their cars, Thorpe pulled aside the man they'd identified as President of Polaris' Eastern

European operations, based in Prague. The two were exchanging terse words, keeping their yells to a whisper but unable to hide disagreement. It was a brief encounter, but passionate enough for Thorpe to continuously jab his index finger into the other man's chest, an apparent effort to drive his point home. Capelli moved the binoculars from the blonde to the two men. She attempted lip-reading but her angle was not suited to see either man clearly.

"What's up with Vance? A little tasteless getting in argument when the dirt's still fresh on his father's coffin."

"Money can't buy class, Capelli."

"Read the bio on this guy from Prague."

Ford fumbled with the FBI folder, and located the appropriate dossier only after spilling the file's contents, scattering everything on the passenger side floor. Ignoring Capelli's 'what's your problem?' eye-roll, he summarized the content.

"Okay. Says here this is Martin Warren. He's been running the Prague operation since its inception five years ago. He's American, with a Czech wife. Looks like he and the late Mr. Thorpe were quite close. They attended Stanford together and Thorpe hired him on as second-in-command once Polaris went public. Warren spent many years in New York but made the move to Prague to appease his wife. He's fluent in Czech, French, and English. The couple has a son studying at the Sorbonne. No criminal record for any of the family members."

They watched as Warren spun on his heel, turning his back to Vance and leaving a large divot in the damp earth – the former apparently had heard enough and strode toward a waiting town car, his face twisted in disgust as though he'd sipped rotten milk. The young Thorpe seemed uncharacteristically flustered, stamping his foot like a petulant child who didn't like hearing 'no.' He pulled the cheap Nokia from his pocket and dialed.

"I'd sure like to know who he's calling."

18

NYPD Sixth Precinct
West Village, New York

The cocky bravado that twenty-six year-old Juan Perez had displayed during his arrest was now long-gone. He sat in a poorly-lit interrogation room at the West 10th street precinct, bouncing his knees up and down, eyes darting back-and-forth like a youngster in time-out. The cops were icing him in the small, unwelcoming room. It was a tactic Tony Pepperidge used with all his arrests. The perps sat there fidgeting, worrying about what the cops did and didn't know and what kind of time they were facing. By the time Detective Pepperidge came in the room an hour later they practically sobbed out a confession – sometimes, anyway. If that didn't happen it was at least enough time to go down the block to White Horse Tavern and catch a few innings of the Mets game.

Pepperidge walked in, smelling of Heineken, and peered in the one-way mirror. The kid looked ready to shit himself.

Perez jumped at the sound of the large, steel door crashing open. He'd been leaning back, away from the door and the pot-bellied officer as far as physically possible.

"So, Mr. Perez, your file tells me this isn't your first time in the cooler. Why are you sweating like a virgin?"

"Look man, I ain't done nothin'. You've got the wrong guy."

"Yeah. I always get the wrong guy. Funny how the evidence always matches with the wrong guy. What was your relationship with Rosemary Valdez?"

"Who? I don't know no Rosemary."

"Then why do we have witnesses who saw you flee her apartment building at the corner of East-Sixth and Avenue A last Monday night?"

"I don't know. People see all kinds of shit. My uncle keeps seeing Jesus in his cereal. That ain't my problem. Besides, I was in Brooklyn Monday night. I can't afford any Manhattan apartment."

"When were you in her apartment?"

"I told ya, I don't know no Rosemary —" Pepperidge cut him off.

"We found fingerprints all over the entry hall that match yours. You see, that's the thing about previous arrests. Those prints are forever in the system – so either you were there or your fingers are going to jail without you."

Perez had fucked up – bad. He knew the job smelled funny the moment he took it. Why would a white guy ask a pot-dealer to beat up an old woman? The stranger had insisted he cop to the crime if caught, that the information he'd given Perez would ensure his freedom. Still, confessing to a beating seemed counter-intuitive to his natural instincts. For now, he'd play the lawyer card.

"Listen, man. This is feelin' like a set-up. I want my public defender before you ask any more questions, accusin' me of shit I ain't done."

"Get him a cheap Matlock, Bobby," Pepperidge muttered to the officer on duty as he huffed out the door.

Three hours later, Ford and Capelli entered the precinct, recoiling at the stench of a homeless man who'd been arrested for squatting on Christopher Street. Apparently his worn-out corduroys had doubled as a urinal. The whole precinct knew the history of Capelli and Pepperidge and now curious stares followed the striking FBI agent as she made her way toward interrogation. They entered the viewing room, Capelli clenching a fist should Tony start with his notorious back-handed compliments.

"Christ, Tony, you eat a small child?"

So much for taking the high-road, Capelli thought to herself – but, fact was, Pepperidge had gained a solid thirty pounds since their last encounter.

"Well, if it isn't the feds. Glad we could do your work for you."

"We'll see about that. Odds are you're wasting my time."

"I'm shocked it didn't last between you two." Ford broke in, then glanced into the holding room. "I'm guessing that's our boy and his rent-a-lawyer."

"You must be a profiler." Pepperidge grumbled.

Sitting next to Perez was a baby-faced towhead that looked like he'd picked up his law degree on the drive to the precinct. According to Pepperidge, this was O'Donaghy's first client and so far it seemed he couldn't tell his head from his ass.

"Catch 'em up to speed, Bobby," Pepperidge sighed to the officer. "She never listened to what I said anyway."

Bobby Delgado, fresh out of the academy, took his job a bit too seriously, the way all new hires do.

"Our friend, Juan, admits to beating Rosemary Valdez last Monday night. Apparently he didn't intend to kill her and, until this afternoon, didn't know he was a murderer. Anyway, he started rambling about being hired to beat her. Since they handed the juicy Thorpe case over to you I thought you may want to speak to him, see if there's anything relevant to your investigation."

"And the lawyer is letting him talk?"

"Kid insists on it, seems to think honesty will get him out of this. I think the lawyer is happy to sit there swimming in his cheap suit and keep quiet."

Perez and O'Donaghy sat up in unison as Capelli and Ford entered interrogation. The room was cold, sterile, and smelled of vomit and evergreen air-freshener. The temperature was more suited to preserving dead bodies in a morgue than to the comfort of the living. Either the heater was on the fritz or the arctic chill was a component of Pepperidge's interrogation stagecraft. The agents each took a seat on the hard metal chairs and made a show of rifling through papers, giving Perez a moment to stop shaking.

"So, Mr. Perez, you get off beating old ladies?" Ford started.

"That's uncalled for," O'Donaghy tried sounding confident.

"What were you expecting? Tea and crumpets?" Ford barked.

The lawyer swallowed hard, not sure which strategy to take.

"It's okay. I already told the detective guy I was hired. I felt bad about it, I really did. But it was twenty g's."

"Hold on." Capelli broke in. "You're saying someone paid you twenty-thousand dollars to kill Ms. Valdez?"

"Not to kill her, just beat her up. Said he wanted her to bleed a lot. If I'd have known she was gonna die I'd have never done it, I swear."

"That's something you can think about as you rot away on Rikers," Ford fumed.

Perez tried to force resolve into his twitching cheeks, then just dropped his face into his hands and started sobbing.

Capelli struggled getting a read on the alleged killer sitting before her. He certainly didn't appear angry or violent, just scared shitless. On the other hand, he admitted beating the old woman which didn't bode well for his character.

"Mr. Perez," she said, offering him a Kleenex. "Why don't you walk us through your version of the events, okay?"

"Okay, but you gotta call me Juan. This whole "Mr. Perez" thing is making me nervous."

That's not the only thing that should be making you nervous, idiot. Capelli kept her thoughts to herself and stared at Perez until he took the hint and started talking.

"Okay, last Sunday I was working on Avenue A..."

"Dealing?"

"Yeah, dealing, okay?"

"Simmer down, cowboy," Ford interjected. "Just trying to get the facts."

"Okay, so I'm *dealing* and this guy approaches me, asks if I can do a job for him. I listened to what he had to say and was ready to turn him down. I'm not big on violence. But then he guaranteed twenty g's and I couldn't say no. I've got a little brother who needs to eat and I've been saving up for a set of wheels... Anyway, all I had to do was go to this lady's place on Monday night, whack her a few times with a baseball bat and leave."

"Juan, I really think we should –" O'Donaghy tried to shut up his client, but Capelli cut the lawyer off.

"You were never told to kill her?"

"No way! And I didn't beat her enough to kill her, either! Maybe someone came in after me..."

"I don't think so, Mr. Perez. The woman you beat was taking Coumadin; it's a prescription that thins the blood, meaning it couldn't clot fast enough so she bled out and died from the beating. It's a terrible way to go."

Perez's face paled. The blood of that woman was on his hands and he'd rot in prison because of it.

"C'mon, yo – you gotta let me cut some deal. I can't spend my life in jail!"

Capelli stood up, turning her back to Juan. She figured it was her chance to play hardball. His meltdown began, the sobs coming faster and faster as his body convulsed in fear.

"You can tell us who hired you, for starters. The more you help up us, the more you help yourself – your cooperation will be noted during the trial."

"Noted with gusto?" O'Donaghy pushed back.

"The more he talks the more we'll note it." Ford responded.

The lawyer nodded at Perez, who tried to compose himself, wiping the tears on his sleeve.

"Okay. Like I said, the guy came up to me on Avenue A. He was a little shorter than I am, maybe five-eleven. He just looked like an average dude, brown hair, brown eyes, maybe forty or a little younger. Definitely older than me though."

"That's describes about a quarter of New Yorkers. Was there anything else distinctive about the man? Did he have an accent? Maybe a limp?"

"Nah, nothing like that. Although... he did smell funny."

"That's good, what did he smell like?"

"Like grease maybe, or car oil."

The agents gave each other a knowing look. Ford immediately left the room to coordinate a line-up with the NYPD. If Perez could ID John Kraft, the grieving father would have a lot of explaining to do.

19

**Doctors Without Borders Camp
Jowhar, Somalia**

Amaka wrapped her small, thin fingers around the Lion bar Turner had snagged from Jean-Pierre's cigar box. She'd not eaten for 48 hours, her temperature was a steady 103 degrees, and severe dehydration had set-in now that the supply of IV fluids had been depleted. Turner hoped the chocolate would spark a little appetite but she simply clutched the bar without taking a bite, looking at him with wide eyes that betrayed great pain despite her brave façade.

Turner had grown increasingly desperate as the yet-undetermined illness wreaked havoc on the camp. The Kenya lab was short-staffed and not making any progress towards identifying the strain of disease. Dr. Abrams hadn't stayed nearby to ensure a more rapid analysis, and while Turner told himself his feelings were irrational, that she couldn't possibly forego her own responsibilities for the sake of his, it still pissed him off.

Their last dinner together didn't help. Over a bottle of South African Shiraz he'd been saving and his old standby – a Moroccan spiced-chicken recipe – they reflected on the past until her throaty laugh and mischievous green eyes drew him into the inevitable. As they clawed the clothes off one another, Turner desperately tried to find a connection with Eva, but for her it was all physical. They feverishly, almost angrily, made love against the kitchen counter, pulling and scratching as if wanting to hurt the other.

After the encounter, Eva immediately dressed; mentioning as she fixed her disheveled hair that she was involved with a colleague in Kenya. She requested Turner not mention anything about the evening should it ever come up. A quick kiss on the cheek was her goodbye as she grabbed her knapsack and left into the blowing dirt, without so much as a backwards glance.

The experience left him confused, even angry – frustrated that he'd allow himself to dream that the past wasn't just that. He knew better, of course, but he'd been more-or-less celibate since arriving in Somalia and the welcome sensation of a woman's touch tapped into deeper needs he'd thought were ignored too long. Now, holding Amaka's hand as she struggled to stay alive, he cursed himself for being ridiculous. This was his priority now.

He felt a light tap on his shoulder and heard Noelle's soft whisper through her medical mask.

"Luc, Jean-Pierre would like to speak with you outside the tent."

"Thanks Noelle, I'll be out in a minute."

He opened the end of the Lion bar so Amaka wouldn't struggle with the plastic wrapping should her appetite return.

Jean-Pierre's hulking figure waited outside the quarantine tent, sitting on a child-sized wooden stool that strained under his mass. Two more people – a husband and wife – had passed on during the night and the dirt from their graves still covered his tattered blue scrubs. The exhaustion caked over his face displayed a look of resignation – the situation was helpless.

"Noelle said you wanted to see me? If it's about the Lion bar…"

Turner's attempt at lightheartedness was cut short by Jean-Pierre's hoarse baritone.

"Luc, this whole camp will die if we don't receive antibiotics soon. I say we improvise, run some of our own tests with what we have – at least to rule some diseases out. Let's try the Mantoux test."

"Mantoux won't tell us much. This is spreading too fast to be TB. Plus, the symptoms are all over the map."

"I can't explain the rapid spread, but the initial respiratory symptoms are emblematic of TB. It's a long shot, but what else can we do? Just watch these people die?"

Turner glanced at the graveyard growing over the savannah. He masked his eyes, tried to think, and in the darkness of his mind he saw Eva in last night's moonlight. He was exhausted, out of answers, and doubt was creeping through the cracks. He looked back to Jean-Pierre and nodded.

An hour later they'd selected twenty patients of varying ages that were displaying a range of symptoms, hoping to get as broad a population sample as possible. One by one, Turner delicately injected the PPD tuberculin between the dermal layers on their forearms. Some flinched at the needle prick, but most were too weak for a response. If the injection site developed a hard, raised area, they'd have to treat the most rampant Tuberculosis outbreak in the camp to date.

20

K&R Mechanics
Queens, New York

"So, you never took your ex's last name? I mean, Pepperidge – that's a little tough unless you're making a mint selling Milano cookies."

"Not that it matters, but no. Always stuck to Capelli, always will. Jesus! That's the exit."

Kate yanked the wheel, cutting dangerously close to a mid-90's Jeep Cherokee in order to make the exit for Union Turnpike.

"Damn! We're not filming Transporter 4 here, Capelli!"

"Sorry, sorry. You distracted me with the talk of marriage past."

"Yeah, well, he seems like a decent guy if you don't mind assholes. Anyway, let's make this as quick as possible – the in-laws are coming for dinner and every time I show up late they use it as an excuse to lobby for a change in my career."

The agents entered the waiting area to find Ronnie resting at the desk. His fat cheek was splayed like a pancake under the weight of his head, a slight trickle of drool trickling from his mouth to the countertop.

"Ronnie!"

Ford slammed his hand on the desk. The chubby receptionist leapt in a panic, wiping his spit-covered cheek in embarrassment at the sight of Capelli.

"Hey, Ronnie. Sorry about Agent Ford, he still hasn't finished sensitivity training. Is Mr. Kraft still here?"

She'd opted not to call-ahead – in her experience people had a tendency to disappear when they were asked to come in for a line-up.

"Um… he actually isn't. He didn't come in for work today. Called around ten and said he'd be out for the rest of the week."

"Did he mention where he'd be? Or give any reason for his absence?"

"Nope, nothin'. Really put us in a tight spot. We were short-staffed to begin with."

"Yeah, I can see you're having to pull double-duty."

Capelli let herself into the garage area, deciding a quick look-around wouldn't hurt on the chance Ronnie was covering for his manager.

The garage was relatively quiet. There was a lanky, dark-haired man munching a sandwich while listening to Mike Francesca's radio sports-talk show, taking obvious pleasure in the fact his manager hadn't shown for work. Across the garage a pair of feet with mismatched socks protruded from underneath an old Ford Taurus that didn't look worth the cost of repair. Capelli strolled over and took a peek under the car, hoping she'd see her suspect changing the brakes. Instead, the toothless grin of an old man – long-past retirement age – welcomed her curiosity. No John Kraft.

21

Kraft Residence
Bayside, New York

"Hey Kraft! Open-up!"

Ford rapped on Kraft's front door, the cracked doorframe shuddering with each successive impact of his fist.

"Stay here," Capelli sighed. "I'll check the back."

She jogged around to the rear of the house, keeping her body close to the cheap vinyl siding and her hand on the Glock strapped to her hip. As she passed the kitchen window, a blur in her peripheral vision froze her. Doubling back, she peered through the glass, her eyes adjusting to the darkness inside. The narrow home was small with two levels and a basement. The main floor was a modestly-furnished kitchen and dining area. It was tidy for a man's kitchen, with floral wallpaper and diamond-patterned linoleum that would have overwhelmed Laura Ashley. Capelli guessed his estranged wife had been in charge of the interior decorating. Along the back wall, a staircase connected the upper-floor to the kitchen and continued down into the basement. Hanging from the kitchen railing she saw what had caught her eye – a thick, brown rope that dropped into the basement stairwell. Her view of the rope's end was blocked, but she feared the worst.

"I think he hung himself!" Capelli shouted, running back to the front door.

Ford fired two shots into the door lock, easily breaking open the shoddy dead bolt. They carefully checked the main level, Glocks cocked.

Capelli descended the long basement staircase, Ford just behind her. She felt blindly for the light switch – fingers stumbling into the dangling rope, ready to feel the cold and bloated flesh of John Kraft. Instead, she made out the rough texture of a thick rope tied into an empty noose. Both agents sighed with the realization this wasn't a crime scene. The calming sensation lasted only minutes as they heard footsteps on the gaudy linoleum above.

"Hey, Kraft! You around? Tried to call earlier, just wanted to see how things were for you."

Capelli could have sworn Joe Pesci was their intruder – his voice a dead-ringer for the actor's. The agents ducked at the stairwell's base, patiently waiting for the plodding footsteps to finish making their way down. Just as the visitor realized he was standing before a noose, Capelli had her glock leveled point-blank to the man's nose while Ford cuffed the squidgy balding man.

"What the hell is all this?!"

"I'm Agent Capelli, this is Agent Ford – FBI. Who the hell are you?"

"I'm John's neighbor, Billy Hayes. Just came by to see how he's doin', maybe grab a cold one."

"The realtor?"

A wide grin spread across the man's face, giddy that she'd recognized him.

"You saw my billboard?"

"No, I didn't see your billboard. John mentioned you were after his house."

"Oh." The man went silent, then, "Hey, Tex, how 'bout you get this jewelry offa me."

Ford grunted but Capelli nodded to set the realtor free, then asked, "Mr. Hayes, do you have any idea where Mr. Kraft may be?"

"I don't know, thought he'd be here. Saw the door open and came to say hi. Is he in trouble? Did he steal somethin'?"

"No, we just need to talk to him."

"Yeah, well... hope ya find him. I've got a date tonight with a school teacher, so I gotta run and clean-up. Always had this fantasy about —"

"Listen, Romeo, why don't you try a little harder." Ford growled, taking a threatening step toward Billy.

"Guy doesn't travel or anything. Only thing I can think is he went to visit his mom. She's got a place in Jersey. Willingboro, I think."

"Alright, thanks. And don't mention this," Capelli gestured to the noose, "to your neighbors."

"Yeah, you got it. Here's my card if you need a home appraisal or realtor. Or a date."

"Thanks, but I rent."

22

Prague, Czech Republic

Frustrated, the albino anxiously paced the quay along the Vltava River as he awaited word from his increasingly feckless colleague. There was an eerie stillness in the dark waters, lapping against the banks only when a tourist boat passed.

The albino kept watch over his hit. His soon-to-be victim was seated on a bench in Kampa Park, one of Prague's more peaceful locales. Most visitors departed at sundown as the air turned from comfortable to cool; now only a few drunks and young lovers remained.

From where he stood the pale man had a clear view of his target between two old stone buildings. To his right, a beer hall smelled of sausages and pretzels, with sounds of clanking glasses and laughter emanating from the windows. The opposite structure held a tourist shop that specialized in simple watercolors of the Charles Bridge and stocked a vast array of Kafka and Neruda novels. The shop had closed an hour prior but an older saleslady remained to take inventory of the cheap trinkets and literature. Mr. A watched as the plump grandmother moved about, a blue sweater-dress straining against her large frame as she bent over to assess the quantity of maps on a low shelf. She made him uneasy, though he couldn't determine why.

An untraceable phone vibrated in the pocket of his tight, black cargo pants. The long awaited text had finally arrived. It simply stated: *green.*

Fifteen minutes later, his mark was on the move, finally coming to the conclusion it was too dark to continue reading Hemingway's short stories. Rounding a narrow alley that led toward a side-entrance to the Charles Bridge, the men began moving in perfect synchronicity, each footfall of the killer's landing in harmony with that of his mark.

The small hairs stood at attention on Martin Warren's neck. He'd become increasingly paranoid since the death of his friend and colleague Edward Thorpe. Tonight he was especially on edge, sensing he was the next to go.

There was a faint rustling off the path to his left. A feral cat had leapt from a tree into a crunchy bed of leaves, and Warren sighed in relief when he saw the furry paws among the ivy. Warren dried his clammy palms on his tailored Italian pants and cursed himself for being such a spook. The paranoid part of him heard what sounded like a footstep a few yards back but he shook the worry off.

Twenty yards from the bridge, his edginess decreased as he saw the pedestrian traffic along the twenty-four hour tourist trap. He quickened pace, eager to be just another face in the crowd.

The albino kept in step along the shadows by the bridge, pulse slowing, his breaths deep now, a veteran in game time. Fifteen feet behind Warren. Twelve. Ten...

The old stone staircase leading up to the bridge was free of witnesses. The only clear view was from the park, which by now was nearly empty aside from a few drunks. The tourists strolling along the Charles Bridge had no visual of the stairway – most of them too deeply in awe of Prague's romantic cityscape to notice anything out of the ordinary.

Warren hesitated, as most do, before taking the first step onto the uneven stone. At that moment the albino took two massive, leaping strides, drawing even. As their shoulders grazed, the albino looked into Warren's eyes, distracting him from the needle prick to his thigh.

"*Promiňte mi pane,*" the albino excused himself, "*hezký večer.*"

As his killer strode passed him, the athletic figure taking the steps three at a time, Warren laughed to himself. If he'd have seen that sinister looking man in the park, with the translucent eyes and black trench he'd have nearly wet himself. It was time for a drink.

By the time he was on the bridge, Warren understood his fate. The pinch to his thigh was not a simple accident – he'd been murdered, just like Thorpe. His breathing went from rapid to strained, contradictory sensations running through his body as it struggled to process the foreign substance. Logic told him this was death, but his mind couldn't fully process the reality. He thought of his wife and the vacation they'd planned for the south of France. Inexplicably, he was momentarily looking forward to the trip, as if he'd be taking it. He remembered Edward and the secret they'd carry to their graves, and of the innocent lives that were soon to be lost.

Martin Warren stumbled aimlessly across the bridge, bystanders parting en masse as if he posed an imminent threat. Finally, he collapsed in a heap of convulsions.

23

Sixth Police Precinct
West Village, New York

White poster board shook nervously in the hands of John Kraft. He couldn't help but wonder how his life had devolved so quickly, his fate now resting on the number three – his line-up number. Two men stood to his left, three to his right. A sour stench of stale alcohol penetrated the air, suggesting more than a few of his fellow linemen were pulled from the drunk-tank. He'd never considered himself an overtly good-looking man, though he wasn't bad looking either. But now he realized just how damn average he was – each man in the room stood within a half inch of his height with the same dull-brown hair and weight around one-eighty, some carrying a little more around the waist than others making them closer to one-ninety. The resemblance was uncanny.

"Number three quit lookin' around. Face forward for identification." Capelli barked.

She was exhausted. The drive to Willingboro and back was not how she'd imagined spending the prior evening. Her plan to open a bottle of Match Book Cabernet – her favorite because it was just expensive enough to not brand her a cheap-skate – get gloriously tipsy, and watch an *NCIS* marathon had been shot to shit when John Kraft went on the lam. Ford had driven, forcing his right-wing radio shows on her for the duration of the trip.

Kraft had come along willingly, claiming he hadn't been trying to evade the cops. Apparently, he'd had a meltdown at the realization he was near suicide and drove off to his mother's before he could do anything irreversible.

"Turn to the right, please."

The men in the line-up turned to their right, except number four who was sweating a bottle of Jaeger and having directional difficulties. Once he got himself straightened out, they were asked to face the wall, and then back to the front.

"Mr. Perez, can you identify the man who hired you to kill – sorry, beat up, Ms. Valdez?"

Perez hardly looked at the men, fidgeting nervously as he considered the situation.

"No, ma'am. He's not there."

"You sure about that? All these guys fit the description you provided."

"He ain't there," Perez said without taking another look.

Capelli used the intercom to alert the officer running the line-up.

"Okay Jerry, you can take 'em back."

Capelli pulled a metal chair in front of Perez; the grating of its legs against the linoleum caused the room's occupants to grimace at the nails-on-chalkboard sound. She sat in front of him, elbows on her knees, chin resting on her hands, and forced herself to speak gently.

"What's going on here, Juan? I'm getting the funny feeling you're withholding information."

"No, ma'am. I've told you what I know."

"Listen, since you haven't been able to identify the man who hired you, the only person that'll be held accountable for the murder of Ms. Valdez is yourself. The prosecutor will accuse you of being the sole person responsible for the crime, suggesting you lied about being hired to try and lessen your sentence. Frankly, it'll work unless you can identify this man. So be straight up with me here, have you been lying to us?"

Perez was feeling pretty damn dumb. He considered himself a smooth kid, able to outsmart the other dealers and neighborhood thugs, stealing their clients and taking over the best street corners. But the FBI was out of his league. He'd murdered a woman and they knew it – there were no aces left to play.

"The guy that hired me wore a mask. Looked like he had a wig too. He told me exactly what to say if I was questioned by anyone, gave me the features and descriptions to rattle off. Said nobody would actually arrest me for anything; guess he was wrong about that."

"A mask?"

"Yeah, it was weird. Didn't look like a mask until he was real close. Musta been custom made for his face or somethin', just kinda distorted it. The wig, or his hair if it was really his, was black, and he wore a long tan coat. The coat was hairy, like animal fur but not the shaggy kind rich old hags on the upper-east wear to Barney's."

Capelli jotted the description with her trusty Bic, thinking how utterly useless this description was.

"Anything else? A limp, an accent? Did he smell like car oil or did he tell you to say that?"

"Told me to say that. Smelled like cologne. Wasn't Cool Water though. That's the only one I know 'cause I wear it around my girl."

"That's nice. Don't wear it in prison. Oh, and you may want to request a change of lawyer." Capelli looked pointedly at O'Donaghy who'd yet to speak up.

The agents left the 6th precinct, bypassing Pepperidge's desk to avoid the inevitable parting shot. They headed to Hudson Street and ducked into Bayard's Ale House for a quick lunch and a pint, Capelli ordering a club sandwich and Ford a plate of loaded nachos. Capelli didn't bother suggesting he switch to a salad.

She stared out the large windows towards the precinct where Perez was being held, tuning out Walt Frazier's colorful commentary of the Knicks game in the background.

"What's on your mind, Kate?"

"Just trying to piece all this together, wishing we had a solid suspect for the Thorpe murder."

"You mean both murders. They're connected. It's obvious."

"So, the killer knew the maid was a potential witness and planned the murder in advance to prevent her from talking?"

"Maybe the killer knew Rosemary personally or had watched the Thorpe residence and followed her home at some point. Otherwise, how would he know where to send the little punk Juan? And why did he just hire him to beat her up?"

"Maybe he knew she was on Coumadin and that she'd bleed so extensively from her wounds they'd be fatal."

"Maybe. Seems like a stretch, though. The Thorpe kill was precise, perfect. No evidence or witnesses, at least not living. Why so sloppy with Valdez?"

"Think about it. The scene was messy, but not the plan itself. Juan has no idea who this guy is and if he didn't know Valdez and he's never been in the apartment, nothing will link him to the murder. If he is a relative or acquaintance, unless we find some motive, there'd be every reason for his prints to be in the home and easy to argue reasonable doubt in front of a jury."

"I don't care if the NYPD has this case. Let's dig a little deeper into Valdez's background. Who knows, maybe Thorpe was killed by an acquaintance of his maid."

24

Doctors Without Borders Camp
Jowhar, Somalia

"I don't believe this… it's medically impossible." Turner was peering over Jean-Pierre's shoulder as he measured the hardened, raised area surrounding the PPD injection on Amaka's forearm.

"Believe it. The site induration is twelve millimeters – Amaka is infected."

The doctors had measured five of the twenty patients tested for tuberculosis. The raised areas – indurations – had all measured between ten and fifteen millimeters: confirmation for TB. The Mantoux Test had it faults – occasionally throwing a false positive – but it was unlikely for all five cases to show inaccurate readings. Odds were they had a TB epidemic on their hands.

"Christ. I've never seen it spread this fast. Let's check the others we tested and go from there."

An hour later they'd determined all twenty of the test patients were infected with the deadly disease – probably the whole camp for that matter. A spread this rampant and severe was unlike anything either doctor had seen – treatments had to begin immediately or there would be scores more graves to dig.

Though tuberculosis was treatable – aside from extremely severe cases – it required at least six months of injections and pills in order for a patient to be cured. That was a tall order for an under-funded camp in Somalia. Even if they received the necessary amount of antidote it would be difficult to convince the sick to return for their continuing treatments once the severe symptoms began to subside. The fact they'd become gravely ill at the camp would not make it any easier – they'd already lost faith in the doctors.

Back in Turner's living quarters, he and Jean-Pierre readied a game plan and cracked open much-needed beers. Both had a sick feeling in their guts – the inevitability they'd be burying many more was a tough pill to swallow.

"What's our exact count in the camp now?" Turner asked.

"Three-hundred, give or take a few."

"I'll place the pharmaceutical order. In the meantime, try to get more Mantoux tests and an X-ray machine from Kenya since ours is on the fritz. I'd like to radiograph at least a few patients' lungs to confirm TB."

25

**Polaris Research Lab
Prague, Czech Republic**

"*Dobrý den.* Skala here." A heavily-accented voice answered the phone, the words mumbled over a cigarette dangling from his mouth.

"Hey, Vaclav. Luc Turner here. How are things in Prague?"

"My friend! Things are the same. Too much shit to do, too little time. Caught my girlfriend in bed with a Russian and…"

"Ouch, I've had my run of bad luck as well." Turner cut him off, not wanting to hear the story's end, fearing he'd be obligated to report a murder. Vaclav Skala had always been kind to Turner, but his temper and dislike for

Russians didn't bode well for the man who'd made him a cuckold.

"Bitches… all of 'em. So what can I do for you, Luc?"

"I've got a situation in Somalia. TB. It's spreading like wildfire. The onset of severe symptoms is unusual and consistent. I was hoping that speaking directly with you instead of entering the request online could expedite the process."

"Sure, sure. Let me check my stock quantities. You'll need Rifampin, Ethambutol, Pyrazinamide… anything else?"

"That should do it for now."

"Okay, let's see here. Luc… where in Somalia are you?"

"Jowhar." Turner took a pull on his beer, relieved that meds would soon arrive.

"You losing it, buddy? You already placed an order for these meds two days ago. They're due to arrive in Kenya tomorrow; a cargo truck should get them to you the following day."

"That's impossible. Jean-Pierre and I are the only ones with access to the system. My staff doesn't place any pharmaceutical orders."

"Don't know what to tell you, pal. Good news is those meds will be there soon."

"You're sure it says the order was placed from Jowhar?"

"Yes, I'm sure," the Czech huffed at being second-guessed.

"Thanks, Vaclav."

26

Mandarin Oriental Hotel
Columbus Circle, New York

Capelli was unsure why she'd caved. Perhaps it was the run-in with Tony Pepperidge. Or seeing Danny with his family. Whatever the reason, it now seemed like a bad one.

She sat in a plush, high-backed chair in the lobby lounge of the Mandarin Oriental Hotel. Her intimate table-for-two was set alongside an all-glass wall on the thirty-fifth floor of the elegant hotel. The sun-setting over bustling Columbus Circle and Central Park South provided such a spectacular, quintessentially Manhattan view that for a moment she'd forgotten about the blind-date. The very late blind-date. He'd picked the time and place, making it inexcusable in the Capelli book of basic decency to be twenty minutes tardy. If Allen whatever-his-name-is stuck

115

her with the $18 tab for her Peach Delight cocktail she had every intention of sending him the bill.

As she was signaling the waiter to bring more dusted almonds a ping from the elevator stole her attention. Off came an impossibly elegant man, mid-forties, so perfectly-pressed and polished he could have been a walking Gucci campaign. He exchanged words with the hostess and began sauntering Capelli's way. Suddenly, the blind-date didn't seem such a bad idea, and she shifted anxiously in her chair.

"Kate?"

"That's me. It's nice to meet you Ad... Allen."

"Likewise. I'm terribly sorry for being late; my last patient consultation ran a bit overtime."

"Oh, no problem at all. I'm enjoying the view. Outside. The view outside of the park."

Pull it together Kate. You're as good-looking as this guy, and much more punctual.

Two hours and three martinis later, Kate was ready to buy Caroline a tennis bracelet for setting her up. Allen Kennedy was the dating trifecta: handsome, successful, and funny. He was a cardiothoracic surgeon and sailed boats in his spare time. Normally such an obnoxious resume would force an immediate gag reflex in Capelli, but this time it charmed her.

The conversation flowed easily, even more easily as the martinis kept coming. Allen was impressed that she was FBI, and once she caught his eyes wandering over her body. His politics were a little right-wing for her liking, and hers a little left for his, but otherwise they checked all of each-other's boxes.

Allen suggested dinner and Kate eagerly agreed. He went into the hotel's lobby to call ahead for a table at Jean-Georges in the nearby Trump International. Capelli leaned back in her chair, blissfully tipsy and looking forward to the dinner ahead. She smiled to herself and read CNN's massive electronic billboard as she waited for Allen to finish his call. The temperature was a cool thirty-eight degrees, the DOW had closed relatively flat, and there was a suicide bombing in Yemen. She had nothing better to do and continued reading until a particular headline made her heart skip a beat. "Body found on Charles Bridge has been identified as Martin Warren, President of Polaris Pharmaceuticals, Eastern Europe."

"Ready to go?" Allen chivalrously held her coat, noting the look of concern on Capelli's face.

"I'm so sorry; I'm going to need a rain-check."

As they walked toward the elevators she dialed Ford.

27

FBI Headquarters
Midtown Manhattan

"**S**ir, you know as well as we do – the odds of two Polaris execs being random vics in a ten-day span is pretty unlikely. We need to get to Prague before the crime scene is wiped. I have no doubt these murders are linked."

Ford was pacing the conference room floor, pleading before the weary director who looked as if he had more pressing matters to attend to. Capelli was still somewhat drunk and knew to keep her mouth shut and let her partner do the talking.

The director scratched his mustache as he considered the options. "Look, things are a little tense with the Czechs right now. I'd rather we show some faith in their forensic capabilities and request they send their findings our way. You go in there like two bulls and trample all over their murder… " Capelli was about to interject but Ford's eyes insisted she stay quiet as Masterson continued. "Besides, the crime scene is on a busy tourist landmark. The evidence will be long gone."

Deputy Director of the Criminal Investigative Division, Matthias Masterson, was feeling the pressure. Just last week, his boss in D.C. had been abundantly clear that Masterson end all frivolous spending and increase their arrest rate by ten percent. The tone of their conversation suggested Masterson was next on the chopping block, despite a successful fifteen year stint at the FBI. He'd noticed a few additional wrinkles on his ruggedly handsome fifty-year-old face and increased his Zantac intake to three a day since the meeting. The last thing he wanted was a wasted trip to Prague on the books to highlight another unsolved case.

"Come on, boss," Ford pressed, struggling to restrain his frustration. "You know that's ridiculous. These are high-profile murders. The longer it takes for us to solve them, the bigger the black-eye on the agency."

Masterson tented his fingers beneath his chin, sizing up Capelli and Ford. They were right, of course, and if it wasn't for his perilous job situation he'd have no hesitation whatsoever to send them overseas.

"I'm not going to beat around the bush here. You two have a good track record and stellar instincts, but your investigation of the Thorpe murder has been less-than-impressive. Kraft was a good lead but now that he's been cleared you have nothing. I'm thinking of adding another team to yours... getting some fresh eyes on the case."

"Oh, come on!" Capelli blurted out. "We've got this thing! Give us another week and let us look into the Warren murder. I personally guarantee we'll have a solid lead when we return."

As soon as Capelli had finished her martini fueled boast, Ford sunk into his chair. "Guarantees" went over like a lead balloon with the boss. She felt Ford's glare mix with the subtle pangs in her temple suggesting the start of a hangover.

Masterson let out a sigh, the late hour finally catching up with the overworked agent.

"I'll give you 48 hours in Prague. I've got a contact there that may be willing to smooth the way for you with local law enforcement. They tend to be tight-lipped when westerners come in to steal their glory. But you better come back with more than just a coffee mug from Prague Castle."

"You won't regret this, boss."

"Fly coach and book the cheapest one-star you can find. And Capelli, take some aspirin before the Grey Goose wears off."

28

Doctors Without Borders Camp
Jowhar, Somalia

A soft rapping on the front door woke Turner. He'd been overcome by exhaustion and fell asleep with his face on the kitchen table, next to his bland dinner of canned beans and rice. A blissful few moments of grogginess allowed him to forget about the epidemic and the fact he was still in this god-forsaken place. Reality hit him soon enough.

The knocking continued and he grouchily yanked open the door to find Jean-Pierre with tear stained cheeks and a wild look in his eyes.

"What happened? Another death? Is it Amaka?" Turner was immediately fully awake, heart pounding at the sight of the emotional Jean-Pierre – he'd never seen the stoic man betray anything resembling fear.

"It's Noelle. She's coughing up blood, Luc! We'd been so careful to wear the masks and disinfect ourselves. I don't know how this happened."

Before meeting Jean-Pierre and Noelle, Turner had thought a marriage like theirs was only possible in the mind of a hopelessly romantic Hollywood screenwriter. As a young woman Noelle worked in the Sierra Leone diamond mines. She'd been subjected to unimaginable brutality and – Turner suspected – rape. After a year of torment she'd run away and sought refuge in a nearby medical clinic where Jean-Pierre was working. He hid her when her employers – or captors – came searching, machetes and all. Since that time they'd been inseparable, moving to Kenya to escape the escalating violence in Sierra Leone. She'd been wary of moving to Somalia, where the government was non-existent and bands of thugs regularly went on murderous rampages. Both Turner and Jean-Pierre had convinced her she'd be safe, that the sick needed them here more than anywhere. Now she was infected with a deadly disease and Turner felt an unbearable guilt. He watched as Jean-Pierre took a seat at the kitchen table, overcome with grief.

Turner couldn't find any words for consolation, but placed his hand on Jean-Pierre's shoulder and a bottle of water in front of him.

"Listen, Jean-Pierre. The meds arrived in Kenya last night. Their small plane isn't working so they sent a truck first thing this morning. By midnight tonight Noelle will have her first round of meds. We'll do everything we can for her."

"I can't lose her, Luc."

"You won't," Turner said, hoping he wasn't telling a lie. "Make sure you're careful around her; keep that mask on at all times. Odds are we're inoculated against this but keep taking precautions to be safe."

29

Ruzyne Airport
Prague, Czech Republic

Capelli cringed as she watched Ford pass through customs ahead of her. He was an awkward traveler, perpetually looking like a fish out of water. Unfortunately for those associated with him, that awkwardness translated into 'obnoxious American' pretty quickly. The customs agent stared in annoyance as the bumbling agent attempted to make small talk about the weather and airport security, beads of sweat forming on his forehead as he realized it was better to just shut-up. If not for the FBI shield, he'd be destined for a cavity search and bomb residue screening.

They retrieved their bags and exited into the passenger pick-up area where a local law enforcement peon held a sign bearing their names. He gave them a curt nod and proceeded to the car, visibly annoyed at their presence. It took a few minutes to wedge themselves and their luggage into the tiny red Skoda Fabia. The packed vehicle resembled a clown car at a circus show; all they needed were the big shoes and foam noses.

Pulling out of the airport drive, their escort introduced himself as Milos Nemec. His bald head and pale blue eyes gave him a cold appearance, thus far proving to be an accurate representation of his personality.

"So, Milos," Capelli started, "What are some Czech phrases we should know?"

"You know English, everybody knows English. You don't need Czech."

"Oh, come on, just a few phrases."

It was evident that Capelli's attempt to ingratiate herself by showing interest in the language was having the opposite effect.

"To greet people say *dobrý den*. To order beer say *pivo prosim*. That should get you by." The words were spoken with finality, suggesting she shut up.

"Thanks." Capelli kept quiet until arriving at the hotel.

After checking into adjoining rooms, the agents made their way to the hotel's lobby café. The Hotel Corinthia had done its best to embrace the look and feel of an upscale business-friendly chain. Still, the vestiges of communism lingered in the slightly shabby lobby sofas, Formica dining table, and the plastic chandeliers. Capelli found it quite charming while Ford was more concerned about finding a McDonald's.

Sitting at a private corner table was Ivan Tesar, the imposing head of the Criminal Investigation Division. Normally, a man so high up the chain of command would not go through the hassle of meeting a foreign counterpart at their hotel. But he reasoned the more he coddled the American agents the sooner they'd depart his country and get out of his thinning hair.

The woman immediately caught his eye. Even in a black business suit, her fit curves were apparent with each purposeful stride. The prospect of working with the Americans became somewhat less dreadful.

He rose as they approached, not out of respect but rather to intimidate. Ivan's six-foot five, broad-shouldered frame and piercing blue stare served as a constant reminder to any colleagues that he was running the show.

"Agents Ford and Capelli, welcome to Prague." He greeted them in perfect Eastern-European English, smiling.

Capelli responded to Tesar's obvious attention.

"Thank you, Mr. Tesar. From what we've seen, it's a beautiful city."

"The world's most beautiful city in my biased opinion. Prague's often called 'little Paris' but I'd argue there's more charm here. Certainly the men are more masculine, no?"

"Well, I haven't been here long enough to decide." Capelli walked a tight-rope between flirtation and professionalism, a tactic that had served her well with men like Ivan Tesar.

"Please," Tesar motioned to the waiter, "order something to drink and I'll fill you in on the case."

"Espresso for me." Capelli smiled at the waiter.

"How European of you," Ford muttered, "I'll take a Diet Coke, please."

The waiter scampered off to retrieve the refreshments and Tesar immediately got to work, leaning in so closely Capelli could feel his breath on her right cheek. The least he could do was pop a mint, she thought.

"The victim's body was discovered Tuesday night, at just around seven pm. There were many witnesses, mostly tourists, who saw him stumble aimlessly along the bridge. Unfortunately, most of them were enraptured by street performers and whatever else it is tourists pay attention to. They were unable to tell us where he came from or if he'd been accompanied by anyone. The local police made the assumption he was just a drunk who'd finally done himself in and focused on getting the body removed and things back to normal as soon as possible. It was the right move at the time – tourism is a major industry for us and dead bodies don't sell Disneyland."

"What about evidence?" Ford pressed.

"Not much. The location, the hurried nature of the clean-up, it all made it quite difficult."

The waiter – whose nametag read Nestor and didn't look a day over fifteen – reappeared with their drinks, nervously placing them on the table with a shaky hand. The manager had informed him of Tesar's stature in law-enforcement and though he was no criminal, being around the man made him nervous. He assumed there was good reason the papers had dubbed him Ivan 'the terrible' Tesar in their headlines. After confirming his patrons were satisfied with their orders he departed as quickly as possible. Tesar frowned at the meek server and continued.

"The victim had no identification on him, or any wallet for that matter. There were a few hundred crowns – which, if you aren't aware of the exchange rate, is a minimal amount of money, about ten of your dollars. Since there was no ID on him, we had no idea he was a high-profile figure. His body remained in the morgue, untouched for the next twenty-four hours. That's not standard policy but our autopsy specialist was away for the weekend. The morning after Warren's death, we received a missing person's report that had been flagged due to the high-profile status of the disappeared individual. His wife had filed the request after he failed to return home and she provided a very detailed description of his physical features as well as the clothing he'd been wearing when he left the house. She identified the body as that of her husband, Martin Warren, later that afternoon. And now here you are."

Capelli appreciated Tesar's to-the-point rundown. It irritated her when colleagues added fluff to their version of events, inappropriately praising their team for a job well-done in order to avoid any scrutiny by the higher-ups. Still, it was disappointing they had no leads and, from the sound of it, no evidence.

"Did she mention if there was anyone who wished her husband harm?"

"Mrs. Warren has been cooperative but hasn't offered anything relevant to the case. She knows about your arrival and is willing to talk to you. Her son flew in last night from Paris and has agreed to be interviewed at the same time – so far we've only spoken to him over the phone."

"I appreciate you arranging that. Maybe the morning will be best. I'd like to see the crime scene tonight and go from there."

Just past six that evening, they piled into Tesar's well-worn Mercedes SUV. Capelli guessed the vehicle had belonged to some cabinet minister when new, then trickled down to Tesar through the bureaucracy as the odometer rang up. It certainly was a welcome change from the pocket-sized Skoda his lackey had greeted them with at the airport.

The sun was making its final descent for the evening, forming a halo of light around the old town's spires and steeples, a welcome distraction from wearying jet-lag. Their chauffeurs – Tesar, with Milos riding shotgun – were severely lacking as tour guides and Capelli regretted not purchasing a cheap *Lonely Planet* guide for reference. The buildings looked pre-historic compared to the uninspired monstrosities that consumed so many American cities and she couldn't help but wonder about the history of each.

"You like our city?" Tesar broke the silence, his gruff voice startling Ford just as the latter had started to nod-off.

"It's nice," Ford blabbered, "like an older Pittsburgh." Capelli frowned at Ford. Prague was nothing like Pittsburgh. "But my wife would drive me crazy sightseeing here. Looks like a lot of landmarks to suffer through." The thought alone increased Ford's exhaustion.

"Prague has many famous sites. Squares, cathedrals, towers, bridges… in fact, the bridge where we are headed it also very famous. Back in the 1600's there was a revolt. When the Hapsburgs put out the uprising, they lined the bridge with the heads of the revolutionaries. Over twenty-seven of them I think." Tesar fell back into a silence, satisfied he'd provided them with sufficient historical information.

During her years in law-enforcement, Capelli developed a few theories as to what drove her colleagues. A large portion began their careers with the Pollyannaish notion they'd catch criminals and 'make the world a safer place.' But there was another disturbingly large group that used the law to satisfy their egos and penchant toward violence. Tesar's demeanor and the glint in his eye as he spoke of decapitated heads suggested he was of the latter. In Capelli's mind, such agents were time-bombs. They were effective and by the book for the most part, but the right trigger would spark a violent outrage that could result in the death of a suspect or the beating of an innocent man. Of course, the police always backed their own, and these rage-prone individuals were allowed to remain on the force, protected by their shields. She just hoped Tesar waited to blow until her case was closed.

Tesar parked the Mercedes in a private lot a few blocks from the bridge and they stepped out, the Americans wobbly on their jet legs. It was drawing near the time of evening when a few of the reliable witnesses had recalled seeing Warren stumble across the bridge. Despite the inky darkness of the late-October sky, there remained throngs of tourists leisurely passing back and forth between Old Town Prague and *Malá Strana* – Lesser Town. As they drew nearer to their destination, Capelli found it hard to fathom the killer would choose this location for a pre-meditated murder. She'd yet to find a quiet, secluded area in the vicinity where a confrontation could take place without multiple witnesses.

Tesar and his lap-dog, Milos, were far ahead of the American agents, waiting impatiently at the bridge's center where Martin Warren had succumbed to death. They'd already investigated the scene and saw this sojourn as a waste of their time – it was seven and there was beer to drink.

"As you see," Tesar began, "it's impossible to collect evidence in a place such as this after the fact."

"Yes, you're right about that. It's unfortunate your cleaning crew didn't do a better job of preserving the scene when they retrieved the body."

A passing teenager bumped firmly into Capelli's shoulder, the stink of body odor following in his wake. It was as if Tesar's instant karma Gods had punished her for her snarky comment – she wanted to slap the satisfied grin right off his face. She headed toward the far end of the bridge where Ford stood, looking out-of-place as ever.

"I'm starting to dislike Butch and the Kid here," she nodded toward Tesar who lumbered ten yards back. Then she noticed Ford's focused stare. "What? What is it?"

"Check out this staircase here. This is the only sheltered area around the bridge."

The two agents descended the stone stairway. It was located on the southern side of the Charles Bridge, about seventy-five feet from the *Malá Strana* entrance with direct access to Kampa Park. They noticed far fewer tourists in

Kampa than on the bridge itself. Most of the shops had closed for the day. The only occupied areas were a beer hall and park where a few local stragglers milled about.

"It's actually nice down here." Ford mumbled as he took in the scenery. "Kinda like Three Rivers Park."

"We should come back in the daylight." Capelli suggested. "Can't see much now."

"Don't have to tell me twice. Let's say sayonara to our friendly escorts and find a hamburger joint."

30

Doctors Without Borders Camp
Jowhar, Somalia

Just three of Turner's nurses and assistants remained uncompromised by the TB virus, increasing the burden on the few healthy workers. The bodies were piling-up and the personnel were no longer able to keep up with the intense physical demand of digging graves. It was just past midnight as Turner took stock of the situation, disheartened to learn another ten patients had passed. The dead bodies were laid in a row outside the quarantine tents, awaiting the dignity of a burial – and to Turner they seemed an indictment of his abilities.

He inspected each of the deceased, ensuring their eyes were closed and limbs straight so they were lined-up with one-another, as was the custom in Somalia. The modest gesture would have to suffice for now. Turner had an autopsy to begin.

Jean-Pierre had prepared the bodies on two metal cots that were nearly touching in the small, ill-equipped operating room. At one time they'd had a large supply of operating equipment, but a series of robberies and vandalism had left the room bare.

Turner entered the space and fought to overcome his emotional and physical exhaustion. It had been the idea of Abukar and Aasha – the couple whose bodies lay before him – to have Turner complete an autopsy in the event of their deaths. It was their hope something of value would be discovered that would save their two sons, now on the brink of expiration themselves.

To speed the process, Turner and Jean-Pierre had agreed to conduct the autopsies at the same time alongside one-another. Each donned their tattered surgical scrubs and masks, though by now both were expecting they'd become infected with the highly contagious disease despite all precautions.

Turner hadn't completed a full autopsy since medical school, a statistic he was pleased with considering he much preferred working with the living. Still, for their purposes, he was confident his skills would suffice.

After noting the date and time of the procedure, the doctors simultaneously retrieved their scalpels and carefully began their Y incisions. Gently, Turner traced the scalpel from Aasha's emaciated left shoulder to her sternum, the blade so sharp that very little pressure was needed to make a clean cut. He then cut the skin from her right shoulder to sternum and proceeded straight down her bloated torso, stopping at the pubic bone. He recalled his med school autopsy, noting how much easier it was to slice into the body of an anonymous cadaver than someone he'd come to know over the last month. The distraught scowl on Jean-Pierre's face suggested he too was having difficulty coping with the situation – made worse for him with the knowledge his wife was infected with the very disease that had killed the couple.

They nodded sympathetically at one another as they peeled back the flaps of skin, exposing the inner-skeleton of their friends that lay before them. The bleeding was minimal, now that the blood was no longer pulsing through the veins of a living person. It simply sank with gravity, allowing Turner to cut into the body with very little mess.

Retrieving shears, the men cut into their subject's chest cavity and began sawing through the lateral sides of the ribs. This process allowed for the chest plate to be removed in one-piece – creating easier access to the internal organs and making reconstruction of the body a much simpler task after the procedure.

Prior to the operation, they'd agreed to remove all the organs at once, allowing them to examine each organ for abnormalities simultaneously. Unfortunately – due to lack of suitable medical care – the doctors had no medical history for either Aasha or Abukar. Should something appear irregular in the organs it would be difficult to determine whether the current TB epidemic caused the condition or whether it was pre-existing.

Turner and Jean-Pierre delicately removed the pericardial sack, and then extracted each heart, placing the two hearts alongside one another in sterilized metal dishes. A rush of sadness swelled up in Turner's eyes as he viewed the un-beating hearts of husband and wife side-by-side on the table. He struggled to control the nausea, coupling deep breaths with attempts to recall happier times, and he managed to proceed.

With the hearts removed, access to the left lung was now much simpler. Turner hesitated before snipping the arteries and veins that stemmed from the lung, unnecessarily concerned he'd cut something he shouldn't and trigger a drop in blood pressure or flat line of pulse. He felt silly at his apprehension, somehow forgetting Aasha was dead and could no longer be hurt.

Each lung was removed and placed in its respective dish. Though their intent was to remove all organs before conducting an individual analysis of each, they couldn't help but be alarmed by the tiny lesions that dotted each of the four lungs. Jean-Pierre was first to address the elephant in the room.

"Luc, I'm not a disease specialist, but these lungs show signs of Miliary TB. Is that possible?"

Miliary Tuberculosis, also known as Disseminated Tuberculosis, only affects about one to three percent of all TB patients and is one-hundred percent fatal unless properly treated in a timely manner. The bacteria erodes into the pulmonary vein and begins spreading throughout the body, giving it the capacity to attack multiple organs including the spleen, liver, lungs and occasionally the lymph nodes. The odds that such a severe form of the disease would develop in both patients seemed impossible to Turner – though at this point, nothing would surprise him.

"The small size and prevalence of the lesions do concern me but I'd rather not jump to conclusions – hopefully it's nothing more than standard TB. Let's examine the organs before deciding conclusively." He did his best to appear unconcerned, for the sake of his friend, but was petrified by the millet-seed sized lesions that dotted the lungs.

In concerned silence the doctors extracted all remaining vital organs in tandem. Their silence spoke volumes as the concern grew with their initial findings. The spleens of both Aasha and Abukar were enormous, suggesting the tuberculosis had begun infecting organs beyond the lungs. The livers were similarly enlarged and flecked with small lesions.

"Luc," Jean-Pierre whispered, "this isn't standard TB."

31

Warren Residence
Prague, Czech Republic

Ana Warren's hand trembled slightly as she poured freshly-brewed coffee from a long-spouted silver pot into hand-painted china. She'd welcomed Capelli, Ford, and a surly Milos into a sunlit den and proceeded to go through the motions of a housewife accustomed to frequent entertaining. Her hair was pinned in a perfectly constructed auburn bun, the plum-colored skirt suit that fit snuggly around her wide hips was recently pressed, and there was not so much as a paper out of place in the perfectly organized room. Despite those appearances, there was a vacant sadness in her eyes that betrayed her newfound widowhood. In a daze, she placed biscuits before the agents, even as they insisted there was no need for refreshments. Capelli wondered if Ana had been taking medication to cope with the emotional loss of her husband;

it was the vogue thing to do these days – especially among the wealthy.

Ford shifted uncomfortably in a blue and gold tapestry Louis XIV style chair. The den's design was more befitting of seventeenth century Versailles than modern-day Prague – it was elegant but far from comfortable. Long drapes hung over floor to ceiling windows that offered a panoramic view of the Vltava River. Between the windows, an exquisite oil painting of a soldier on a rearing black horse in battle dominated the wall. After adjusting his hefty body in the narrow chair, Ford raised an eyebrow to Capelli, signaling her to bring Mrs. Warren back to reality before she began cooking a roast in her depressed haze.

"That's excellent coffee, Mrs. Warren," Capelli complimented after taking a sip and scorching her tongue, "why don't you have a seat and we can talk?"

"Oh, yes. Of course." The woman distractedly sat down, smoothing her skirt and avoiding eye contact with the agents.

Eric Warren, Ana and Martin's son, took a seat and placed a hand on his mother's arm in a comforting gesture. A mop of dark hair fell messily over his ice blue eyes – eyes that seemed more suited to a wolf than a man. Despite its intensity, his face had kind features and an easy smile, even in the glum circumstances. He sat tall, with posture suggesting a readiness to take over the man's role his father had left behind.

"You feel okay, mom?"

"Yes, honey, I'm okay." She whispered with the subtlest hint of a Czech accent, most of which had faded during her twenty-five years in New York.

"Mrs. Warren," Capelli began, "I know you've already spoken with the local investigators so I'll do my best to keep our visit brief. Agent Ford and I have read through the statements you made after the death of your husband. Is there any additional information you can recall? Any strange visitors? Was your husband behaving normally?"

"As I told the other agents, I thought everything was fine. Martin has been depressed for the past year, but he always said it was because he missed Eric while he was off at school. When Edward Thorpe died he became even more morose but the loss of a friend does that to a person. When my best girlfriend, Irina, passed a few years back from cancer it took me months to feel like a normal person again."

The garish sound of techno club music came blaring from Milos' phone – startling everyone in the room. He'd been standing in the corner, leaning against the wall and munching on the plate of cookies Mrs. Warren had placed on the ornate coffee table. He left to take the call – probably from Tesar who'd claimed he was pursuing a lead that morning – with the plate of cookies still in hand.

"Sorry about that, Mrs. Warren. He should have quieted his phone. How about you, Eric? I know you've been off at school but has anything seemed out of the ordinary lately?"

"No, not before... before it happened." He shifted nervously, looking for the right words to avoid upsetting his mother. "But I went on his computer today to email a professor, and when the screen turned on, it displayed his most recent document and... I don't know... It just seemed weird."

"What seemed weird? What was the document?"

"He'd been drafting a letter of resignation."

"Resignation from what?"

"Polaris, I think. It was addressed to Vance Thorpe but the letter was unfinished. Maybe he changed his mind."

"Had he mentioned problems at Polaris to either of you? Or maybe a desire to retire?"

"Dad really didn't talk about work to either of us. When I was a kid he did, though. He'd get all excited about a new drug trial or research breakthrough. I remember being eleven or twelve when they'd come out with a new blood pressure medication. It was all he could talk about, said it was revolutionary. But lately he'd just ask about my schoolwork and try to pry information about girlfriends from me." A sad smile washed over Eric's face at recalling the ribbing his dad always gave him over girls. It was all in good fun between them.

"Eric, was there anyone your father confided in other than yourself and your mom? A best friend or someone he worked with who may have some insights into what was going on?" Capelli had given up on Mrs. Warren. Her eyes were fixed on the wall and she seemed to have slipped into a catatonic state.

"I really don't know. That's terrible, isn't it? Like I don't even know my own dad."

"No, no it's very understandable. A lot of times our parents don't want to burden us with their problems or discuss their friends. Your young friends were probably a more interesting topic of conversation for him." Capelli smiled, trying to lighten the mood.

"I suppose. I do know he and Mr. Thorpe were best friends. We were always with him in New York and they'd drink scotch and smoke cigars, play golf, the whole thing. But since moving to Prague, I'm not sure who he spends time with."

After another twenty minutes of questioning – which produced no helpful insights – the agents thanked a tuned-out Mrs. Warren and her son for the coffee and excused themselves. They passed through the ornate foyer in a frustrated silence, both feeling as though there were more questions than answers in the Polaris deaths.

The clicking of boots-on-marble prompted Capelli to turn around to find a somewhat flustered Eric Warren following behind them.

"Sorry, Mr. Ford and Ms. Capelli. There's something else I wanted to tell you away from my mother. Do you have a few more minutes?"

"Of course, Eric. What's on your mind?" Capelli offered a supportive tone, hoping he'd feel comfortable enough to open up.

Eric Warren took a seat on a chaise lounge in the foyer. Ford was perplexed as to why anyone would need formal seating in an entry hall but he'd stopped trying to understand the extravagances of the wealthy. Eric rubbed his hands together as if trying to warm them and nervously began to ramble.

"This probably has nothing to do with the case. I mean… I don't how it would. But, I just felt like you should know since nobody else does." He paused and looked away, staring at the front door as if contemplating escape.

"What is it Eric? Any little bit can be very helpful."

"Can you keep what I'm going to tell you out of the press? My dad was a great father and businessperson; I don't want his name slandered when he's no longer able to defend himself."

"I'd be lying if I said I could guarantee privacy but I'll do my best not to disclose unnecessary information to the press or my colleagues for that matter." Capelli hated privacy demands. These days it was impossible to keep anything quiet no matter how vigilant she was, especially if it was a nugget of scandalous information. The press had a keen nose for that type of dirt.

"Okay... I guess that's all I can ask for." Eric stopped for a moment, considering one last time whether to continue. "Awhile back I learned my dad had another son, born long before my mother and he were ever together. Apparently, when my father was young, he had a fling and got the woman pregnant. According to dad, neither he nor the woman wanted to be parents at the time. My dad was very career focused and didn't want the burden of raising a child with a woman he didn't love. So, they gave the child up in a closed adoption and went their separate ways."

"Does your mother know about the adoption?"

"He never told her. They met so many years later he didn't see any reason to. He loved her very much and didn't want to do anything to turn her away. Over time, I guess it was just easier to keep the secret."

"How did you find out?"

"About three years ago, dad came to visit me in Paris. He seemed distracted – like there was something he needed to tell me. I asked him about it, thinking maybe my parents were divorcing or mom was sick. I knew something was really bothering him when he ordered scotch at lunch. He could hardly look me in the eye when we toasted one another."

Eric Warren had sunk into the chaise, the manly bravado he'd shown in front his mother was nowhere to be seen on the now child-like man who sat before the agents. He seemed lost in thought, as if he were still trying to comprehend the fact he had a brother out there somewhere his dad had kept secret for so many years. He cleared his throat and continued, eyes welling slightly.

"It took awhile, and a few more scotches, for dad to come out with his secret. He told me he'd mostly forgotten about the 'situation', especially after I came along. Can you believe that? To call your son a 'situation'? Anyway, apparently the guy hired a private investigator to find his parents, which is supposed to be impossible with a closed adoption, but he was successful and found dad. At the time, dad had been going back and forth between Prague and New York quite frequently and his... his son, I guess, approached him outside of Polaris' headquarters after work one day."

"Did they keep in touch at all?" Capelli asked, doing her best to sound empathetic given the situation.

"I don't know. I'll be honest; I was freaked out by the whole thing. What kind of person gives up their child because they are too busy with their career? It changed how I saw my father – the man I knew would never think to do such a thing. Plus, I guess I was jealous. I thought I was the only son – his pride and joy – and all these years he knew there was another one out there."

"I'm sure you were his pride and joy. Another child out there he'd never really known wouldn't change that," Capelli offered, trying her hand at a little psychotherapy in an effort to keep the kid from clamming up.

"Maybe, I don't know. He could tell the whole thing was a lot for me to take so he didn't go into too much detail. Actually, I don't know why he bothered telling me. He never told my mother – it would have absolutely crushed her. She's a great woman but has some trouble with her emotions, as you probably noticed. It doesn't take much for her to become depressed. I guess he just needed to unload on someone and I was the lucky guy."

"That means he trusted you with the most difficult and personal issues in his life – which says a lot about your relationship and how much he respected you as an individual." Dr. Capelli continued her coddling.

"Maybe, or he was just being weak and couldn't get up the courage to tell my mother."

"What did he tell you about this… this person from his past?"

"Not much. I made it pretty clear I didn't want any details. I guess the guy's name is Nathaniel, though dad didn't pick the name, the adopted parents did. He works in finance or something; he's gotta be forty by now."

"Do you know his last name? Or where he lives?"

"No, no idea. Dad mentioned something about London but I'm not sure if he lives there or grew up there or what. By that point in the conversation I was just trying to shut him up, I really didn't want details."

"That's understandable. You say this took place three years ago. Was there ever mention of this Nathaniel again?"

"No, I think dad felt it best not to say anything. I feel bad now; he probably really needed someone to confide in. But we just swept it under the rug. Things were never quite the same between us."

Milos impatiently tapped his worn leather boot on the cobblestone while chain-smoking Pall Malls. He gave a curt nod to Capelli and Ford when they emerged from the Warren residence and didn't inquire to the substance of the interview. "Let's go. Ivan has news."

32

Doctors Without Borders Camp
Jowhar, Somalia

Aggravated, Turner flipped across the lumpy twin mattress from his left to right side, hoping the change in position would resolve his insomnia. It did not. Dwelling on the fact he desperately needed a good night's rest after a week of three-hour nights and cat naps made it all the more difficult to shut down his worried mind.

The first round of TB medication had been administered that morning but it did little to calm his nerves. Another fifteen people had died overnight and Turner unreasonably blamed himself for not getting them treatment sooner. Each time he bordered on slumber a vision of the dead bodies awaiting burial jolted him back to consciousness. In his vision, the faces of the dead twisted in pain as animals gnawed at the newly dead flesh.

Insomnia was preferable to the gruesome scenes haunting his subconscious.

Around 4:00 a.m., Turner accepted that rest was a luxury not to be had so he strolled sleepily across the groaning floor boards to the kitchen in search of late-night leftovers. Moments like this made him long for the comforts of a fully developed society with its 24 hour delis and on-demand cable. He settled for some leftover chicken – which may or may not have spoiled – and a Heineken. His doctor friends overseas always saw to it that there was a steady supply of beer that arrived with the medication and food for the camp – something for which Turner was eternally grateful. He opened his battered copy of Hemingway's *A Moveable Feast* and spent an hour escaping into the life of 1920's Paris. The book had accompanied Turner on his many journeys and never grew old, though it could do with a new binding.

At five, he donned light khakis, a long-sleeved grey t-shirt that desperately needed washing, and his brown Wellie's, then set out for a walk. The morning air was still and cool, the sun had yet to begin its ascent.

Turner cursed himself for leaving his hunting knife behind – his only defense against the vast array of malnourished creatures that lived nearby. Rather than go back he skirted the perimeter, close by the tents, just in case a hungry critter was craving doctor for breakfast.

The quiet of the first quarantine tent surprised him as he walked by. He heard an occasional cough but otherwise his patients seemed to be sleeping comfortably. For a fleeting moment he was jealous at their slumber, a thought which immediately made him feel foolish as he considered they were all on the brink of eternal sleep.

He paused by the second tent, where Amaka was housed, and debated whether to check on her. There was a slight tremble in his body as he considered what he might see – it was possible that in her weak condition Amaka had died in the night – the mere thought of which caused bile to rise in Turner's throat and his heart to pound. Bracing for the worst, he peeked his head inside the tent for a brief look.

The young girl's back was facing him, her body so still it was impossible to discern whether she was breathing. Then, as though she sensed his presence, the little girl turned over and faced the tent's entrance – a small action but one that she'd been too weak to make only a day prior. Relief washed over Turner as he realized she was still alive, followed by shock when she gave him a wide, slightly buck-toothed grin and held up a yellow object for him to see. It was the now-empty wrapper for the Lion bar she'd been too weak to consume.

He placed his hand on her head, both shocked and grateful to realize she no longer had a fever.

"It was very good. Is there more?" She spoke quietly, still weak, but a glimmer in her eye suggested she was getting her feistiness back.

"I'll find you another one," Turner smiled as he went about examining her, "but first you have to eat some healthy food so you can fight the disease off."

She nodded in reply, cooperating as Turner took her vitals and recorded them on the file near her cot. The improvement was remarkable. It had been less than twenty-four hours since she'd received the antibiotic cocktail and already there was a night and day change in her condition. He retrieved water, hoping she'd feel well enough to drink since she remained terribly dehydrated.

Amaka raised her bony arm which was back to an emaciated state, and sipped from the plastic cup. She coughed as the liquid hit the back of her throat, but after a few more tries, she was able to drink the whole glass and requested more. Turner obliged, and then whispered, "Get some sleep Amaka." With a tender smile he left to examine the other patients.

33

Prague, Czech Republic

Milos took massive, urgent steps down the winding, old-town streets, with Capelli and Ford jogging to keep pace.

"Why do I feel like this guy's trying to lose us?" Ford huffed.

Still, this torture was better than having to endure Milos' reckless driving.

The walk from the Warren residence through Prague's Újezd district where the Olympia pub was located should have taken them ten minutes, but they made it in six and a half. Panting slightly, they entered the pub and spotted Tesar at a corner table with a beer mug and a half-eaten plate of sausages sitting before him.

"Nice of him to wait," Ford mumbled to Capelli. "This guy might be on my top-five all-time assholes list."

"Yeah, with Milos coming in just ahead of him."

As if reading their minds, Tesar took the trouble to wipe his hands and stood, motioning for the two Americans to join him, but didn't go so far as a smile.

"Good afternoon. I trust your meeting with the widow went okay."

"It was fine. As you suggested, we didn't learn much new from her."

For some indiscernible reason – perhaps it was the competitive spirit with their Czech counterparts, or a suspicion of their investigative capabilities – neither Capelli nor Ford felt the need to inform Tesar of Martin Warren's secret son, or the fact he'd considered resigning from Polaris. For now, they'd hold that information close to the vest until determining its relevance.

A pretty waitress approached the table with a warm "dobrý den," her presence bringing out the rarely-seen charm of Ivan Tesar. The investigator took the liberty of ordering a round of Pilsner Urquell for the table and a vast array of sausages whose titles sounded far from appetizing. Capelli would have preferred to order on her own, like a big girl, but figured if there was one thing the native Czech knew it was beer and sausage. She suffered through a few moments of awkward small talk ranging from the opulent Warren home and the chilly weather, until the beers arrived and Tesar got to business.

"I have news from our medical staff." He opened with in an unnecessarily ominous tone; he may as well have been saying the world was heading to nuclear war within 24 hours.

"That was quick work. Did they determine cause of death?" Capelli sipped the beer, which was without a doubt the best she'd ever had – not that she'd admit it to her host.

"Yes. It appears snake venom was injected into Mr. Warren via needle and syringe. They are working on determining the type of venom and amount used as we speak. I'll admit, this is a first for me. Usually we have pretty standard gun and knife murders."

"That's the same murder weapon as used on Edward Thorpe. If it wasn't obvious already, I'd say it's looking more and more like these murders are connected – and we have no credible suspects in either one."

Tesar just nodded, piling a heaping spoon of sauerkraut into his mouth. He'd only half-heartedly investigated the Warren murder, assuming correctly that the Americans would swoop in since the victim was part of a major US-based company. Let them solve the case, he figured – they'd take the glory either way.

Capelli savored another sip of the crisp pilsner, relishing its delicious taste. She normally stuck to wine or the occasional vodka but this beer was as good as it got. Setting the heavy mug back on the old wooden table, she got to business.

"Were there any trace fibers on the body? Or the victims clothing?"

"Nothing, Miss Capelli. Nothing unusual." Tesar seemed distracted, and it only took Capelli a moment to realize why.

The pretty waitress arrived with large platters stacked with sausages, her bony arms ready to snap from the weight. Tesar flashed a smile and the waitress responded in kind, apparently flustered by his attention. Ford smirked at Capelli, curious what the waitress saw in Tesar the Terrible.

After a few moments the sausages and utensils had been dispersed and the waitress – whose cheeks were now an embarrassed shade of magenta from Tesar's attentions – left their table.

"Anyway," Capelli cleared her throat, "I'd like to take a look at the autopsy and evidence reports, if that's not a problem."

"It's not a problem. But I'm not sure why you'd waste your time when I've told you there's nothing helpful to the case."

"Never hurts to have a fresh set of eyes glance over things." Capelli did her best to sound friendly, but her annoyance with Tesar was not well-concealed.

"Whatever makes you happy, Agent Capelli. How do you like the sausages? This is one of Prague's best gastronomical pubs; you won't find better Czech food anywhere."

Capelli had yet to take a bite, but Ford, whose plate was nearly licked clean, chimed in with ready praise.

"Amazing. I love a good New York hot dog but these sausages are special. I've got a whole new appreciation for Europe."

Tesar simply gave a satisfied nod and continued eating. He'd not looked either agent in the eye since they'd arrived at the pub and it was becoming evident he was keeping something to himself.

"So, Ivan. Is there anything else about the case you can share? We're flying back to New York tomorrow and I fear we'll be empty-handed." Capelli's words were neutral but her tone threatening.

After a moment of deliberation and a show of wiping his mouth and hands, Tesar finally spoke.

"Actually, there is some news. I was waiting to tell you until the tip is verified but you seem impatient. As you know, Interpol offered a reward for any information related to the murders of Edward Thorpe and Martin Warren. A call came in early this morning reporting a suspicious character who bought a place, in cash, on Nerudova Street. Apparently, he'd leave a little money every time he visited in return for the landlord's silence. I guess the reward money was a bigger payment because the landlord called in to report the man. Now, there's nothing yet linking him to either murder – more than likely it's a prank to get some easy money. That's why I didn't mention it. Nonetheless, we are to be at the building in a half hour to have a look around."

Capelli was disappointed. These types of quacks always called in, hoping for an easy couple thousand dollars. Odds were high that their trip to Nerudova Street would prove fruitless.

34

Nerudova Street
Prague, Czech Republic

The pale man stood halfway down a steep, brick-stepped alley that jutted off of Nerudova Street. In the dark shadows he remained hidden, even in the light of day, and from there he studied the Nerudova Street traffic. Various trinket shops lined the long, snaking alleyway, each offering the same garbage with a special twist – some knick-knack's were a few pennies cheaper, others came with a free map or bottled water – whatever trick the owners thought would help beat the competition.

The man stood beside an old, wooden door with iron knockers that looked more suited to the Middle Ages, though he guessed the tourists found it to be quaint. Beyond the door was a courtyard that housed a buzzing pub whose gimmick was to serve a fresh-baked pretzel with each beer order, operating under the assumption that the salty food would keep patrons drinking. The pub's exterior offered a perfect view of his aparthotel's front door, while keeping him sufficiently concealed from sight. Should anyone come looking for him down the passageway, he'd duck in amongst the tourist families and backpackers who'd filed in during the lunch rush.

With his Ghurka messenger bag slung over his shoulder, he studied a Frommer's guide to Prague he'd picked up at the corner shop a few minutes before – his effort at blending in. Flipping through the book, he stopped on a page detailing nightlife. While pretending to read the pages, he simmered inside, angry for not leaving town sooner. His instincts were better than this.

Earlier that morning, as he was packing for a return to Gstaad, the albino heard a tentative rap on his door. Never in his various visits to the apartment had anyone disturbed him. Retrieving his rarely-used butterfly knife – he found killing with his hands more satisfying – he checked the peep-hole to see his pathetic, filthy landlord, Jaroslav, standing outside with sweat beading on his forehead. The unkempt man, pot-belly stretching his worn overalls, knew better than anyone not to disturb this particular resident. Something had to be wrong.

Slipping the knife into the waist of his black cargos, the albino slowly opened the door two inches. Jaroslav stepped back and bowed his head slightly, as if ashamed.

"I very sorry, sir." Jaroslav muttered in broken English. "Make horrible mistake."

The albino just nodded in a mechanical fashion, urging the landlord to continue.

"I very short on money. Interpol offer reward for people that help solve case. I know you good person, but thought you be gone by now – you never stay so long – and it do no harm to let them look. I know you hide nothing, they not find anything bad here, but maybe they give me money anyway, so…" The man stammered on, finally stopping when his resident's hand rose, cutting him off.

The story was a lie, the albino knew. Jaroslav was terrified of him, cowering each time they'd pass one another in the halls. They only spoke during the initial purchase of the apartment. The killer's reclusive temperament was enough to draw suspicion, and coupled with his striking physical attributes it was not surprising that Jaroslav would suspect him of acting outside the law. Still, he'd assumed the frequent payoffs he'd slipped under the office door would be sufficient to buy silence. Unfortunately, it seemed the intelligence community had offered a bit more, and the pale man knew better than most that greed trumps all – even if it goes against one's better judgment.

Now here they were. The silly man had realized his error and came to warn him, an unspoken plea to let him off the hook – spare his life. Luckily for Jaroslav, a dead body in the building would only validate the tip – but this deed would not go unpunished.

It was only fifteen minutes before a dark suburban pulled up in front his aparthotel building, the *U Zlate Podkovy*. Cars were no longer allowed on the tourist-jammed streets but, as with everything, a special accommodation was made for law enforcement.

The albino recognized Ivan Tesar and his lapdog, Milos, from his research on the local authorities. According to his inside sources, there would be no trouble buying off Tesar – he had a loose interpretation of right and wrong that tended to sway with the amount of money being pushed his way. Two additional agents exited the SUV. The man was clearly American: if his unrefined demeanor didn't give him away, the red, white and blue tie certainly did. With him was a woman, stunning and elegant despite her stiff black suit. The look of her, and the fact she was American law enforcement, aroused him. So he made himself a promise – he'd have her. More than once.

35

Nerudova Street Apartment
Prague, Czech Republic

The wooden door opened before the agents knocked. The landlord had obviously been standing on the other side, awaiting their arrival.

Tesar and the man who'd introduced himself as Jaroslav exchanged what Capelli guessed were pleasantries, though he could have been calling the landlord a thief and a moron and she'd have been none the wiser. If Jaroslav was trying to remain calm and collected he was doing a terrible job of it, sweat pouring from his forehead as he stammered in Czech. With nervous backward glances, he led them up a winding set of hundred-year-old stairs to a third floor apartment. His hand grazed the railing on the trek up for stability, but it trembled the whole walk up.

Tesar's face must have gotten around on the local evening news or in the morning papers because the landlord did everything in his power to better please the investigation. He'd only nodded to Capelli, Ford, and Milos who, as always, straggled about ten feet behind. But with Tesar he was nothing other than an amenable, helpful host – so much so that even with a language barrier, Capelli and Ford rolled their eyes at his overly-accommodating behavior.

Jaroslav fumbled with his key ring, which held upwards of twenty keys, and after dropping them once and using the wrong key twice, he successfully opened the door to the apartment in question. Ford, always a little tactless at concealing his initial reaction, let out a long whistle at the sight of the little studio. The stainless steel Bosch appliances, perfectly made bed adorned in the latest Sferra sheet set, and elaborate techno-geek command center, surprised all the agents. Perhaps the smarmy Jaroslav was on to something with his tip.

"Listen, Ivan. We're in your jurisdiction here, so we'll follow your lead." Capelli offered. She didn't mean it, but thought an appeal to his ego would be beneficial. "You can take a first sweep and we'll follow behind you."

"Fine, Miss Capelli. But anything you may discover is to remain in Czech jurisdiction until we conclude our investigation."

Plastering a friendly expression on her face, Capelli agreed.

It was a half-hour before Tesar's crime scene techs arrived. The group entered the hall from the stairwell, giving Capelli and Ford their first look at a rather motley trio of characters. There was a balding, slack-faced man who was probably forty but due to his haggard appearance could have easily passed for a retiree. His dark-blue work overalls hung loosely off his thin frame, suggesting he'd recently lost weight or had borrowed a colleague's work-wear for the excursion. Next, a student-type not a day over twenty whose innocent face, with it's perfectly clear skin and bright blue eyes, did not belong investigating crimes. Capelli doubted he'd even started shaving. Bringing up the rear was a woman – the only one of the group to formally introduce herself – named Svetla. Her dark hair was cut in a blunt bob, adding to the severity of her already angular face. She was a pretty woman, and seemed social enough, but wore the tough expression of a woman working in a man's world.

The techs spent an hour dusting and swabbing the apartment. After their initial sweep Tesar finally allowed the American agents into the studio. Capelli and Ford made a bee-line for the high-tech set-up on the far side of the apartment, opposite the small bed. These days, people's whole lives were stored on their computers and they assumed this guy would be no exception.

Ford hit the enter key on the silver MacbookPro computer, not expecting anything to happen. The screen lit-up along with a pinging sound alerting them the computer had awoken from its slumber. Ford looked at Capelli and shrugged; surprised the machine had turned on and wasn't demanding a password.

"There's something wrong with it." Tesar's voice boomed from across the room. "Tech will need to access it."

"Probably nothing there, anyway. So far it looks like this guy's just a neat-freak with a nosy landlord."

"He signed the lease as Sir Paul McCartney. He's obviously looking to remain anonymous." Capelli interjected.

"That's suspicious, yes. But not solid. Maybe this is his crash pad with a mistress and he doesn't want the missus finding out and pulling a Heather Mills."

Capelli just raised her eyebrows and sighed. Ford had a point.

The computer's desktop space was empty aside from two folders, neither of which had been named. Ford tried clicking on both and a message appeared on the screen in Russian. Nobody knew exactly what it said, but the bright red X was an internationally understood symbol – they were denied access.

Accepting defeat, they left the computer with its blinking message and began scouring the rest of the apartment. The countertops and the small kitchen table were completely free of clutter, leaving no paper trail for them to rifle through – no mail, bills, or any other identifying papers were to be seen anywhere. Even the bathroom was meticulously clean with the uniform bottles of shampoo, shave cream, and toothpaste all in their designated place behind the mirror of a medicine cabinet mounted on the wall above the pedestal sink. According to Svetla, there was not a hair to be found in the bathroom, not even the shower drain which would suggest they were dealing with someone whose tidy tendencies went beyond those of a neat-freak – this was a man who didn't want to be found.

After determining the bathroom was a dead-end, the agents searched a small but modern armoire that stood against the wall near the foot of the bed. There were six size large, slim fit, black Italian T-shirts hung in a row on six stainless steel hangers spaced exactly one inch from one-another. To the right there was a small drawer that held six pairs of men's briefs, carefully folded and stacked atop one another. There were no shoes, suits, or casual wear that would normally be found in a man's closet, suggesting this was a short-term crash pad or the man had been tipped off and departed with his belongings. But then why leave the computer?

Ford, determining there was nothing interesting in the armoire, began looking through the kitchen cabinets. The cupboards were empty aside from one complete set of white dishes. He assumed they were Ikea until Capelli joined him and pointed out the Raynaud china was worth more than his beat-up Ford Explorer. He just shrugged; figuring Caroline would be impressed with the man's taste.

Ford opened the refrigerator door, half hoping to find a snack, but instead found twenty bottles of Volvic bottled water lined up in perfect rows.

"Guilty or not, this guy is definitely a freak."

"So what? He's tidy and hydrated. Maybe you should take note." Capelli raised an eyebrow his way, but paused when she noticed an object wedged near the refrigerator. Crouching, she strained to reach the half-hidden item, eventually grasping it with her fingertips.

Her heart pumped fast and the blood drained from her face, she couldn't believe it.

"What is it?" Ford asked, Capelli's body still blocking his view.

"A syringe."

"Maybe he was diabetic." Svetla, who was now seated on the lone kitchen chair, chimed in.

"Maybe. Or it's our murder weapon."

36

Doctors Without Borders Camp
Jowhar, Somalia

Jean-Pierre leaned against the counter in Turner's ramshackle kitchen, waiting as his colleague shuffled through notebooks documenting the previous few weeks. Turner had asked him over to help develop a timeline of the disease's progression based on the doctor's daily notes. Its sudden onset, rapid evolution, and now the immediate decrease in symptoms after only one dose of medication, were incongruous with what Turner knew of TB. He was a natural skeptic but thought if he could trace it back to the beginning then perhaps something would jump out that would help connect the dots.

Jean-Pierre had left Noelle's quarantine tent, arriving at Turner's residence just as the power went out – an almost daily occurrence at the camp. Still, despite knowing he'd be spending the evening reading Turner's chicken scratches by candlelight, he was the happiest he'd been in years. The heavy burden of helplessness and fear had finally lifted from his shoulders as Noelle's condition began improving – he wasn't going to lose her.

"Okay, this should do it." Turner huffed, placing a stack of composition notebooks on the rickety wooden table. "Grab a beer and have a seat."

Jean-Pierre did so and laughed. "You know, Luc, these days people use computers. I know there's a perfectly good one sitting around here somewhere, gathering dust."

"Yeah, but when the power goes out there's still work." Turner said, tossing a notebook over to Jean-Pierre.

"Okay, so what details should I be looking for in these diaries of yours?"

"I want to read through the entries just before the outbreak to see if we had any new patients arriving around that time that could have been the carriers. If so, we may be able to pinpoint where the first infected individuals came from and see if there's another community out there in need of antibiotics."

"Easy enough." Jean-Pierre took a swig of his beer, ready to dive in.

"Also keep an eye out for any cases that don't jive with TB. I'm having a hard time accepting the Mantoux results – both you and I should be sick if this was TB."

"My friend, you are being paranoid."

"Probably, but something isn't adding up."

37

Nerudova Street
Prague, Czech Republic

The killer couldn't fathom what was taking the agents so long, considering there was nothing to find. One of his best decisions had been to burn the tips of his fingers, rendering the smudged fingerprints he left behind worthless – not having to wipe down fingerprints saved a lot of time if a quick getaway was necessary. His only worry was hair, or perhaps some other scrap of DNA being left behind, but he had enough confidence in the ineptitude of local law enforcement that it was only a minor concern. He crossed the shadows to a nearby teahouse, fearing one of the meddling trinket-shop owners would grow suspicious of his presence in the alley.

The agents, looking dejected, left the apartment and hastily entered a black SUV just as a slight pinging sound alerted the killer. He smiled to himself as he watched the attractive agent carrying his computer under her arm, not realizing he'd installed a tracking device into his disk drive that would keep him aware of his pursuers' movements – at least until they dropped it off with a tech specialist for analysis. The pale man had created a destructive virus which already had erased his stored data and would melt the hard drive in minutes should anyone try and recover the missing information. It would be impossible to get beyond the flashing red X on the desktop.

Tapping his iPhone to life, he watched the moving red dot as GPS tracked his computer, then motioned for his bill. The rotund waitress responded with an annoyed eye-roll – unhappy at being pulled from the latest salacious headlines on *Hello* magazine. Awaiting the unhappy waitress, the man patiently finished his Oolong tea. He'd let them have a head start.

38

Fiumicino Airport
Rome, Italy

Turner sipped a strong, frothy espresso at the airport bar, marveling at how quickly he re-acclimated to the civilized world. The rich coffee coupled with the throngs of attractive, always-stylish Italians making their way through Rome's Fiumicino Airport instantly perked him from a sleepy malaise caused by too-many connections as he made his way to Prague. The flight from Mogadishu to Nairobi had aged Turner a solid ten years. As a general rule he gave himself a 50/50 chance of surviving the short but perilous trip with poorly trained pilots and airplanes whose wings seemed duct-taped together. Still, it was a necessary evil to catch the Alitalia flight to Amsterdam which would eventually get him to Prague by way of Rome. The exodus felt like something from *Planes, Trains, and Automobiles*;

leaving Turner to wonder when John Candy's ghost would make an appearance.

A gorgeous dark-haired woman passed close enough for Turner to absorb the lavender-scented breeze that followed in her wake. She wore a fitted skirt and low cut sweater with a red silk scarf serving as a dose of color to the otherwise black outfit. Immediately his mind went to an impure place and he realized what a sad state of affairs his personal life had become. The woman didn't so much as peek back at him, which chipped at his ego considering his looks usually garnered him a glance or two. But now, after being in-transit for over fifteen hours, his floppy hair was a mess and his rumpled khakis a crime in the eyes of an Italian woman.

"Peroni, per favore," Turner ordered.

The Roman bartender popped a frosted bottle and slid it to Turner.

Sipping the cold brew, he turned his attention back to the *International Herald Tribune* cover story detailing the death of Polaris Pharmaceuticals executives.

Turner hadn't planned on taking this trip, but his review of events with Jean-Pierre had raised more questions than answers. On top of that, the Kenya lab claimed to have lost his specimens. Katrine Johansson had apologized profusely for the mix up, blaming a recent outbreak of malaria for the irresponsible oversight. He'd asked to speak with Eva but she was otherwise occupied, adding to his aggravation with his former flame.

As luck would have it, Turner hadn't sent all his samples to Kenya and a number remained stored in Jowhar. He decided it was a good time to call Skala and cash-in the IOU he was due. Two years ago at a conference in Berlin, Skala had taken a liking to a pretty German girl. Unfortunately, the girl had a big German boyfriend who had a solid fifty pounds on the scrawny – and very drunk – Skala. Turner threw in a right hook just in time and dragged his friend from the bar before He-Man could reappear. He figured requesting his colleague to analyze a few samples wouldn't be too much to ask.

As they discussed the outbreak and the odd presentation of TB symptoms over the phone, Skala had grown curious. He recalled a similar rapidly-spreading TB outbreak in a children's camp in Shatoy, Chechnya six months earlier. Since the camp was some distance from the town, they were able to contain the disease. However, the medication did not arrive in time and all twenty-two children perished within two weeks – an unheard of progression for TB. Skala had inquired about the incident, wanting more information on the strain, but his calls and emails had gone unanswered. Since Shatoy was a remote village, and twenty-two deaths are a small footnote in a war-torn country, the tragedy never made news and was swept under the rug.

The case in Chechnya immediately had Turner's radar on alert. From the little information they had, it seemed the disease was similar to that in Jowhar. Moreover, it pissed him off that those kids never had a chance – so he was personally escorting his samples to Prague in search of answers.

39

Ruzyne Airport
Prague, Czech Republic

"**C**ome on, Ford. They're boarding already!" Capelli, always punctual, hated running to the gate. She was more of a seating-group 2 type of woman.

"Yeah, well, if and when you have kids, you'll understand. Anytime you take a trip, you gotta come back like Santa Claus."

"So who's the Absinthe for – Brian or Lucy?"

"Hey, this stuff isn't legal in the states," he defended himself, juggling a two-foot long chocolate bar for Brian and a purple duck for Lucy.

"Spoken like a real FBI man."

Grabbing some rumpled Czech crowns from his pocket, Ford came up a few bills short. His eyes pleaded with Capelli for a loan to buy his deal-of-the-century Absinthe. She tossed the last of her monopoly money on the counter.

"Don't come crying to me when you go blind from that stuff."

Capelli settled into her middle seat, uncomfortably wedging herself between Ford, who was looking out the window like a kid at Christmas, and a heavy-set balding man who desperately needed a stick of Mitchum. She considered breaking open the Absinthe to get through takeoff. Hell, she owned a third of the bottle.

"I can't believe Masterson wouldn't give us another day." Ford griped. "We started making progress."

"I wouldn't call it progress yet. We'll see what comes of the syringe analysis and if Tesar's able to dig up more info on the apartment owner. Otherwise, we didn't do enough to justify staying."

"I suppose. Wake me when we're stateside. I'm gonna catch some shut eye before I return to the house of chaos."

With Ford snoring softly beside her, Capelli reflected on the connection between the deaths of Warren and Thorpe. She never noticed the tall albino man sitting two rows back.

40

**Polaris Research Lab
Prague, Czech Republic**

It was 10:00 p.m. and an exhausted Turner was finding his way through the dark halls of Polaris Pharmaceuticals' satellite lab on the outskirts of Prague. The facility was a far cry from the showy office building located in the center of town. The brilliant, but less presentable, scientists were housed here to conduct their research without interruption. The lab itself was state-of-the-art, but the office wing was in dire need of fumigation and a thorough paint job. He followed his nose and eventually came upon the office he'd been seeking.

"Jesus, Skala. How do you get away with smoking in here?"

"You don't have to call me Jesus. Vaclav will suffice." The Czech man rose from behind his paper strewn desk and flashed a yellow-toothed grin. "Great to see you, Luc. It's been far too long my friend. We must drink." He pulled a bottle of vodka from his desk and poured generous shots into dirty paper cups.

The last thing Turner wanted after traveling was a shot of vodka from Skala's coffee-stained Dixie cup. But since a shower and hot meal were a few hours off he decided one shot may not be a bad idea.

"Salut!" Vaclav cheerfully raised his glassed. Judging by his glassy eyes and the fact it was after 7:00 p.m. Turner assumed this wasn't Skala's first nip. Most scientists with Vaclav Skala's proclivity towards hard liquor and the occasional round of paid-for sex would be too much of a liability for a pharmaceutical company. But, as luck would have it for Skala, the Prague office hadn't adopted the West's personal conduct standards, and his brilliance was such that he'd been deemed a necessity. It didn't hurt that he knew the dirty little secrets of his boss one rung up. As long as Lenka Kovar – genius scientist and adulteress extraordinaire – was his boss, there was nothing but job security in his future.

"So, Luc, how's our friend Eva?" Skala always preferred speaking of women rather than medicine.

"Let's just say I'd rather discuss a severe strain of tuberculosis than that woman." Turner, knowing he'd regret it, held out his Dixie cup for another shot.

"Ah, I see. Well, my friend, I think what you need is a trip to a little place I know off Wenceslas Square."

Turner knew the place from a night two years ago when he'd crossed paths with Vaclav. No shot in hell was he going back to that rat-hole – even Hefner would blush at the scene.

"Sounds great, but I'm beat. Let's get these samples in a fridge and call it a night. Tomorrow we can get a bite."

"Ah, I see those little grey hairs are catching up to you." Skala laughed as Turner inadvertently picked at the grey wisps in his sideburns. "It is okay, my friend, you've had a long day. Tomorrow we play." Skala grabbed the samples to place in storage. "Ah! I forgot to mention that I left a message with the doctor assigned to the Chechnya camp during the outbreak. Apparently she quit shortly after the children died – understandably had enough of the whole thing."

"How many others were stationed with her?"

"She was the only permanent doctor. There was so much fighting at the time they were concerned for safety. From what I've gathered, they rotated local nurses and other doctors would come for a few weeks at a time from nearby villages. Unorthodox, but I guess necessary. I'm trying to track down those names, but the records have been difficult to obtain."

"Those assignments will all be in the Doctors Without Borders database. I'll get in touch with someone tomorrow."

"That's who I contacted – utterly worthless endeavor. Maybe they'll show more love to you, pretty boy."

"I'm sure you managed to say just the wrong thing, Vaclav. We'll try again tomorrow. The more we can learn about the Shatoy outbreak, the better."

41

FBI Headquarters
Midtown Manhattan

A weary Danny Ford rapped on Capelli's office door at 8:57 a.m. They had exactly three minutes to trek down the hall for a progress report with Masterson, an update that Ford was dreading. He'd spent his commute on the L train steeling himself for the dressing down they'd get for wasting company funds on a two-day jaunt to Europe that produced little to no results.

Ford gave her a minute and then opened the door, fearing she'd fled to avoid the impending meeting. Instead, he saw her cradling a phone and scribbling feverishly with her Bic. Her wide-eyes screamed *don't just stand in the doorway, you idiot – get in here.*

"Okay, that's great. Thanks for your call, Ivan. I appreciate you keeping us in the loop. You'll be the first to know if I get a hit... right... okay... goodbye."

"Come on, we don't want to be late for our flogging," Ford whined, already heading out the door. "What's super cop want anyway? I thought for sure we'd never hear from him again."

"Let's just say I think we'll avoid Masterson's guillotine for one more day. I'll catch you up in the meeting."

As the agents entered Masterson's office he didn't so much as glance up. Capelli felt for the man – he'd been such a nice guy until his promotion. Now the weight of his position in an agency with some recent black-eyes and a bloated budget under scrutiny had turned him into a curmudgeon, to put it nicely.

"Ah, my favorite agents." Masterson muttered, still staring at his computer screen. "How's Prague this time of year?"

"Lovely, you should take the wife," Ford replied, forgetting Masterson was mid-divorce.

"Cute, Ford. Sit down you two and give me an update."

Capelli jumped right to it, eager to prove herself. "Well, we found a few interesting things. First, Martin Warren had a secret son he gave up for adoption. The records are sealed but I'm working my contact at the adoption agency to get more information. He reached out to Warren a few years back so I figure it can't hurt to talk with him."

"Probably nothing." Masterson straightened his back, preparing to give a lecture.

"I agree. But this may not be. A reward was offered for information related to the murder of Warren. A landlord called in a tip about a suspicious tenant, which we assumed was unrelated – an attempt at easy money. Well, we investigated anyway and found a remarkably clean, print-free apartment."

"Interesting…" Masterson cut her off. Ford just slumped his chair, figuring this was going nowhere.

"It is, most people don't wipe a place down unless they're running from something. We also found a syringe wedged behind the refrigerator." Capelli paused, allowing the possible connection to sink in. Masterson leaned in, now hanging on her words.

"Well, Ivan Tesar just called and informed me that the syringe was clean. There were no prints and it wasn't possible to identify if there'd ever been a substance in it. But they were able to obtain DNA from a pillowcase. Apparently the person in question wasn't aware he drools in his sleep. The sample matched with an individual who had once been entered into the Interpol database – but – listen to this – the records were pulled from Interpol and are sealed with FSB. According to Tesar, they weren't interested in cooperating with him on the issue. He'd like us to throw our weight around and see if we can convince the Russians to share their information." Capelli sat back, feeling satisfied with herself.

"The FSB? Cooperate? Not within the next decade." Masterson stared at the wall, thinking. "You know, this may have nothing to do with your case."

"True, but it's hard to brush it aside. This guy is obviously a criminal and there was a syringe in the apartment. It's at least worth a call to Russia."

"I'll see what I can do. Meanwhile you guys keep at it. The media's having a field day with these high-profile killings and we're starting to look inept. If you don't catch me a killer soon I'll frame one of you for it. Somebody's gotta burn."

42

Chelsea Hotel
New York, New York

The albino made it to New York without incident, traveling under the name Hans Bruun with his falsified Swedish passport. He set-up shop in the Chelsea Hotel where Bob Dylan seduced Edie Sedgwick, Janis Joplin charmed Kris Kristofferson, and Charles Bukowski wrote about ham, eggs, and women. But the glory days were long gone and the hotel was now bordering on dilapidated and undergoing much-needed renovation. A work stoppage order was plastered over the doors until the Landmark Preservation Commission could come to an agreement with the developers on the hotel's new look.

Though the Chelsea came far from meeting the albino's standards of cleanliness, the fact it was completely devoid of security and personnel made it the ideal locale for him to work in peace. He'd chosen a room with a queen-sized bed and small living area – a sad excuse for a suite – and thoroughly wiped it down before setting up his computer and scrambling gear, then managed a rare smile to himself as he thought of his colleague, Mr. B. For the past twenty-four hours Mr. B had been trying to reach Hans, who had grown weary of his partners constant nagging and ineptness. From now on, Hans would run the show and establish contact on his terms. Grabbing one of his untraceable burner phones, he dialed Mr. B. It only took one ring.

"Jesus, where have you been! Tell me you've not been arrested…" The voice burst through the receiver.

"Relax, Mr. B. The Martin situation was a success. Things are back on track now." Hans didn't bring up the search of his Prague apartment – that would cause Mr. B a coronary.

"You should have discussed that with me. I don't appreciate learning about unplanned murders on the local news!"

"It had to be done. You know that."

"Fine. No more improvising, unless I clear it. Where are you now?" The tremble in Mr. B's voice began to subside.

"No need for you to know that. There's been a small change in plans but everything remains on track." Hans guessed it would not go well if he revealed his plans for the female FBI agent to his nervous colleague.

"You better still be in Europe. There's a problem in Prague that will need to be addressed."

"What?"

"I'll tell you when it's necessary."

43

Kate Capelli's Apartment
New York, New York

Kate climbed the four flights of stairs to her quaint Murray Hill townhouse apartment. Most New Yorkers wouldn't brag about living on 39th and Madison – these days it was all about a posh Tribeca loft or the tree-lined streets of the West Village. But Capelli was happy with her little Midtown oasis, a confused blend of the business world and cozy residential streets.

Entering her foyer, Kate immediately felt the absence of Oscar, her beloved Boxer mix she'd rescued as a puppy. The large dog had taken up half her square footage but she'd trade the extra space any day for his wagging tail at the end of a long day. He succumbed to old age six months before, yet she expected to hear his bark as her keys slid into the door lock.

Disconcerted by the new silence that greeted her; she shucked her Theory blazer over the sofa and traded it for a cold glass of New Zealand Sauvignon Blanc, then set her ancient Blackberry on speaker to listen through the many voicemails from the day.

The first was from Marcy Travers, her nasal North Dakota accent still distinct as ever despite living in New York for ten years. Travers was third in command at the New York State Adoption Service and had been helpful to Capelli on prior cases when children were involved. *Hi Kate, it's Marcy. Sorry I didn't get back to you sooner, it's been a real zoo here. I'll do what I can for you on the Warren adoption but, without a court-order, there's only so much... Anyway, one of these days you've gotta come visit me in Williamsburg, a great little wine bar just opened in the neighborhood.* Marcy continued rambling until Kate finally jumped to the next message. *Hey Kate, Allen here. Hope everything is okay with your case. Or – if that was an excuse to get out of dinner – you were very convincing and I promise this will be my only call. But if f you'd like to get a bite one of these nights, give me a ring. I'd love to see you.*

The case had kept her so preoccupied that Kate had almost forgotten about Allen. One of these days she'd figure out how to manage a date without being called to a crime scene. Work-life balance existed only in dreams for Capelli.

She stood, topped off her wine, and looked out the living room's large picture window – her favorite feature of the apartment. While the idea of seeing Allen made her a little giddy, nothing could take her away from a hot bath and take-out couscous from the nearby Moroccan restaurant. Nothing, that is, that was in her control. One man could change her plans for the night – or forever – and he was carefully watching her every movement from the building across the street. Just watching and waiting for the perfect moment.

44

Aria Hotel
Prague, Czech Republic

Turner's alarm buzzed promptly at 7:00 a.m. The warm morning sun peeked through the curtains and landed squarely on his face, nearly blinding him as he silenced the bedside clock. His whole body ached, forcing the realization that with middle-age comes longer recovery time from torturously small airplane seats.

Without sitting up he reached for the phone and dialed room service, hoping that eggs and large pot of coffee would make him feel half-human. Gazing out at the red rooftops of *Malá Strana,* he congratulated himself on making the fiscally irresponsible decision of shelling out for a fancy hotel.

Rather than take a quick shower before his breakfast arrived, he opted for an extra thirty minutes under the plush comforter, clicked on CNN International, and hunted around the bedside table for his phone. He was expecting an update from Jean-Pierre.

"Ugh." Turner groaned to himself. Four missed calls and a voicemail, one from Jean-Pierre, the rest from Vaclav Skala. Maybe he'd kept the party going last night and needed bail money. For all his brilliance, the scientist remained a liability.

The first message was a simple update from Jean-Pierre. *Luc, hope all is well. Things are still improving remarkably fast here. Maalik has a case of diarrhea but it doesn't seem related to the illness, probably just dehydration. Amaka says hello, she's been working on quite the art project for you. It's a strange creation with grass and sticks. I have no idea what it's supposed to be but I guess it's the thought that counts. I'll check in tomorrow, enjoy the civilized world.* The thought of Amaka brought a smile to Turner's face. She was notorious for her artwork, always diligently working until achieving her version of perfection. Most of her pieces took a lot of imagination to appreciate.

The remaining messages were from Skala. Five in the morning: *Luc, wanted to let you know I'm going to start growing the bacteria now. Thought it was best to get an early start.* Turner was grateful his phone had been on vibrate – that was not a call worth waking for. Next message: *Listen, Luc. I'm not sure we're dealing with TB here. The cultures seem to be growing faster than normal.* Interesting, but probably nothing. Final message: *Luc, get here now. This is unbelievable!*

The urgency in Skala's voice caused Turner's heart to skip a few beats. If the samples were so fascinating to the scientist then surely they were worth ditching a shower for. He pulled on a pair of jeans, a cream colored turtleneck, and his worn out brown boots, grabbed his wallet and hurried out the door, right into the room service cart. Apologizing profusely for a near disaster, Turner signed a generous tip to the waiter, grabbed a croissant from the tray, and longingly eyed the fluffy scrambled eggs.

"I've gotta run, the breakfast is yours if you want it." Judging by the young man's wide smile the eggs would not go to waste.

45

Polaris Research Lab
Prague, Czech Republic

Vaclav Skala stared through the lens of his Leica AS Laser Dissection Microscope and grew increasingly fascinated by the tube-like bacteria currently on the slide. While the size and shape of the bacteria looked like tuberculosis, it wasn't acting like it.

Skala arrived early to grow the bacteria in Petri dishes. It was a necessary step to proving with one-hundred-percent certainty the illness Turner had been dealing with was, in fact, TB. Bored by the thought of such an uninteresting disease, he took his time prepping the dishes, applying the sputum samples, controlling the oxygen in the bacteria's atmosphere.

He'd been somewhat surprised at the extensive cord factor the bacteria displayed: a serpentine 'cord' formation that occurred only in the most virulent, drug-resistant strains of TB. That little tidbit had been the cause of his second voicemail to Turner. But it was the realization that after only one hour the bacteria had begun to divide that prompted the third call. Typically, it took anywhere between fifteen and twenty hours for M. tuberculosis to begin division, an extremely slow rate of growth compared to other bacterium.

"Morning, Vaclav. What's the urgency?" Turner walked into the lab, nodding his thanks to the secretary who had escorted him to Skala's workspace.

"Luc! Lovely case of bed-head. Nice of you to show." Skala never turned away from his microscope, but his guess about the bed-head had been a good one.

"It's 7:48 in the morning. I didn't know we were working on China time."

"What can I say? I'm an early riser." Vaclav entered commands on the large high-definition computer screen which displayed with unparalleled clarity the slide sample sitting under the microscope.

"Impressive, Skala. I see your toy fund has increased."

"The Polaris buyout was fantastic for the budget. And so far they've been too disorganized transitioning to notice my personal habits." He winked at Turner, finally peeling his eyes from the scope.

Turner carefully eyed the worm-like bacteria shown on the computer screen, recalling that lab-work had never been his strong suit in med school

"What's this little nodule here?" he asked Skala, pointing to a nearly invisible spot that had attached itself to the ends of each bacteria strand.

"Don't know yet. Frustrating little bugger is adamant on remaining attached to his friend TB. I've tried to dissect the organisms with the laser but, even then, they stick together. A first for me, I have to say." Skala popped Nicorette gum, a preemptive strike on an inevitable nicotine craving. Even he wouldn't smoke in the lab.

"Is it possible it's just part of the M. tuberculosis bacteria?"

"Possible, I suppose. But I've done a little research and haven't found anything of this nature." He spun on his chair, gesturing for Turner to follow him.

"The cells began division during the first hour. With a normal TB division wouldn't occur until almost twelve hours." Skala carefully moved a microscope over one of the Petri dishes. He leaned his sweaty forehead into the machine, peeking through the lenses. The cells had divided yet again. He was officially perplexed.

"May I have a look?" Turner asked, trying to sound patient.

Skala stepped aside and popped another Nicorette while Turner took his turn.

"These samples have that same little nodule." Turner rubbed his chin, unsure what to make of the bacteria.

"Don't jump to conclusions, Luc," Skala was anticipating Turner's next question – it was the same question that had kept Skala up at night. "I'm going to try and separate the common TB bacteria and the nodule and see what I find. One more thing: was there any point when the samples could have become compromised? Were they properly preserved, even while you travelled here?"

"I followed protocol by the book," Turner paused, thinking. "Perhaps this isn't TB but some other bacteria that responds to the drugs. And this kind of cell division would explain the impossibly fast progression of the patients' symptoms."

"But then your antibiotics wouldn't have been effective. And –"

"And, they worked too well. Not that I'm complaining. The whole camp was cured within a matter of days. Symptom relief was nearly instant."

"Should have taken weeks. Look, go to my office and dig through the medical journals pertaining to bacteria. Meanwhile, I'll stay here and try to separate these bacteria."

The thought of working in Vaclav's disheveled, smelly office made Turner's stomach flip. He thought to himself how ridiculous it was, that he was comfortable in war torn countries with limited plumbing but not in his colleague's workplace.

"I'll give you some space to work, no need for me to be a distraction. My hotel is nearby. You've got the number if you need to reach me."

"It's a deal, my friend. Sausage and Pilsner tonight?"

"Sounds great. I owe you."

46

FBI Headquarters
Midtown Manhattan

"**A**hhh…" Ford grumbled into the phone. "Hang on a sec, baby. Lisa's at the door."

"Go, go. I'll see you tonight. Don't forget the potatoes. Love you." Caroline had grown accustomed to Lisa interrupting their conversations.

"Love you, too." Ford hastily replaced the phone in its cradle. "Come in, Lisa." He called.

Lisa Stiles entered the drab office chomping on a wad of gum. Her dark curly hair fell messily over plump shoulders as she leaned against the doorframe. Her technical title was receptionist but in reality she served as mother and office manager to the agents working on the 2nd floor. They often joked amongst themselves that she was the one irreplaceable person at the bureau and had dubbed her "Wonder Woman" long ago. She'd keep correspondence, answer phones, hold meetings and remind forgetful agents of their wives' birthdays. For all this she was paid little more than a Dunkin' Donuts employee.

"Hey, Ford. Some guy – calls himself Babineaux, line two. Claims to be Interpol." Her strong Brooklyn accent was spoken in a flat monotone, sounding as if she found everything mind-numbingly boring.

"Yeah, I'll take it. Thanks, Lisa."

"Yup." She blew a large green bubble, popping it as she left the office.

Ford clicked on two, readying himself for the "here's why we can't be of any help to you" spiel typical of agencies like Interpol.

"Nikolas, Ford here. How are things in Lyon?"

"It's late and rainy." Typical French, always complaining, Ford thought to himself.

"It's past your bedtime over there. What's keeping you up?"

"I have some information for you, but it has to remain between us," he said with a Pepe Le Pew accent.

"Fair enough." Ford wished he'd get to the point, he had potatoes to peel.

Nikolas Babineaux ignored Ford's tone and continued. "The man whose DNA you found in Prague... I may know who he is. Well, not who he actually is but I'm familiar with an alias of his. I was around a few years back when some files went missing. It was pretty clear to us that the FSB was involved."

"How did the FSB delete files from the Interpol system? Don't you guys have better security than that?" Ford chided.

"We had a mole about eight years back. Don't let that get around." Babineaux dropped his voice an octave to stress this embarrassment was not to be made public.

"Lips are sealed."

"Anyhow, he was using the alias Erik Richter. Interpol was after him for the assassination of a British parliament member ten years ago. He's been off the grid since – which is pretty stealthy for a six-foot-four albino."

"So you have a photo?"

"Had. It was deleted with the file. But he's physically distinctive, not an average Joe as you Americans say."

"All right. What else do you know?" Ford was surprised how helpful his French counterpart was being. They'd crossed paths before and had done nothing more than butt heads, mostly at the fault of Ford and his colorful remarks about French socialism.

"There's speculation he spent time in Russia. We believe the FSB suspect him for a series of attacks against Russian politicos and oligarchs, a few years back. They'd like to bring him in before we do."

"Hence the deleted files."

"Exactly. But their mole only deleted the information in the file, not the file itself with Richter's name. Doing that would have raised a red flag. So when you ran the DNA through the international databases we still got the hit. At least now I know he's still out there."

"Well, it seems we've helped each other then," Ford said without sarcasm.

"I suppose we did. It's possible that Richter has nothing to do with your case, though. But at least you found his hideout."

"I'm still going to put out an international BOLO. I want this guy brought in."

"I'll help if I can, but this guy's a shadow. You shine a light on him and he's gone."

"Thanks, Nikolas. I'll keep it in mind. Now, get some sleep."

47

Aria Hotel
Prague, Czech Republic

Turner was feeling proud of himself, having finally mastered the task of setting up a Skype account. He was preparing for a video conference with Edyta Zajak, the Polish doctor who'd been in charge of the Shatoy operation during the disease outbreak that killed so many children.

The past forty-eight hours had been frustrating. While Skala worked diligently in the lab, Turner tracked down Zajak and began reaching out to infectious disease specialists for help. Skala had been unable to determine what the foreign organism was that had attached to the bacterium and was running out of ideas. Increasingly, the evidence was pointing to something more sinister than a simple strain of TB.

Eyeing the glowing red digits of the hotel clock, Turner was surprised to see it was nearly noon, the scheduled time for their video chat with Dr. Zajak. Skala had promised to arrive a half hour ago. Turner cursed Skala's quirkiness as he spiffed up his room. He felt silly making the bed and folding his clothes but wasn't sure what his computer camera would pick up during his chat with Zajak.

Finally, sitting in front of his computer, Turner poured the last bit of room service coffee into a white porcelain cup and restlessly waited. After only a minute, the round face of Dr. Zajak appeared on screen. She looked to be in her early fifties, had blonde hair giving way to vibrant silver, and bright blue eyes surrounded by crow's feet. Her plump frame and warm smile gave the impression she'd be more suited to baking cookies and reading bedtime stories to her grandchildren than facing the daily rigors of running a Doctors Without Borders operation.

"Luc Turner, I assume?" she asked with a thick Polish accent.

"Pleasure to meet you, Dr. Zajak. I appreciate you taking the time." Turner felt a little awkward speaking at the computer."

"No problem at all. I'm sorry to hear about the outbreak in Somalia. What's the status there?" Zajak asked with genuine concern.

"We suffered a lot of casualties but it seems the medication has done its job. I've not been there for about four days now but my colleague assures me things continue to improve."

"That's great news. I wish we'd have been so lucky in Shatoy. I'll never forget having to dig those twenty-two little graves." There was emotion in her voice but she maintained a tough expression as she spoke – she was a woman who didn't crack.

"There's nothing worse." Turner immediately thought of Amaka, grateful she'd cheated death. "A colleague of mine – he's actually supposed to be here with me – was the one who told me about the Shatoy outbreak. A lot of the symptoms are similar to what we saw in Somalia. Can you tell me what happened?" Turner worried he was being pushy, but Edyta Zajak didn't seem into small-talk.

"I'm surprised your friend found out about Shatoy. Everyone aside from me did their best to keep it quiet. Nobody wants to lose their reputation over some dead kids." She shook her head and pursed her lips, more angry than sad, then looked off into the distance, as if deciding where to start. "The whole outbreak lasted less than two weeks. By that time all the children had died."

"No adults were infected?" Turner interjected.

"Only a nurse. One of the adults came down with the flu and naturally we worried about it spreading. The children were very malnourished with weak immune systems so we quarantined them in a building away from the adults, to prevent illness. But twenty-four hours later the kids all began coughing and developing fevers. Initially I assumed they'd contracted the flu, despite our best efforts. But after a few days their symptoms became progressively worse. None of them would eat, they were too weak to walk, and the fevers spiked even higher."

"Did their symptoms ever begin to differ from one another?" Turner asked.

"Yes, actually. The first week it was a fever, cough, and extreme weakness in all the kids. By week two, some were coughing up blood, others had severe diarrhea, and some just seemed to completely shut down right away. It's like their bodies gave up."

"That sounds familiar. How did you manage to stay healthy?"

"The first week I stayed with the adults and a nurse went with the children, since they were healthy at the time of separation. She didn't tell me the kids had become ill until the second day of their sickness. As I knew I was walking into a contaminated area, I wore a mask and gloves at all times and never had a problem. My nurse, however, died along with the children." Turner recognized the disaffected tone in her voice when she mentioned the nurse's death. It was common among people in their profession – if you didn't develop emotional armor you wouldn't make a month in the field. Death had to become a cold fact in a timeline and nothing more. Still, it always surprised him to hear such tragedy spoken of in the same neutral way they'd talk about buying groceries.

The sound of two abrupt knocks caused Edyta to turn her plump face from the computer.

"I'm sorry, Dr. Turner. My appointment is here, I must go. Please call if you have any more questions."

Before Turner could reply the screen went blank, Edyta disappearing at the click of a button. "Good bye to you, too." Turner mumbled to himself. Between Skala's no-show and Edyta's hang-up he was feeling unwanted, like he'd been stood up at the school dance.

As Turner considered another pot of coffee, the shrill ring of the hotel's phone startled him.

"Hello, Vaclav?"

"Hi, Dr. Turner. This is Renata Kubova from Polaris labs. I'm a colleague of Dr. Skala." Her English was passable, though muddled with a thick Eastern European accent.

"Oh, yes, hi Renata. What can I do for you?"

"Well, I'm wondering if you've seen Dr. Skala. He didn't come in today and the MGIT has produced some results I know he'd be interested in. He specifically asked I call him once the results were ready."

"Ok, I'll tell him. He's probably just off on an errand." By errand Turner meant sleeping off an epic hangover.

"Thank you. He's normally the first one here when he's working on a project."

Turner detected a touch of worry in her voice, the type of concern suggesting she was more than a colleague to Skala.

48

FBI Headquarters
Midtown Manhattan

"**C**ome on guys, I can't put an international BOLO out for a tall albino guy." Masterson rubbed his eyes. Washington was on him to cut his costs by ten percent. Again. And now Capelli and Ford sat in his office requesting he put an unwarranted BOLO on an individual whose identity remained unknown. It was only Tuesday.

"Look, I've got a hunch on this. It feels right." Ford paced across the nubby carpet with conviction.

"Your last hunch cost me five grand for you to sightsee in Prague Oh, and Montreal. Let's not forget Montreal."

"Come on, Sir. That was a year ago. And as I've proved to you my credit card was cloned and those

213

whorehouse charges weren't my doing. Prague will still pay off if you sign off on the BOLO."

Masterson glared at Ford, considering how to shut him up. "Look, get me more information on this guy. Homeland Security jumps on my ass every time we put an innocent Mohammed on the no-fly list. Infringes on civil rights blah blah blah."

"But this guy isn't innocent. Besides, if we can pick him up it will be good for our relationship with Interpol." Ford went out on a limb.

"Hey, it's not my job to wipe Interpol's ass. Besides, all you've got is a decade old alias and physical description." Masterson began shuffling papers, suggesting he was busy and that the agents should leave.

"There's not a lot of 6'4 albinos out there. I googled it. The guy will stick out like a sore thumb." Capelli rolled her eyes at Ford's increasing desperation.

"Great, so every tall Swede who goes through TSA screening will be pulled aside. That'll look real good for us. Prove he's a part of your case and I'll consider it. Now get out!"

Masterson's tone suggested the agents were two minutes from being placed on forced leave of absence. Both exited without further complaint.

"What a load of shit," Ford whined.

"Cut him some slack. He's been getting a lot of heat from D.C. lately. Let's go get a cold one at Conelly's."

Hans Bruun waited as the agents drank two rounds of Guiness. The Irish bar was crammed with throngs of rumpled suits and weary expressions. Miserable people leading miserable lives, Bruun thought to himself. He watched Ford say goodbye to his lovely colleague and head west toward the subway. As Capelli stepped onto Madison and started south he was confident she was heading exactly where he wanted her to go.

49

Aria Hotel
Prague, Czech Republic

Turner listened with mixed emotions as Jean-Pierre gave him what had been dubbed the Doctor's Daily Briefing. He was relieved to hear the disease hadn't reappeared and no other major crisis had occurred. Aside from another guerilla raid, things were running smoothly in Jowhar. Between Jean-Pierre's medical skills and Noelle's organization they kept the place ticking like a Swiss watch.

"Oh and Luc, before you go, have you heard of a group called Angels of Africa?"

Turner ran through his mental Rolodex of NGO's which had pledged their support to end disease and poverty. He knew most began as tax deduction schemes for the wealthy; and nothing was more popular on the gala circuit than boasting about philanthropic good deeds over champagne and caviar. That attitude towards charity had once bothered Turner, but no more. He'd learned to accept that good things could be done even if for the wrong reasons.

"Angels of Africa doesn't ring a bell. But all those fluffy, optimistic titles run together in my mind. Who runs it?"

"Not sure. Eva sent me the information yesterday. Apparently they are sponsoring twenty African orphans for study-abroad programs. School, housing, and other living expenses are all taken care of."

"Sounds great. Maybe Rafi would be a good candidate. She's bright and her English is coming along well."

"No, Luc. They want youngsters that will be able to receive a lifetime of good education. The idea is that one day they will return home and put their skills to good use improving things here. I was thinking of Amaka."

The suggestion threw Turner, a rush of adrenaline coursing through his body. He'd grown so close to Amaka he'd started to think of her as his own daughter. The thought of sending her overseas pained him.

"I know what that silence means, Luc. But this would be a great opportunity for her. You know what happens to the girls who stay here. There's no future for her. And I'll have my Lion bars to myself again," Jean-Pierre said with a laugh.

"Yeah, absolutely, you're right. It's perfect for Amaka. And don't worry; I'll raid the duty free shop for Lion bars to bring back."

After another worried call from Renata and a series of unreturned calls to Skala, Turner grew concerned. He obtained Skala's address from Renata who was near panic, confirming to Turner she did more for Skala than just answer phones and clean slides.

Turner exited the hotel, a chilly breeze alerting him to the fact he'd forgotten a scarf. According to Renata, Skala lived in Prague 4 located on the opposite side of the Vltava from Turner's hotel. The concierge provided him with a map and explained the quickest route.

Rather than take a tram packed with tourists, Turner opted to take the fifteen minute pedestrian route. As he crossed the Charles Bridge, Turner considered Jean-Pierre's idea for Amaka, and reprimanded himself for even hesitating. It was clear she was special – intelligent, kind, and vibrant, despite all the adverse conditions of her surroundings. The chance to leave and receive an education would be the perfect opportunity for her.

By the time he neared Skala's address, the sun had completely set, leaving an inky blackness in its wake.

Looking around he was surprised by a pretty residential neighborhood with well-kept streets and rows of elegant old apartment buildings. According to the concierge's roughly-marked map, his destination was just around the corner. Passing a cozy Italian restaurant, small boutiques, and dinner party laughter from a flat above, he marveled at Skala's choice of neighborhood. It seemed like an uncharacteristically mature choice for his party-loving colleague.

Skala's building was a mid-sized walk-up with wrought iron balconies and a pinkish limestone façade – no doubt the architect had been inspired during a walk along the banks of the Seine. Turner buzzed 3A and wasn't surprised when there was no response. After a few more half-hearted attempts, he randomly rang the other buzzers. Within seconds a prolonged buzzing sound unlocked the front door, granting him entry.

"Skala, you here?!" Turner yelled to the door after pounding his fist repeatedly on the door marked 3A. Turner tried the knob. The heavy wooden door gave way to an apartment worthy of architectural digest, if Skala were to clean it. Turner marveled at the high ceilings and crown moldings while avoiding the clothes and research journals strewn across the apartment.

A noise from the bedroom caught his ear.

"Skala?"

A rancid smell forced Turner to pull his sweater over his nose – he hoped it was rotten trash but feared far worse.

Lights from a television flickered in the bedroom and Turner again called out to Skala, but the only reply was a heavy English accent updating the days Premier League scores.

Then, in the ruffled shadows of the bed sheets, Turner spotted Skala lying on an undone mattress. If it weren't for the heavy stench of decaying flesh Turner would have thought his colleague was taking an evening nap. He circled the bed until he came face to face with the cold, dead eyes and bloated face of Vaclav Skala, frozen in an expression of pure terror. A stream of vomit was dried and caked where it had drained from his mouth. Turner had seen the faces of death a thousand times – and they never looked ready to leave life – Skala certainly wasn't.

The body showed signs of end-stage rigor. That, coupled with the timeline of his last conversation with Skala, allowed Turner to establish an approximate time of death at thirty-six hours prior. Still stunned, Turner gently closed Skala's haunted eyes and leaned against the wall, eventually allowing himself to collapse on the floor. Was it suicide? An accident? Murder?

Though Skala had a penchant for alcohol and the occasional joint, Turner hadn't known him to do anything overtly self-destructive. He rose and began shuffling through the bedside table, in the bed sheets, and on the bedroom floor, looking for anything of relevance. There were no drugs present, prescription or otherwise, and no suicide note.

This is a crime scene, Turner told himself. Call the cops. Instead, he rifled through bookshelves, flipped over sofa cushions, looking for something – he didn't know what. He knew with every second he remained in the apartment, with every additional print he left, he was making himself the prime suspect – but he needed answers – answers that he couldn't rely on the local Czech cops to unearth. As he flipped through Skala's notebooks, Turner wasn't thinking how he'd explain all this or whether the Czech system would allow him a fair trial – all he wanted was to find justice for his friend.

50

Kate Capelli's Apartment
New York, New York

"**Y**ou've reached Allen. You know what to do."

As she waited for the beep, Capelli had the sweaty palms and fluttery heart of a woman who'd been long out of the dating game.

"Hi, Allen. Kate here. I'd love to take you up on that dinner one of these days – maybe we can pick-up where we left off."

Good. To the point, friendly, not rambling – though possibly a little winded since she was climbing a third flight of stairs. Still, Capelli congratulated herself for improving on her usual dithering voicemail.

The last flight was made extra difficult by Tom, the three-hundred pound Irish bartender who insisted on a parting whiskey shot every time she went to Connelly's. He was hoping that one day a shot would turn into five and she'd give him a chance. It wasn't a likely scenario but she appreciated the free Jameson nonetheless.

As Capelli placed the key in her front door lock, an uncomfortable feeling came over her. The little hairs on her neck stood on alert as she glanced down the hallway. Aside from Mrs. Laningham's loafers missing from her doormat down the hall, nothing seemed out of the ordinary. Whiskey always made Kate a little paranoid. Still, she wished Oscar was on the other side of the door to keep her company, on nights like this.

After fidgeting with the sticky deadbolt – a daily annoyance that reminded her just how much wasn't getting checked off her to-do list – Capelli began her after-work ritual. Her black kitten heels were shucked haphazardly across the entry hall, a well-worn black blazer flew in somersaults to the couch, and her Blackberry and pocket change went scattering across the glass coffee table. Each item was removed quickly as though it was on fire, signaling the end of another work day. On a normal evening she'd turn on the news, get the daily dose of corruption and world squalor. Today was different – she was spooked. Her Spidey-sense was on full alert, listening carefully for anything abnormal. Footsteps, a breath, the creak of floorboards – anything suggesting she wasn't alone. Her inner ten year old wished someone would come and check for monsters.

When she'd entered the police academy over a decade ago, a part of her assumed the gun and badge would render her fearless. But after working NYPD homicide and seeing the disgraceful acts humans could inflict on one another, she'd grown hyper-aware of her own mortality. And that meant living with a hard truth – an acceptance life would do with her what it pleased and that, ultimately, events were out of her control. Surely none of her homicide vics had planned on leaving the world at the hands of sadistic killers.

After a few moments of standing silently in her living room, waiting for the boogeyman, Capelli began feeling foolish and dug out the sauvignon blanc bottle from her fridge. As she poured what remained into a glass, her Blackberry buzzed loudly from the living room, jingling nearby coins on the glass coffee table. Sighing, she went to check on the call, hoping it wasn't work related. It was Allen. Smiling to herself, she paused before answering. Immediately her smile dissipated as she saw a shadow creeping across the far wall. Her fear mixed with pride – her instincts hadn't dulled... if only she'd have listened to them.

The shadow stopped. Capelli noticed the polished black Roper boots and knew she was dealing with a sizeable male. The adrenaline forced her mind into turbo mode, letting her sort her options within seconds. She could kick backward, hoping to snap the intruder's knee. If she missed, she'd lose balance and give him an easy mark. She could turn and throw a punch to the throat, but without looking at the man she had no idea his height and where to aim for maximum impact. The man remained still and so close she could feel him almost exhale against the back of her neck. Slowly, Capelli held her hands out to the side, fingers splayed, showing she meant no harm with her movements. The intruder stayed put, his close proximity prohibiting her from making any aggressive moves. She slowly completed a one-eighty and came face-to-face to with a haunting pair of translucent eyes set in a ghostly white visage. Capelli knew immediately that his physicality would pose a problem. He had a clear height advantage, and through his tight black shirt she could see the muscles wrapped over a lean frame.

Capelli realized she was face-to-face with the man sometimes known as Erik Richter. If what Babineaux had said was true, this man was a trained killer – and despite her skill in hand-to-hand combat the odds weren't in her favor. She stopped her mind to a standstill, trying to focus on her first strike, but too many thoughts ran through her head. How was this man tipped off? Had he followed her back from Prague? Was he responsible for the Polaris deaths? And, most importantly, what did he want with her? Surely he could have killed her by now if that was his plan. A bullet to the head would have finished her off immediately. Would he kidnap her? It would be at least twelve hours before anyone realized she was gone, and she had the unfortunate knowledge of what that meant when it came to capturing kidnappers.

A slow grin came across the albino's face, his stillness taunting her.

Capelli threw her knee towards the albino's groin and thrust the palm of her hand towards his face, hoping to break his nose. Nine times out of ten, one of those attacks would have connected. But with warp speed he dodged both moves, a near impossibility, and grabbed her by the neck, restricting her airway and rendering her a pathetic, flailing victim.

Her senses began growing dim but she forced herself to think, knowing she'd soon be unconscious. Through the growing haziness, she noted his free hand to retrieve a syringe from his left pocket. Fear rippled through her as she imagined lying in a pool of her own vomit with the same frightened look as Edward Thorpe. She felt her heart racing, which only meant she'd lose oxygen sooner. With the last bit of strength left in her weakening body, Capelli dug her nails into the man's neck, drawing blood. As the syringe was plunged into her neck, she smeared the blood across the living room wall just as everything turned to black.

51

Vaclav Skala's Apartment
Prague, Czech Republic

After finding nothing of relevance to Skala's demise, Turner sat on the bedroom floor and groaned – a guttural cry of sadness and exhaustion. What had he gotten into? As he prepared to call the police and report Skala's death, he realized he didn't know what number to call.

He tried dialing 9-1-1 on his cell phone and heard a wrong number tone. He searched for a tourist guide or a phone book with emergency numbers. He dug through the low bookshelf in the bedroom by the TV, still blaring soccer highlights. The noise distracted him from the horrible stench of decay.

As he dug around on the lower shelf, Turner noticed something wedged between the wall and bookshelf – a spot he'd missed when ransacking the place. He reached behind the books, through the open back of the shelf, and retrieved Skala's computer. While a certified slob, Skala valued science and technology above anything and treated his equipment accordingly. Turner couldn't imagine he'd store his computer so haphazardly.

As the laptop powered up, a prompt required a password. *Great,* Turner thought to himself. He ran through a variety options, ranging from Polarislab, to Skala, to names of bars that he remembered his late colleague frequenting. Finally, he tried Renata and the computer came to life. Turner wasn't going to enjoy breaking the news of Skala's death to the young assistant.

The desktop was a collage of folders. Turner scanned the file names, not knowing what he was looking for. One particular title caught his eye – Shatoy. Turner opened the folder and saw various documents with vague headings. Some were supply order forms, others accounts of the disease outbreak that had occurred, and still others of unknown relevance. Why would Skala have so much information about the Shatoy outbreak? He wasn't a part of Doctors Without Borders and, as Edyta Zajak had made clear, most everyone had attempted to sweep the incident under the rug.

The sound of loud footsteps and laughter echoed from the marble hall just outside Skala's front door. The noise put Turner on alert and he realized it was time to report the death and leave before residents grew suspicious of him. He used Skala's computer to look up the emergency services number and dialed 112. It was a surreal feeling, reporting a death in a foreign country, but the police promised to arrive in minutes and Turner agreed to wait and give a statement. Before the authorities arrived, Turner slipped Skala's computer into his backpack. The strange location where he'd found the machine suggested to Turner that his friend had been hiding the computer – he wanted to find out why.

52

35,000 Feet Over the Atlantic

Capelli came to, groggy and confused. For a blissful instant, she expected to wake in her own bed. Then, she recalled the syringe plunging into her neck – but here she was awake. Alive. If this was the Polaris killer, he'd spared her the Taipan venom. But why?

Her mouth tasted of bile and felt like cotton balls, so dry it induced a craving for water unlike any she'd ever experienced. Her neck felt sore and bruised from the vice-like grip her captor her had applied to incapacitate her. Panic flooded through her body as she tried to raise her arms and legs. She couldn't move. Had she been given a paralytic? How long had she been under? Would it ever wear off? She recalled reading about the Curare arrow poisons used in South America for so many years to paralyze animals while hunting. Some more unsavory characters used the plant to render people helpless to this day.

Suddenly, a large jolt was followed by a few smaller bumps. Turbulence. She was on a plane. The surprise of the first bump had caused her to let out a slight groan, unintentionally letting it be known she'd awoken. Heavy steps approached. The man hovered over her, then gently moved her onto her back and turned her head left, allowing Capelli a clearer picture.

This was unlike any plane she'd seen. Nothing like the cramped economy seating she'd grown accustomed to flying. Expensive wood paneling, plush leather seats, and a large flat-screen TV adorned the cabin. Her paralyzed body lay on a queen sized bed, fitted with red silk sheets that would make the Heff proud.

Her captor assisted Capelli over to a mahogany dinner table set for two. She noted champagne chilling on ice, caviar, and candles. At some point after the kidnapping Richter, or whoever he was, had changed into a tailored navy suit complete with a checkered pocket square, looking every bit the gentleman if it weren't for his clear, snow-cold eyes.

Capelli watched the man savor the caviar. After each bite he meticulously wiped his mouth with a silk napkin. Despite herself Capelli thought of Anthony Hopkins as Hannibal Lecter and hoped this freak didn't desire her liver for dessert.

Her own thirst became increasingly severe as he sipped Dom Perignon from a crystal champagne flute. He smiled a smile of someone using unfamiliar muscles.

"I apologize you weren't well enough for dinner, I'd rather hoped you'd be able to join me." He stood, and walked toward her, revealing a syringe.

Capelli watched him plunge the needle into her arm as blackness took over.

53

Aria Hotel
Prague, Czech Republic

Turner returned to his hotel long past midnight. For the last 3 hours, chief investigator Bohdan Soldat had questioned every detail of Turner's story until the CSI finished their analysis. Soldat made no effort to hide his suspicion that Turner was guilty of murder. The investigator had broad shoulders and a large belly that made his presence imposing even while sitting at the cluttered dinner table in Skala's kitchen. His bald head was covered in sweat and he held a well-worn handkerchief over his large red drinkers' nose, evidently uncomfortable with the stench of death.

Soldat had repeated the same few questions, altering the phrasing. He grew increasingly frustrated at Turner's consistent answers, the inspector developing a steady crescendo from whisper to an aggravated shout. Turner was aware he'd done himself no favors with his nervous behavior, but he was petrified they'd discover the computer in his knapsack was the victim's and not his own. Soldat had made Turner power up the device, and when he correctly entered the password, the inspector was satisfied. Still, Turner worried Soldat might think to check the contents of the hard drive – at which point Turner would undoubtedly be taken into custody.

Luckily, it was getting late and everyone was getting drowsy. Finally the body was removed, the interview concluded, and Turner sent on his way – though Soldat was crystal clear Turner was to remain in Prague until his name was cleared.

54

FBI Headquarters
Midtown Manhattan

"Hey Capelli, it's me again. I know how Connelly's hangovers can be, but you should probably get your ass into work. Masterson is especially menopausal today and ready to can the next guy to piss him off."

Ford clicked 'end' on his cell and sat back in the ergonomically correct desk chair that gave him constant back pain. He'd thought more than once about suing the shoddy furniture maker but they had a government contract and it would look bad for the agency. Bureau politics never ended.

It was unlike Capelli to no-show. The only time she'd been late was when Oscar was alive and had a backed-up colon, needing an extra five to complete his morning ritual. He gave her the benefit of the doubt, hoping she'd finally gotten some action and would lighten up a little, but it was now eleven and he was starting to worry. Perhaps it was his father instincts making him increasingly paranoid, but something felt off and he didn't like it.

After another hour of half-assed bureau work and unreturned phone calls, Ford decided enough was enough. He stopped by Lisa's desk, gave a bull story about taking Brian to the doctor, and headed home to pick up Capelli's spare set of house keys.

Ford knocked on Capelli's door for the third time. While unsuccessful in waking his work partner, the neighbor, Mrs. Laningham, came into the hallway wearing a purple and pink floral muumuu to investigate the disturbance. They'd met once or twice before, but she still insisted on doing her best Colombo routine to fish for gossip. She'd long assumed any man in the vicinity of Capelli's apartment was a potential suitor.

After assuring Mrs. Laningham that nothing was wrong, and showing off the crumpled pictures of his kids stored in a worn-out Fossil billfold, she finally returned to her apartment. In order to get rid of the old widow, he faked departure and waited silently at the bottom of the stairs until he heard her door shut.

Ford crept back up the four flights and silently slid the key into the deadbolt lock. It took a few moments to finally click, but eventually the bolt slid. Inside, everything looked normal, typical Capelli. She kept her place just clean enough that an unexpected guest wouldn't make her blush, but just messy enough that it felt lived in.

Ford noticed the lights were on and the fridge door was slightly open. He called for her again, and again received no response. After shutting the fridge, he checked the living room. Her blackberry was on the floor beside a few scattered coins. He finally felt justified in assuming something was wrong – no agent went anywhere without their crackberry these days. He bent over to retrieve the phone, his belly straining against his belt. As he stood, cursing the extra 'dad weight' he'd gained, he saw blood smeared across the living room wall. His pulse quickened as he dialed Masterson.

In twenty minutes, a CSI team had set up shop inside Capelli's apartment, collecting and processing evidence with just a bit more urgency than usual. For the most part, government agencies were not to be praised for their efficiency – including the FBI. But when one of their own was at risk there was no better outfit to have on your side.

Ford leaned against the black and white tile countertop in Capelli's kitchen, Masterson sipping coffee beside him. Both men brooded in concerned silence, frustrated by their current uselessness to the equation, stuck in the waiting game. Ford checked his watch once more.

"Hey, guys. I know protocol is you swab everything from the kitchen to the panty drawer but can one of you get back to the lab with that blood sample sometime today?" Ford barked, ignoring Masterson's "don't piss off the science geeks" look.

"We'll be finished here in another ten, Agent Ford. We'll rush the blood through ASAP." CSI Thomason was fresh out of John Jay College and looked like he should be worried about a prom date, not blood analysis. Ford and he first met at the Thorpe crime scene. Despite his youthful looks and Washington Heights swagger, Ford had been impressed. The kid was smart and efficient. He suspected that, like most guys, Thomason had a thing for Capelli and meant it when he said he'd push her case to the front of the line.

Before CSI had arrived, Ford had found Capelli's blackberry; he'd gone through her call log and found nothing of great interest. There were nearly two dozen missed calls from Ford but otherwise the last call was from Allen at 7:18 the previous evening. Grasping at straws, with nothing to do but wait, Ford decided it wouldn't hurt to give the surgeon a call.

"Allen Kennedy." A smooth baritone answered the phone after several rings.

"Allen, hey, Danny Ford here. I'm Caroline's husband. We've met at a few events."

"Yes, of course! How are you and Caroline?" He asked with genuine interest.

Ford had done his best to dislike the wealthy Clooney doppelganger. But, despite his best efforts, he found Allen Kennedy to be one of the few tolerable individuals at Caroline's social functions.

"Doing well, thanks. It's actually Kate Capelli I'm calling about. Did you happen to see her last night?" Ford asked, feeling awkward.

"Unfortunately not. I haven't seen her since we had drinks last week."

"Did you speak with her recently?" He felt terrible questioning an acquaintance but everyone was a suspect for now.

"No, we played phone tag. Actually, I returned a phone call from her yesterday evening and she hung up on me immediately. I thought she'd call back but never did."

"What time was that?" Ford knew, 7:18, but wanted confirmation.

"In the evening. Seven-ish maybe? Look, Danny, I don't want to get into the middle of something messy. If you two have a thing I'll step aside. Though you'd be an idiot 'cause you've got a great woman."

"Oh, no, nothing like that. Kate didn't come in for work today and I'm a little worried about her. That's all."

Ford left the blood stains out of it. No need to worry the guy.

"Really? I don't know Kate well but it doesn't sound like her. We haven't had a proper dinner date since her work always seems to get in the way.

"Tell me about it. My kids don't even know what I look like anymore." Ford gave a little grunt of a laugh, trying to keep the call lighthearted. "I've got to run but I appreciate you taking my call, Allen. I'm sure Kate will pop up here soon."

"No problem. I hope everything is okay."

55

Gstaad, Switzerland

For the second time in twenty-four hours, Capelli awoke in a disoriented haze. She lay in bed, thinking she'd tied on one-too-many at Connelly's, the excessive thirst and pounding headache suggestive of a bad hangover. Cracking her eyes, she had no sense of where she was or why the hell her limbs wouldn't move.

The encounter with Richter at her apartment, the airplane, everything about the kidnapping came rushing back to her as the cobwebs cleared. As the paralytic weakened, she felt a tingle in a few toes; straining with all her effort, she managed to turn her head several inches and assess the surroundings.

To her relief, she was alone. No doubt she was being monitored, but at least he wasn't looming over her for the moment. She tried to keep her mind from racing ahead.

Though she'd not personally worked any kidnapping cases, Capelli had heard the horror stories. People, usually kids, locked up in cell-like basements or barns with chains wrapped around their bodies, sometimes not seeing daylight for weeks or months.

As her senses calibrated, it seemed she was being held in the Ritz-Carlton Aspen. The room was large with white walls and a limited amount of stark, modern furniture that created a sterile feel. One whole wall was glass – an interesting choice for holding a person captive – and revealed a breathtaking view of snow-capped mountains. Capelli wondered if she could smash the window with a chair and escape. Of course, she still couldn't move her legs properly to even walk, and if her captor was savvy enough to smuggle a kidnapped FBI agent onto a private plane he was probably smart enough to use shatter proof, one way glass.

A water bottle, aspirin, and a small bowl of almonds had been placed on a bedside table. Extreme thirst and hunger overcame any fear that the items had been tampered with. If this man wanted her dead she'd already have been six feet under. Slowly, she managed to get her left arm off the bed and onto the water bottle, only to have it go limp and send the bowl crashing to the floor. The room echoed with the harsh sound of shattering porcelain. She looked around like a child in fear of scolding, but several minutes passed and nothing happened.

As the first few sips of water hit Capelli's empty, severely dehydrated stomach, the liquid immediately came back up. After a few deep breaths she was was finally able to keep the fluid down. Dropping her limp arm to the floor, Capelli picked up an almond and painstakingly raised it to her mouth, hunger overcoming any germ phobia she may have once had. The almond settled in her stomach without issue and she proceeded to eat the remaining nuts from the floor, too ravenous to realize how pathetic she appeared.

The food and water gave her just enough of an energy boost to make her think she could get out of the bed. She tried lowering her body to the floor and ended up falling in a heap. Sharp pain attacked her knees as they landed on small fragments of porcelain, but the pain gave her an idea. While on her hands and knees, as subtly as possible, she tucked a few pieces of broken bowl under the bed and into the frame – hoping any possible hidden cameras didn't pick up on her actions. She then crawled toward a lone chair in the room, on top of which was placed a pair of silk pajamas. In her experience, criminals wanted their subjects to behave in a certain way. If they didn't, the result usually ended negatively for the victim. Since her host was offering food and clothing, she figured it best to use his offerings for fear of angering him. Plus, her clothes stank of sweat and vomit and she had to admit the silk pajamas looked very appealing – even if the idea of changing in front of cameras was not.

She managed to pull on the pajama top over her own clothes and then shimmy out of them without exposing herself. Quickly she pulled the bottoms over her still uncooperative legs and struggled into the chair that faced the majestic expanse of snow-capped mountains.

Head still pounding, Capelli recalled the aspirin. Slowly, she rose to her feet, stood behind the chair, and used it as a walker. Capelli made her way to the bedside table where the medicine sat. The label read Ecosprin, a generic Swiss brand of aspirin. It hit her – she was thousands of miles away from New York, probably in some unmapped village in the Swiss Alps. Dread welled-up inside her and she couldn't stem the tide. The NYPD and FBI had no valuable information on her captor or his whereabouts. It was unlikely they'd discover her location in the Alps – if that's in fact where she was – and, if they did, it was even less likely that a rescue would be staged while she had a pulse. This was going to be her fight.

56

Aria Hotel
Prague, Czech Republic

After three fitful hours of twisting in his sheets, interspersed with only brief moments of sleep, Turner acknowledged that a deep slumber was not in the cards. He watched the red digits of the bedside clock slowly tick towards 6:00 a.m., each sixty-second interval feeling like an eternity.

Walking through the lobby, Turner looked as shitty as he felt. A thin-framed, pillow-lipped front desk agent – who'd been more than a little flirtatious at check-in – now eyed him with a mix of fear and disgust. Evidently word had gotten around about the previous night's police escort. Feeling like a man with a target on his back, he headed down the hill to Segafredo Cafe to get a better look at Skala's computer.

"Ah... *dobrý den,* I'd like a double espresso and the ham and eggs, please." Turner ordered with a strange accent, as if distorting his voice would miraculously translate his English to Czech.

"Hemmenex?" The waiter asked, his lips unmoving as though he was practicing for a gig in ventriloquism.

"Yes, sorry, the hemmenex," Turner replied, having no idea what hemmenex was.

Three hours, four double espressos, and countless dirty looks from the ventriloquist later, Turner had only scratched the surface of Skala's collected information and analysis. He'd always known the man to be a sensationalist, searching for scandal and conspiracy at every turn, but he'd not realized just how deeply the skeptic indulged his suspicions.

Most of the files were dedicated to political mischief, CIA and military scandal, government overthrows and the like. Had Skala lived in the U.S., Turner had no doubt there'd be a Homeland Security surveillance van parked outside his home.

Several theories had been fleshed-out into articles submitted anonymously to various outlets, undoubtedly published on a blog beside a picture of Nessie. Turner forced himself to dig through the nonsense to hopefully locate medically-relevant folders, particularly anything relating to the disease outbreak.

Now he sat, jittery from too little sleep and too much espresso, with two files open on the desktop. One labeled 'Shatoy', the other 'Somalia.' Beginning with Somalia, Turner dissected the contents one-by-one. The first five documents were supply orders made from the Jowhar camp to Doctors Without Borders during the course of the previous three months: everything from band-aids and antibiotics to rice and powdered milk. There must have been a reason Skala had gone through the hurdles of obtaining the records, but what was he looking for? A part of Turner felt invaded – deceived, even – that Skala had been digging into his business and never discussed any of this during the past few days.

Turner closed the order form document to search the other files in the computer. He looked through the time codes for each file, carefully searching for the one most recently opened by Skala. That document, dated right around his time of death, was simply called 'notes'. There was only one 'note' in the file but it felt like a gut punch to Turner. It read:

-MGIT tests show the standard antibiotic cocktail used in the treatment of tuberculosis is NOT effective against the strain samples from Jowhar, Somalia This supports my hypothesis that the as-yet-to-be-determined disease outbreak in Jowhar, and likely that of Shatoy, could not be tuberculosis but a genetically manipulated super-strain of the bacteria.

Turner leaned back in his chair and uttered a louder than expected groan; eliciting yet another dirty look from the waiter. This was bad news.

Skala had insisted the Mycobacteria Growth Indicator Tube would produce the most timely results in testing the tuberculosis drugs on the strain Turner had brought from Somalia. MGIT grew the bacteria in a liquid solution and combined that with tuberculosis antibiotics. If the bacteria didn't grow, the drugs would have been determined effective in fighting the disease. Since – according to Skala's notes – the bacteria had grown, it meant the strain was not treatable with the typical course of antibiotics. *That's not possible,* Turner thought to himself. *The drugs worked at the camp, but not in the MGIT?*

Questions began flooding his mind, both relating to the disease itself and Skala's demise, but the abrasive sounds of roaring sirens jolted Turner back into the moment. Four police cars rushed by the café in the direction of his hotel.

Through the café's window, he watched the cops swarm the Aria hotel. Surely they had other business in the area; this had nothing to do with him... and then Turner's pulse jumped.

The imposing Bohdan Soldat emerged from his vehicle, the large gut and drinker's nose even more prominent in the bright morning sun. He slammed the car door and hiked up his pants, taking in the surroundings.

The other officers did the same, as though playing a game of Simon Says with the superior officer they so obviously revered. Pants adjusted, Soldat walked purposefully into the hotel, his underlings filing in closely behind like ducklings behind their mother. The whole crew looked very OK Corral to Turner – and he knew his next move had to work.

The waiter seemed oblivious to the show. Instead his attention was focused on two pretty Spanish tourists currently practicing their Czech language skills on him, giggling each time they butchered a word. Quickly, Turner gathered Skala's computer, his notes, and nonchalantly slipped on his jacket as though heading for a relaxing stroll. He settled the bill with the barista, whose annoyed glances toward her co-worker suggested a frustrated work-place crush. Taking his change Turner realized he'd been over-charged, but let it go. He had bigger worries.

Fifteen years ago, a more naïve Turner would have gone back to the hotel and cooperated with Soldat, trusting that justice would prevail and a simple misunderstanding would right itself. That Turner was long gone.

The US embassy was only a block and a half away on Vlasska Street. If he could get there, at least he could obtain some form of legal counsel to defend his rights. Odds were the Bohdan Soldat type – a corrupt-seeming cop with a chip on his shoulder – didn't care who hung for the crime as long as somebody was put away – even if it meant that someone was innocent.

Outside the embassy, armed marines were checking an arriving vehicle for explosive devices.

"Good morning." Turner smiled warmly to a State Department officer stationed in a small vestibule outside the embassy doors. Several marines a few feet away watched Turner with interest, their combat training no doubt sensitizing them to Turner's subdued anxiety. Despite his conscious attempt to remain calm, he couldn't resist glancing in the direction of the police activity.

"Good morning, sir. Your passport, please." The embassy official was young with dark, intelligent eyes, a buzz cut, and perfectly pressed suit. He wore an American flag pin on his lapel and didn't offer a smile.

"Unfortunately I've lost my passport, that's why I'm here." Turner lied. He'd wait to mention the local police had confiscated it until he was on American soil. "But I've got a driver's license, here, and my identification for Doctors Without Borders, my employer." He displayed both ID's and waited as the man inspected them.

"One moment." The brusque sentry turned off the microphone and made a call, presumably to a higher-up within the embassy walls. Turner kicked a pebble like a man not in any rush, trying to hear the discussion inside the booth. Up the street, he could see a Czech cop looking his way and speaking into his walkie-talkie. A marine followed Turner's gaze and noted the cop, then went inside the booth. As the sirens grew louder, Turner avoided making eye contact with the other marines, who were now watching him with interest.

The embassy official stepped out of the booth and handed back Turner his IDs.

"Are you in some kind of trouble, Dr. Turner?"

"I don't know. I was hoping that replacing a passport wouldn't be too much of an issue –"

"Dr. Turner – in the next minute, the Czech police will arrest you for murder. A lost passport is the least of your worries."

"The man who was murdered was my friend. Whoever wanted him dead wants to frame me."

Two police vehicles urgently parked on the curb. Soldat stepped out and made a beeline for Turner.

"I'm an American citizen. You verified that. I want to see the ambassador."

Soldat stormed toward the booth, barking in Czech, as the embassy officer studied Turner's eyes. Nodding to one of the marines, the officer ordered, "Get the doctor inside."

57

FBI Headquarters
Midtown Manhattan

"**H**ey, your wife's here." Lisa said, leaning into Ford's office while smacking on a piece of bright green gum.

"Huh? What?" Ford asked, wholly focused on whatever was on his computer screen.

"Caroline, ya moron. She's downstairs going through security. Just thought I'd let you know."

"Yeah, thanks." Ford stuffed another bite of cold pad-thai in his mouth and continued sifting through security tapes from JFK airport. He raised his arm and sniffed his pit, cringing at the stench. Without taking his eyes from the computer screen he grabbed a bottle of Giorgio Armani Aqua Di Gio from his desk drawer and squirted liberal amounts around his neck and wrists. The cologne had been a secret santa gift at the bureau Christmas party a few years back and was a last resort when the deodorant was outmatched.

After searching Capelli's place the day before, Ford had returned to headquarters and pulled an all-nighter, digging through anything that may prove relevant to her disappearance. He accessed her old case files, re-read current case files, and carefully dissected her personnel file. There was no mention of any stalkers so he dug through the collars she'd made, wondering if someone was coming back to even the score. None of her major arrests had been released from prison recently and those that were had been small time pick-ups from her early NYPD days. Ford found nothing.

Then, close to midnight, CSI Thomason called with good and bad news. The blood on the wall had not belonged to Capelli. It did, however, match the DNA sample from the Prague apartment. *Good girl,* Ford thought. It had been Capelli's way of leaving behind some evidence for Ford to work with. Now he would do everything in his power to make that one clue pay.

He called Masterson at home, waking up his boss, shouting that Capelli's disappearance was a direct result of Masterson's refusal to issue a BOLO for the suspect. To Masterson's credit, he allowed Ford a moment to vent, talked him down to a more logical state, and suggested they work out a plan of action.

They contacted Babineaux at INTERPOL, requesting he reach out to anyone familiar with the Erik Richter case. Then they reached out to Tesar – who was less-than-pleased at the early wake-up call – and convinced him to bring in Ricther's landlord, Jaroslav, for questioning. In exchange, Ford promised the agency would make Tesar a guest speaker (thereby qualifying him for all-expenses-paid status) at the next international law enforcement symposium in San Diego.

Ultimately, Jaroslav wasn't much help, despite Tesar's interrogation methods. The only valuable tidbit was confirmation that the suspect had been in Prague at the time of their search, having left just moments before the agents showed up. Unless Jaroslav had provided the suspect with the names and physical descriptions for Ford and Capelli – which seemed too technical for the bumbling landlord – it was plausible the suspect had personally watched the agents arrive to search the apartment. One thing was for sure: Richter had entered the United States sometime in the past week. This small sliver of information had Ford carefully watching tapes from customs and arrivals at JFK and Newark, hoping to get a glimpse of their suspect.

As Ford's eyelids began closing for the second time in ten minutes, exhaustion doing its best to overcome him, Caroline knocked on the door.

"Hey, baby, come on in."

"Any luck?" Caroline asked, placing a venti coffee on the desk.

"Nothing yet." Ford took a long pull on the coffee. "Thanks for this, I needed it bad."

"I figured. I brought you some sandwiches and fruit, too, so you don't have order in. I don't need a missing friend and a husband with a blocked artery in the same day." Caroline tried to sound lighthearted but tears had welled in her eyes. It was both fear for Capelli – who she'd grown to be close with – and the constant worry that something like this would happen to her husband. She hid her stresses well, but this incident with Capelli had all those feelings rushing to the surface.

Ford stood and wrapped her in a hug, reading her thoughts. Caroline wiped her eyes, pushing her concerns back into the vault.

"I'm going to find her, I promise that much. And Capellil's a tough nut. That guy kidnapped the wrong woman, that's for damn sure. She's probably got him hanging upside down, begging for mercy by now."

"I hope you're right."

"Hey, wait a minute. There I am!" Ford pointed to the computer screen showing him clumsily dig for his passport at the customs window.

"And there's Kate."

"Oh shit." Ford's face paled.

"What?"

"Hang on a sec." Ford stopped the tape and, through a series of keyboard commands, blew up the screen, then panned through the line of people at customs.

"Son of a bitch." Ford banged on the table with his fist.

"What? Is that the guy?" Caroline asked.

Ford zoomed in on a pale face partially disguised under a New York Yankees baseball cap. He used the ruler tool on the recognition software to get a height approximation. Six-foot four give or take a few millimeters.

"Description and timing both fit." Ford ran a hand through his hair, pulling in frustration. "Jesus that bastard followed us here! He was only three people behind us in line and we never even noticed." Knowing he'd been so close to the subject made Ford sick. If he'd seen the man earlier none of this would be happening.

"Well, one thing's for sure. This guy's mug is gonna be plastered all over the place. There won't be one cop, border guard, or TSA agent who won't have seen his BOLO by the time I'm finished. And when I catch the son of a bitch, he won't know what hit him."

58

American Embassy
Prague, Czech Republic

"**D**r. Turner. Come on in, sorry for the delay. Your case has caused quite a stir with the local authorities." Ambassador Richard Timmerman spoke with a polished New England accent, waving his hand in a "follow me" gesture as he moved from the waiting area back to his plush office.

"Have a seat." The ambassador commanded rather than offered. He had the aura of success and confidence radiating from his blue eyes. Without reading Timmerman's bio, Turner would have placed his age closer to late forties than his actual sixty years. Tanned skin and a fit physique suggested he'd managed enough free time to log a proper vacation and time in the gym. The only flaw Turner could spot was a small scar above his upper lip, most likely acquired during his tenure as a marine.

Timmerman toggled the intercom.

"Karen, can you get us some coffee in here, please? Hold the cream for me this time. And uh… hang on." Remembering his guest he looked to Turner and whispered, "How do you like your coffee?"

"I don't need anything, thank you." Turner was uncomfortable using Karen as a personal barista. She'd been the one to take his information and relay it to the proper personnel around the embassy. With a law degree, fluency in three languages, and head turning looks he couldn't imagine why she didn't tell him to pour his own damn cup of coffee.

"Bring it black for Dr. Turner. Sugar and cream on the side." He hung up the phone without a thank you.

"Okay. Let's get down to it. I've sent one of our diplomatic attaches over to the police station. He'll meet with Soldat and his crew to review the evidence against you. According to your statement – other than the fact you discovered the body – there shouldn't be much to hold against you. It's best if you tell me now whether there will be any surprises."

Timmerman's words were expected, but his tone bordered on accusatory. Turner knew he'd be thrown to the wolves if it meant avoiding a potential international conflict with the Czechs. The truth was, nobody had his back. If Soldat had doctored evidence, or through some round about logic came up with a motive for him to kill Skala, Turner would be given a windowless with cell within 48 hours – Soldat personally slamming the barred door shut.

"I didn't harm my colleague. There's nothing to find. If everyone does their job properly I'm sure this will all be seen as a misunderstanding," Turner said defensively.

"Well, let's hope so, Dr. Turner. It doesn't look good for me when American citizens start killing brilliant Czech researchers."

Before Turner could throw his right fist, adding symmetry to Timmerman's wounded face, Karen entered with the coffee.

"Ah, perfect. Brewed fresh I hope?" Timmerman asked, gazing down Karen's red blouse as she arranged the coffee on his desk.

"Yes, as always," Karen replied with gritted teeth. Turner couldn't help but think this embassy posting was a big resume builder.

"Thank you, Karen. And thanks as well for all your help earlier. You've been a lifesaver."

"No problem, Dr. Turner. There's a group of us working hard on your behalf. You'll be cleared in no time."

Karen offered a genuine smile as her cheeks grew a deeper pink.

"Thanks, Karen." Timmerman's words and tone again meant two different things.

"Sure." She said, and left slamming the door slightly so it seemed accidental but still made a point.

"Listen, Dr. Turner. I'll give it to you straight." Timmerman spoke with a deep voice, as if just now getting down to business. "Our team will be objective, no bias for or against you. If there's any evidence linking you to the murder I'll be obligated to turn you over the Czechs. However, if you come up clean, I'll get you out of here and on a plane to the States as soon as possible."

"That's all I'm asking for."

Timmerman spent another half hour volleying between his good and bad cop roles while Turner dutifully answered his questions. Then Karen showed a mentally haggard Turner to a room where he would await news of his fate. He settled in at a worn mahogany desk and made the questionable decision of retrieving Skala's computer from the knapsack and hacking into the research files of the man he was accused of killing.

59

PremierJets Global
Westchester, New York

Patrick Janovic entered the luxury hangar at PremierJets Global – a high-end private jet rental company – grateful this was his last night on the graveyard shift. Two weeks before, he'd made the fireable offense of booking the Gulfstream V-SP rather than the G-550 for one of the VIP's last minute larks to "do Vegas," as the high-roller put it. To Patrick, a laid back kid from Nebraska who'd only trekked east in pursuit of a girl, a private jet was a private jet. But to Oleg, the son of a Russian oligarch, there was a big difference between the two and he'd bombastically threatened to take his business elsewhere.

Football, of all things, had saved Patrick. He'd been a third-string college fullback who only saw the field for a combined total of three-and-a-half minutes the same year his boss's brother was setting touchdown records for the team. His boss didn't have the heart to fire a Husker and sentenced him to two weeks on the night shift – and a cut in his already minimal vacation time – as punishment for his mistake.

Worse than the dismal late-night hours were the last-minute, book-a-plane-on-a-whim customers who had him scrambling to find sober pilots at 1:00 a.m. for their trip to an exotic locale with the latest bimbo.

He settled in to the creaky back-room desk chair and logged on to the computer while un-wrapping the sandwich Amanda had made. He dreaded the meal but didn't have the heart to tell his girlfriend that her tuna salad was repulsive even to their golden retriever. Just the thought of the half jar of Miracle Whip that went into the concoction made him gag.

Although Amanda was probably deep into her school work at the Columbia University library, Patrick still felt her presence and couldn't will himself to chuck the sandwich. He cursed himself for being a pansy as he choked down the last bit of ciabatta and tuna. The final bite required extra chewing to keep the gag reflex at bay and, as a distraction, he logged onto the company server and opened the terror watch list file. He was outlining his first novel, a thriller, and his mind ran wild every time he had a chance to scan through the latest no-fly list and terrorism alerts. It was silly he knew, but certainly the best way to get through a twelve hour shift.

PremierJets Global walked a fine line between following the TSA guidelines and turning a blind eye for their wealthiest of clients. Being a charter company, they were obligated to check their passengers against the no-fly list and scan all baggage that was intended to board the planes. On Patrick's watch, such precautions always took place. He'd been raised to believe that rules were there for a reason and there was no shame in following them despite what a colleague may say. There had been certain occasions where his boss had called in and insisted he rush the client through without the typical precautionary measures, personally vouching for them. Such calls had always raised a red-flag in Patrick's mind but the consequences of causing a stink and losing his job were too great. Amanda was a grad student with a two-night-a-week bartenders' income and he was left to scrape for the rest.

Scanning the recent alerts, a particular photo caught his eye. The alert was grainy; an airport security shot that had been blown up beyond its pixilation, but unmistakable. His pulse quickened slightly and he tried to temper his nervous excitement.

Patrick opened TIDE, the Terrorism Identities Datamart Environment, a secondary watch list to no-fly, and saw the same grainy photo with the name Erik Richter as an alias. He continued opening the various watch list databases that the company had access to. In each one the same man's face appeared alongside an urgent alert. Though he knew it meant he was probably twenty-four hours away from filling out a Starbuck's application, Patrick dialed the FBI contact number.

"Ford here." The voice jolted Patrick from the netherworld between sleep and consciousness that he'd been drifting in and out of as his call was transferred throughout government agencies and personnel.

"Uh, hi, sorry. Are you the person dealing with the Erik Richter case?" Patrick stammered, unsure what to say and operating under the assumption he'd be transferred again.

"That's me." Ford said with the voice of a man expecting to waste the next three minutes of his life.

"Hi, Mr... sorry, Agent Ford. I'm Patrick Janovic. I work at PremierJets Global in Westchester and I'm pretty sure the guy you have the BOLO out on chartered a flight the other night."

Ford straightened in his chair. It made sense his suspect would charter a jet. He certainly couldn't go through security with Capelli slung over his shoulder.

"Hi, Patrick, I appreciate you calling in. The photo is pretty grainy; can you give me a physical description of the man who chartered the flight?"

"Sure, yeah. He was pretty tall, maybe six-four or five I think. Really pale, kind of freakish actually. His hair was almost white and his eyes really pale blue. He dressed pretty sharp, wore a nice suit."

"Did he have anyone with him?"

"No, he was traveling alone."

"How many others were on the plane, including your personnel?"

"Just the pilot. Usually for long flights we insist on two pilots but it was a last minute job and he didn't want to wait for us to find a co-pilot. I had him sign a waiver authorizing use of only one pilot. He didn't want any cabin attendants either, just required his dinner be brought on board before take-off." Patrick was pleased he had such clear recollection of the night – he couldn't help but get excited at the notion of aiding a police investigation.

"Did he have any luggage with him?"

"I don't remember exactly how many pieces but definitely a few."

"Were they heavy?" Ford had a hunch this kid had come face to face with Capelli's kidnapper. He attempted to steady his voice, not excite the kid, but he was growing anxious. If Capelli wasn't on that flight the odds were favorable she'd been left for dead somewhere in New York.

"Not sure, sorry. I don't usually handle the baggage." Patrick gave a little belch; either the stress or the Miracle Whip was getting to him.

"Patrick, do you still have the flight logs? I'd like to know what name he chartered the flight under and his destination."

"Sorry, Agent Ford. I tried to look the information up while I was on hold but no name was listed."

"So you just let strangers come take millions of dollars worth of aircraft without asking for their personal information?" Ford was testy. Still operating off no sleep, the only thing keeping him conscious was his body odor that was no longer covered up by the Acqua di Gio.

"Of course we require that information. It must have been deleted or inappropriately logged. I was the one on duty though and haven't made a mistake yet, so I don't think that was the case. His first name was Hans, I remember because he corrected my pronunciation. The route logged was to Switzerland and with his pale skin and foreign accent it all made sense. Nothing seemed suspicious; most of our clients are a little eccentric."

"Can you recall where in Switzerland?"

"I wish I could, I'm sorry."

"Has the pilot returned yet?"

"Yeah he came back with an empty bird. Client only booked one-way."

"You have the pilot's contact info?"

"Yeah, sure. Think Teddy Baldwin took that job. Hang on a second and I'll give you the details."

Patrick relayed Baldwin's phone number and New Jersey address to Ford, who had already sent out an interoffice message to the task force charged with finding Erik Richter. The lead was thin and needed follow-up, but Ford had a hunch his partner was 4,000 miles away in Switzerland. He only hoped she still had a pulse.

60

Gstaad, Switzerland

Capelli's first thirty-six hours of captivity had passed as a groggy blur while the drug slowly lost its grip on her system. Drifting in and out of consciousness had made it impossible for her develop any type of escape plan. She barely recalled changing into the silk pajamas and eating the plate of food from the bedside table until she stepped on a shard of porcelain still scattered across the wood floor. She faintly recalled her captor entering, pulling the thick feather duvet off of her body, and hungrily taking her in as she struggled to summon the physical strength to defend herself for the attack. But, before Richter was able to proceed, a cellphone buzzed urgently from his pants pocket and he stormed from the room.

Capelli estimated Richter had been away at least two days since the last encounter. In his absence she put herself through a rigorous series of push-ups and boxing maneuvers to sharpen her senses and prepare for the inevitable fight. Sleeping with Eduardo the boxer had been a colossal mistake, but his classes were now useful. Along with honing her jab and upper-cut, he'd included a plethora of self-defense skills meant to be used outside the ring. The FBI required self-defense courses, but those were the equivalent to a community-college entry course whereas Eduardo's lessons were Ivy League. For over an hour Capelli kicked and punched the air, pouring sweat, imagining Richter's pale face grimace in agony as she bludgeoned him into submission with her fists. Boxing him to death was a nice idea, but she knew more help would be necessary.

From the recesses of her mind Capelli recalled her father's stories of innovative prisoners – "Evil MacGyver's" – as he called them. She knew there was a way to fashion a knife from a Styrofoam cup and toilet paper rolls but that required heat and a thorough search of her own luxury cell had not turned up any incendiary devices.

From the bed frame Capelli retrieved the porcelain shards she'd hidden, careful not to cut her fingers. She then fully removed a drawer from the bedside table. Using her fist she smashed the back panel out of the drawer, splintering wood into long, sharp pieces and placed them to the side, then carefully inserted the drawer back into its slot – it appeared completely unharmed.

Capelli then searched the small bathroom. There was a shower, toilet, and sink, but otherwise the room was bare aside from a bar of soap. It was a substantial block and, as enticing as a sudsy shower sounded, it was instead added to her pile of goodies.

An overwhelming pressure came over Capelli as the reality of the situation pushed its way into her mind. Gasping for air she sat in the chair and took in the breathtaking expanse of mountains on the opposite side of the glass. It seemed a cruel joke that just a sliver of shatter-proof glass was all that separated her from freedom in those mountains. That thought – along with anger at herself for being kidnapped in the first place – sparked a resurgence of adrenaline, pushing the fear out and kicking the survival instinct into high gear.

Capelli refocused. Her time window to attack would be short. She'd need something severe enough to incapacitate him with a quick blow, yet small enough to keep hidden until the very last moments. For maximum impact she needed to draw blood as well inflict pain. No matter how well-trained an enemy may be, the sight of one's own blood was known to shock – and that could provide Capelli a much-needed extra moment to throw a second blow as Richter got his bearings.

After shredding her old vomit-stained t-shirt into long strips, she began tying it tightly around the bar of soap in order to keep the bar from crumbling as she pressed the porcelain shards into one side of it. It was a menacing looking little weapon, the shards long enough to inflict a semi-deep flesh wound and the wrapped bar just big enough for Capelli to keep a firm grip of it as she pushed into Richter's flesh.

She used the same wrapping technique on the wooden shards, forming a tight little bundle that would be able to stab or club, depending on her needs. Then, using one of the remaining slivers of porcelain as a make-shift screw driver, she removed one of the four wooden balls that served as feet for the large chair. Unless he tried to sit in it, Capelli doubted Richter would notice the missing leg. She stuffed the heavy ball into her sock, swinging it like a mace.

The sparse décor of the room made hiding the weapons difficult. Putting them all into the bedside drawer wouldn't do much good if he attacked her near the chair, or in the bathroom. She tucked the soap shiv under the bed pillows, placed the wooden club under the cushion of the chair, and the heavy mace into the tank of the toilet.

Feeling somewhat prepared now, Capelli considered the remaining obstacle – the door lock. On both sides of the door was an electronic lock which required a password and thumbprint to release the door. Her recollection of Richter's last visit was hazy, but she had attempted to watch him enter the code. He appeared to press four digits moving from left to right and then down. If his body didn't block her view on the next visit, it may be possible to see which numbers were pressed when he sealed the door behind him. If not, her efforts to incapacitate him would be pointless.

The nearly silent *whop whop whop* of a stealth helicopter alerted Capelli to the return of her captor, the residence shivering as the small chopper touched down nearby. Rather than fear, Capelli felt anticipation at the thought of turning Erik Richter from abductor to victim.

61

American Embassy
Prague, Czech Republic

Turner listened to the dull beep of a ringtone as his line connected with Edyta Zajak. He'd heard nothing from Timmerman or Karen regarding his status as a murder suspect and was doing his best to productively pass the time, which at present was loudly marked by a grandfather clock in the corner. The massive old antique was taunting him with its relentless ticking, marking the moments until he was arrested in a foreign country for a crime he didn't commit.

"Halo?" Edyta answered with her nasally foreign accent.

"Edyta. Luc Turner. I received your email requesting I call?"

"Yes, Dr. Turner. I heard about Skala. Such a shame. He was the only one I trusted with my theory but now that he's gone I believe you're the best person to turn to." Her voice shook tentatively.

"I'm happy to talk but I have to warn you, I'm calling from the embassy and am not sure it's allowed. If we get cut off I'll try and reach you later." Turner had the strong feeling his call was breaking embassy rules.

"I understand." She was silent for a moment, awkwardness seeping into the phone lines.

"What did you want to discuss, Edyta?" Turner gently urged.

"It's about the Shatoy outbreak, actually. I thought it strange that only the children contracted the disease, aside from the nurse tending to them. So while I was still at the camp, before the disease had taken all their lives, I began retracing the events of the previous few weeks. Every person had been in contact with exactly the same foods, people, animals and other environmental factors. There was only one outlier, and that was the vitamin supplement given on the last shipment. Regular pills were brought for the adults, but for the children they were experimenting with new aerosol nose sprays for the vitamin dosage. To me it was a great idea since it can be difficult for kids to get medications down orally."

"And the children contracted the illness after you administered the medications?" Turner's mind flashed back to the day he and Jean-Pierre administered their supply of aerosol vitamins. He too had found the spray a welcome change, the youngsters complaining far less than normal.

"Yes, that's correct."

"Do you remember the products' name?"

"Geno-Vyt. It's not on the mass-market yet but has gone through lab testing and was labeled safe and effective for human consumption."

"Edyta, what drug provider sourced your shipment?" Turner too had administered Geno-Vyt just before the outbreak in Somalia, an unlikely coincidence that had red-flags waving like the Chinese New Year.

"The same lab Skala worked for in Prague. Polaris Pharmaceuticals acquired it a few years ago, but before that it was some obscure little company that did groundbreaking research. They've always been great to work with."

"Were any of the Geno-Vyt sprays tested for contamination after the outbreak?"

"Unfortunately not. I sent back a few of the sprays to the lab and requested they be tested, noting my concerns. After a few weeks of hearing nothing I began calling and kept getting shuffled around from person to person. Finally I contacted Skala directly and he claimed no such sample ever reached his lab. His team would have been responsible for carrying out the testing and he promised to do some checking around. After two days he called and told me nobody had received my package, that it must have been lost in the mail. I received a delivery confirmation so I think someone made a mistake at Polaris." She paused for a moment, before continuing with an unsure voice. "Or they knew it was contaminated and didn't want word to get out that their product had killed more than twenty children."

"You told Skala of your suspicions?"

"Yes. Initially he didn't seem share my concerns but promised if the package arrived, he'd personally test the products. Since a package never arrived, nothing was tested. It wasn't until you came to him about the symptoms associated with the Somalia outbreak that he grew suspicious. I received a call from him the night before he died. He'd gone looking for the Geno-Vyt they had in stock so he could test it for contamination and there was none on the shelves."

"Why didn't either of you tell me about this? You two acted like you didn't know one another, and nobody ever mentioned the Geno-Vyt connection." Turner was a calm-natured man, being played like a puppet between two colleagues didn't sit well with his ego.

"It was Skala's request. I think he wanted to test the product first to see if there was anything to be concerned about. Before the takeover, the lab was his responsibility and much of the useful research was his doing. He was quite concerned with protecting the reputation of his work."

"I'm not exactly *The Daily Mail*. I could have been trusted with this information."

"I know, and I'm sorry. What do we do now?" Edyta was all business.

"We need to get that drug tested. The full shipment was used in Somalia so that's not an option. And you said Skala couldn't find the drug at Polaris? How is that possible?"

"Apparently there's a different storage building for the drugs used on humanitarian missions. Many of them are still in the testing process and to avoid mix-ups they prefer to keep it all separate. Skala lost his keycard months ago and didn't replace it since he never organized the shipments. I guess he was going to have someone let him in the next day but... well, you know what."

Turner thought for a moment, considering how he could get his hands on a sample of Geno-Vyt for testing. It was no easy task, considering the tight security pharma companies practiced. Plus, he was a murder suspect holed up in the embassy, no small road block. Still, there was one possibility.

62

Over the Atlantic

"**H**ey, boss, you got any of that Dramamine?" Ford pleadingly asked Masterson as he wiped sweat from his forehead, swallowing hard to keep his fast-food dinner from making an ugly comeback.

"The idea is you take it before the flight, which is why I suggested you have it an hour ago." Masterson passed the pills over to Ford and leaned as far away from the nauseous agent as possible.

Neither man was too keen on taking the company jet over the Atlantic. It lacked the 'safety in numbers' sense of security that commercial air travel offered. Very rarely did a Boeing 747 carrying two hundred passengers crash, whereas the private jet variety didn't have nearly as stellar a track record. But time was of the essence and when it came to locating Capelli there was none to be wasted.

After Janovic's tip, Ford had reached out to Teddy Baldwin. The pilot had confirmed he'd flown an overnight job to Bern, Switzerland. He provided a passenger description that jived with the man on JFK's security tapes. Like Janovic, he hadn't seen a second passenger but didn't discount the possibility. He'd managed a clear look at the luggage, confirming at least one piece was large enough to hold the body of a woman curled in the fetal position. The thought of Capell stuffed into a suitcase had been the original source of Ford's nausea. However, if she was being transported it was likely she was still among the living. Ford couldn't imagine the kidnapper carting a dead body over the Atlantic – the stench alone would raise suspicions.

After speaking with Baldwin, Ford rang Babineaux. The French Interpol agent had grown frustrated with middle-of-the-night inquiries, spewing a multi-lingual chain of profanity when he heard Ford's voice on the line.

Despite his grumpy demeanor, Babineaux had come through. He quickly summoned the help of his colleagues involved with the Richter case years ago. A lead investigator recalled a possible safe-house located in the Swiss Alps. It was suspected that after one of the oligarch murders Richter had been in hiding there. Technology was not nearly as efficient a decade before when the team was hot to catch the albino assassin. By the time they'd pinpointed the chateau's location, another killing had taken place in Britain with Richter sighted at the scene. Local Swiss authorities had been sent to search the home but found it unoccupied and nothing suspicious enough to warrant further investigation.

The Gstaad safe house was a soft lead, at best. No sightings of a man matching Richter's description had been reported, but nobody had been looking too closely over the recent years either. It was ultimately Baldwin's statement that had convinced Ford there was a credible link to Gstaad. At the airport in Bern, the pilot went to say his goodbyes – part of PremierJets Global customer service guarantee – and he'd overhead the man request the small shuttle service drive him to the helicopter hangar. This nugget of information had been what ultimately convinced Ford and Masterson that Gstaad was a lead worth pursuing. The distance from Bern to Gstaad was enough that a helicopter would be an efficient mode of transportation, and the charter flight to Bern could be a ruse on Richter's part to throw off authorities.

Only two hours from their destination, Ford and Masterson sat in silence, their nervousness evident in quick breaths and fidgety fingers. Both men knew if this was a bad lead, they'd wasted precious hours and let Capelli down. On the other hand, they could be walking into a death trap if a trained killer such as Richter got a whiff of them coming. Babineaux was scrambling a team of Interpol's finest to accompany them from Bern to Gstaad. Nonetheless, confrontation on foreign turf was something no agent of sound mind was enthusiastic about.

63

Polaris Research Lab
Prague, Czech Republic

Renata Kubova was not a stereotypical tough-as-nails Eastern European woman. She'd been raised mostly in Britain by a father who lectured at London School of Economics and a mother who dithered in fashion but mostly attended society parties and carried on affairs behind her husband's back. Renata's passion for medical science had been born from her grandmother's lifetime struggle with leukemia. Becoming involved in medicine to save the life of a family member sounded cliché, even to Renata – like the plot of a bad television movie. Still, despite the fact her grandmother passed away when she was sixteen, Renata's interest in eradicating disease remained strong, and her mind capable of handling the rigors of medical school.

Now the always responsible Renata found herself in the middle of a strange scenario that had her risking her career before it had fully begun. Earlier in the day Luc Turner had reached out, asking her to locate a bottle of Geno-Vyt and send it to a colleague of his in New York for testing. A born skeptic, Renata was not about to start smuggling pharmaceuticals from her workplace at the request of a man she'd only had limited acquaintance with. Still, he'd convinced her with explanation of possible contamination and, more than that, informed her that Skala had the same suspicions.

Her romance with Skala had been in the early stages, a series of after-work drinks and the occasional dinner. He spoke with such passion about his research Renata knew a woman would always be a distant second to his work. Still, their conversations excited her, reigniting her occasionally waning enthusiasm for disease research and sparking a new passion for Skala. At their most recent dinner, just before his death, Skala had spoken excitedly of his collaboration with Turner. In Skala's memory, she decided to continue that partnership and see where it led.

Now for the second time in an hour Renata attempted to enter the pharmaceutical storage room that stood separate from the main lab. Her first attempt had been unsuccessful. The universal keycard she'd been issued proved to be not so and she was repeatedly denied access. Sensing something awry – there was no reason for the magnetic code to have been changed – Renata switched tactics.

Leo King, a lecherous British colleague, had been in hot pursuit of Renata since his arrival at the Prague lab a year prior. He was the man in charge of boxing and sending the humanitarian pharmaceutical orders so there was little doubt his keycard would be active. Unbuttoning a few notches of her clingy white work blouse, Renata entered King's office and informed him there was an appointment waiting in the downstairs lobby. Flustered by her presence and the forgotten appointment, a pink-faced King scurried from the office leaving his key ring behind.

Renata approached the storage building, waving King's card at the lone-guard posted outside. He failed to notice the ginger-haired, freckled male face on the card was not that of the blond-haired, blue-eyed Renata and gestured her past without scrutiny.

Waving the keycard over a sensor turned the red light to green, granting access. Renata sighed in relief as she entered the building. The space was cold in temperature and sterile feeling, resembling a mini-airplane hangar with its cement floors, high ceilings, and metal shell. The shipments had all been sent earlier in the day and now the space stood empty of employees. Renata strolled down the aisles, scanning the pill bottles and vials stored in glass refrigerators, her heels clicking loudly on the floor.

The vitamin storage area was at the end of the first row of cabinets. Quickly, she located the Geno-Vyt and used one of King's silver keys on the stolen key ring to unlock the sliding glass door. The lock clicked but the door refused to budge. Inspecting the door track for a blockage of some sort she came upon a secondary lock. The silver key did not work; the door was still not moving. Feeling harried, anxious to get the stolen keys back in King's office, she tried each of the other keys. A small golden one that stood out from the rest finally did the trick. She grabbed the bottle, re-locked the door, and hurried from the building.

King's office was empty when she returned to the main building. Renata figured he'd gone to report his missing keys at human resources or had been distracted by some short skirt in the lobby. She tossed the keys on the floor beneath his desk, hoping he'd blame his own clumsiness, and went back to her own cubicle.

Placing the Geno-Vyt in an overnight mailer, she hurriedly scribbled the New York address of Dr. Sheldon Greyson onto the envelope and left for the post office.

64

Gstaad, Switzerland

Capelli sat in the fetal position against the door, listening carefully for footsteps while giving herself a third pep talk in as many hours. Since the helicopter had arrived, the place had gone mostly quiet once more. An hour earlier, she could hear fists beating a heavy bag, but she'd yet to see her captor. Days without a visit from her captor had meant days without any real food and she hoped her physical strength wouldn't fail her when the killer finally made his appearance.

Over and over Capelli went through the plan of attack in her head. She'd developed a strategy, practiced possible assaults with her home-made weapons, and considered the best means to restrain him once she had knocked the kidnapper out. Of course, all this planning meant nothing when she couldn't anticipate her captor's moves, wha weapons he may be carrying, and whether he may have company. Even worse, if surveillance cameras recorded her constructing the weapons, she'd have no element of surprise.

Distracted by her grumbling stomach, it took a moment for Capelli to realize that the man sometimes known as Erik Richter was walking towards her room. He made no effort to conceal his approach as the heavy boots clunked loudly down the hall. Quickly, Capelli slid between the sheets in an effort to look sleepy.

There was no knock, no warning. The man barged into the room and closed the door behind him. Capelli watched carefully through one barely-opened eyelid as he punched the keypad to lock the door. The numbers were laid out like those on a phone, with one on the top left, three on the top right, a zero at the bottom. From her vantage point, it appeared Richter had typed 1-3-5-9, but it was impossible to be sure. At least the pattern was correct, she thought. Her mind began processing the vast array of possible combinations and she quickly stopped herself to focus on the fight ahead.

Sitting up, feigning grogginess, Capelli got the first clear look at her captor and didn't like what she saw. His pale body was chiseled and lean, designed with a multitude of pink scars made extra obvious by the stark contrast with his skin. It appeared his whole body had been shaven and each white hair on his head was perfectly trimmed. He wore no shirt, only black leather pants and heavy boots. In his hand he carried thin ropes and long leather whip. The look in his eye was carnivorous and frighteningly animalistic – she was prey ripe for hunting.

Capelli nearly vomited, the acidic bile making its way into the back of her throat before she managed to swallow it down. Mind reeling, she considered distracting him, trying to reason with him, but no words would come out. He just leered at her silently for a moment before he spoke.

"Finally, I get to have some fun with you. Take off your clothes." He stood at the base of the bed, touching himself as she undressed.

The feeling of total violation overcame Capelli but she remained focused, playing to his desires until the moment was right. Slowly the silk pajamas came off and she looked him in the eye, waiting for her instructions.

"Lie down on your back."

Naked on the bed, Capelli lay exposed and vulnerable, hoping he didn't incapacitate her with another paralytic before she could defend herself.

Hovering over his victim, Richter rubbed his hands between her thighs, then over her taught stomach on the way to her breasts. Her body trembled uncontrollably to his touch despite her mind's admonitions to stay calm. He groaned a little as he sat atop her, rubbing his hands through her hair, and then viciously pulling her brunette locks. Instinctively Capelli pushed against his chest, feeling his aggression increase the longer he fondled her. He slapped her across the face as punishment for her resistance, the stinging sensation momentarily incapacitating his prey.

"Bad girl, Kate. That's what these are for." Richter grabbed the white ropes that lay next to him on the bed, then snagged her left arm and pushed it against the bed post, wrapping the rope tightly around her thin wrists. Capelli knew she had to make her move before being fully restrained. His focus on the knot provided the perfect distraction as she slid her right hand underneath the pillow and grabbed her soap weapon.

One knot completed, Richter looked at her and smiled for the first time. It was a wicked smile.

"That's a good girl. One to go and we'll get started."

As he reached for the second rope, Kate whipped her hand through the air towards Richter's face in a swift motion, the porcelain shards piercing into his left eye. Stunned, Richter screamed as she pulled the weapon from his face and thrust it again, this time into his neck. Unfortunately she'd just missed his jugular and despite the blinding severity of the eye wound, Richter's strength didn't falter. He punched at her face, but only managed a glancing blow as his vision was blurred by the blood coursing down his face. Simultaneously Capelli thrust her knee into Richter's groin and rammed the soap shiv into his gut. The move drew blood but the shards had been pressed further into the soap with each blow and were no longer causing maximum damage. He grabbed her hair, pulling with such ferocity Capelli feared he'd scalp her by sheer force. She pushed the fingers of her free hand into the bloody neck wound and managed another kick to the groin. The combination of painful attacks finally put him on the defensive as he instinctively reached for the painful neck injury. Capelli threw a punishing right hook to the temple and Richter crumbled atop her.

Using her body weight Capelli rolled Richter off her, the dead-weight of his mass thumping loudly as it hit the wood floor. The knot restraining her left wrist proved difficult to loosen with her sore right hand, now fractured from the harsh blow – but she managed to get it loose enough to slide her left hand free.

Capelli quickly put the silk pajamas back on. Knowing Richter wouldn't remain unconscious long, she gathered the ropes and prepared to tie him, her hopes for freedom swelling inside her. As she leaned down, looping the rope around Richter's ankles, he suddenly jerked his foot up, hitting her square in the nose. She fell back, with a crushing pain in her skull; as Richter struggled to get up, Capelli forced herself to crawl to the bathroom on her hands and knees. A woozy Richter slowly rose and followed in pursuit, getting to the bathroom just behind Kate. Standing now, Capelli made a move for the toilet tank but not before Richter grabbed her by the neck and thrust the back of her head into the mirror, causing it to shatter. Overcome with rage he continued slamming her into the mirror as she flopped back and forth like a rag doll, growing weaker with each successive impact.

In his blind rage Richter failed to notice as Capelli grabbed a chunk of the mirror from the broken counter top. Using her unbroken left hand she thrust the piece into his torso, puncturing a lung as it traveled through his ribcage. He dropped Capelli suddenly at the pain and she managed to push past him and lift the lid of the toilet tank. He spun around to face her, wheezing as he tried to get a satisfying breath, blood spewing from his neck, left eye hacked to pieces with a porcelain shard still protruding from it. Before he could reach her, Kate swung the heavy wooden mace, perfectly connecting with Richter's face and he fell back into the sink, head crashing into the broken mirror. Ready to end it for good, Capelli took the heavy toilet tank lid and beat it against Richter's head until he was bordering on death.

Five minutes later she'd successfully hog-tied her captor and toyed with the idea of smothering the unconscious man before her. Despite his evil, she didn't have the make-up to kill a debilitated man.

The door code was not 1-3-5-9 as Capelli had guessed, but after trying a series of combinations she finally hit pay dirt with 2-3-7-8. A green light appeared indicating the correct code had been entered and the screen requested a thumbprint. She dragged Richter's body toward the door and yanked at his hog tied limbs, nearly dislocating his shoulders in an effort to raise his hands to the touch screen.

She wiped the blood off his thumb and pressed it into the pad, exhaling in relief when the words "access granted" lit up in green.

Capelli pulled Richter into the bathroom and closed the door. On the outside handle she stacked glass shards from the mirror to serve as an alarm on the off-chance Richter regained consciousness and managed to escape his restraints.

Confident her captor was no longer a threat; Capelli left her cell and entered into the main room of the spacious house.

65

Gstaad, Switzerland

Capelli walked quickly through a vaulted living room towards the kitchen. Placing her head beneath the water faucet she gulped from a steady stream of ice cold tap water, wiped her chin, then found a large stack of protein bars in a cabinet, three of which she ate in quick succession before realizing they tasted like chewy sawdust. Somewhat hydrated and nourished Capelli began searching the expansive house.

The stark white living room had no cupboards, shelves, or any nooks and crannies to be used for hiding places. The sparse furniture and clean lines made it impossible to hide weapons, computers, or even a phone, which Capelli desperately wanted to find.

A glass staircase led up to another large open space furnished only with a king-sized bed made up with a single white fitted sheet. The closet was arranged in the same obsessive-compulsive fashion of the Prague hideaway. T-shirts, cargo pants, even underwear were perfectly pressed and hung equidistant from one another – organization that would make a marine proud. Not finding anything of interest, Capelli took the glass stairs down two levels to a basement. There was little doubt in her mind that somewhere in this uber-modern safe-house there was means of communication with the outside.

The base of the staircase emptied into a long corridor with a solid wall along the right and bedrooms to the left. Each of the three rooms stood empty, without a single piece of furniture or evidence of use. Pausing a moment, Capelli considered the home's layout. Above her was the living room and kitchen, three-quarters of which had to be above the walled-off area before her. Running her hands along the wood-paneled wall, painted in bright white to complement the stark interior décor choices, Capelli felt for a handle or knob. Nothing. She made another pass back down the wall, this time pressing harder. As she continued down the far end, still pushing her palms firmly into the wall, a portion of the wood four feet high and two feet wide receded six inches. It displayed a keypad similar to that of her cell upstairs. The idea of dragging Richter downstairs was not an appealing one, but his fingerprint was necessary to open the hidden door.

After bounding up the stairs two at a time, she dug through the kitchen drawers and found what seemed to be the sharpest knife. Entering the cell, Capelli carefully removed the glass shards from the bathroom door-handle. Richter was still out-cold, his hands and feet turning unpleasant shades of blue at the lack of blood flow due to the hog-tied position. Wincing, she held the tip of his thumb with her left hand and began sawing it off at the base with her right. Hatred spurred her on as the blood spewed onto her hands.

It took longer than anticipated for Richter to awake from the pain. Not until the thumb was nearly removed did a piercing scream emit from his hoarse throat. Capelli immediately swung the mace at his head, silencing him once again. She placed ice over the stump where his thumb once was, wrapped it with a towel from the kitchen and hoped he wouldn't die before interrogation. Patting him on the head, she muttered, "Sorry, buddy."

Back downstairs Capelli typed in the same 2-3-7-8 code as was used to access the cell. She then pressed the severed thumb into the keypad and the door slid open to the right, exposing an assassin's play room. There were vast arrays of guns ranging from simple pistols to military grade automatics hanging behind a locked glass case. Behind another glass case were over twenty knives polished and sharpened to a deadly gleam – some sterile and efficient in appearance, others ornate and beautiful with carved ivory hilts and gold embellishments.

Atop a stainless steel desk sat two computers alongside technical equipment unfamiliar to Capelli, but that would undoubtedly impress Jimmy the techie back at the bureau. Hitting the space bars brought each of the computers to life, but, predictably, both required passwords.

Capelli scoured the room for a phone, finding nothing until coming upon a large stash of GoPhones in the bottom desk drawer. She powered on the phone and impatiently waited for it to register and retrieve a signal.

An unfamiliar sound shot a jolt of adrenaline through Capelli – the possibility of Richter's escape, or the potential presence of an accomplice – momentarily held her in the grips of fear. Turning towards the noise she came face-to-face with the hissing fangs of a large snake. Capelli was tolerant of roaches, rats, and most other varieties of unpleasant city dwellers – but not snakes. Fortunately, the slithering creatures were one of the few things a New Yorker didn't have to fear. But now she stood in front of two five-foot long snakes with only a sliver of glass as protection. Logic told Capelli she was safe from the reptiles, but her neck hairs stood at attention nonetheless.

The snakes were a deep olive green color with a chevron pattern running down their bodies that Capelli could almost call beautiful if not for the fact the filigree adorned such grotesque creatures. She'd need confirmation from Dr. Yamaguchi but had little doubt these were Inland Taipan – their lethal venom responsible for the deaths of two Polaris execs.

The phone buzzed in her hand, indicating its readiness. Punching in Ford's number she kept one eye on the snakes, just in case. It dawned on her, while waiting for the line to connect, what a sad state she was in. Filthy, sweat and blood-stained pajamas hung from her mashed body while she gripped the thumb of her captor in her left hand and the phone in her right.

"Hello?" Ford's voice came on the line, muffled sounds of men yelling and helicopter blades in the background.

Tears sprang to Capelli's eyes at the sound of Ford's voice.

"Hello?" He sounded frustrated, ready to hang up.

"Danny... its Kate."

"Kate? Jesus, Kate, are you okay?! Where are you?" His voice was a shout of excitement, shock, and fear. Only now did he realize a part of him never expected to hear his partner's voice again. Frantically, he waved his hands in an attempt to silence the swarm of Interpol agents readying for the mission.

"It's Richter, Danny. He took me from my apartment. I'm such an idiot to..."

"I know, Kate. Richter stalked us from Prague to New York. I should have noticed. Just tell me that you're okay."

"I'm okay. Masterson will have me on the bureau shrink's couch for the rest of my career but I'm still breathing. Richter's tied-up in a bathroom but knowing that son-of-a-bitch, he'll find a way out."

"Where are you?"

"I'm not sure. There aren't exactly cable bills with his name and address lying around. Definitely in the mountains, guessing somewhere in Europe."

"Switzerland perhaps?"

"Maybe. Actually…" Kate thought back to her first night in the plush cell, "the aspirin was a Swiss brand, but it can probably be bought anywhere." The snake hissed again and this time Capelli it gave it the finger, feeling emboldened by impending rescue.

"Babineaux had a lead on a possible safe house in Gstaad. I'm in Switzerland now, ready to come in with an Interpol team. Stay on the line and I'll trace your signal. Hopefully you're not in Colorado."

"Hey, you'll only hear this once – but I can't wait to see your ugly face."

"That's sweet."

"Okay, enough of that. How did you get a lead on Switzerland?"

"We circulated a picture of Richter from JFK security footage. Young kid from PremierJets Global called in a tip. Were you on a private jet?"

"Yes and the experience is not all it's cracked up to be, let me tell you."

"Hang on Kate, Masterson has the trace."

"That was quick."

"Babineaux got it right." Ford made no effort to hide the excitement in his voice, "We've got a chopper ready and will be there in under an hour. Is there anywhere nearby you can wait, away from Richter?"

"I haven't been given the town tour but I get the feeling this is pretty middle-of-nowhere. Besides, I'm not leaving this asshole alone. I've found his weapons cache – he tries to run I'll stab him with his own fancy knife."

"Just be careful, Kate. We're coming to get you."

66

Greyson Residence
New York, New York

As Turner waited in the gaudily furnished foyer of Dr. Sheldon Greyson's Upper East Side townhouse, it was easy to recall why he'd never liked the man. Framed photographs with celebrity clients, news clippings mentioning his practice, plaques and trophies from various medical institutions doubled as evidence of his insecure narcissism.

Medical school colleagues, the two had always been in fierce competition, disliking one another with such passion it bordered on obsession. Greyson had been the teacher's pet of the program. Turner, who actually was the best student of his class, found Greyson to be unbearable with his misused eight-syllable words and insistence at showing up professors. Nonetheless, Greyson had proven to be highly talented in the area of infectious disease and Turner had no other choice but to have Renata send the Geno-Vyt to his long-time rival while under embassy-arrest.

Two days before, Ambassador Timmerman's stunning assistant Karen had entered Turner's room at the American Embassy waving his passport with a victorious smile. She'd personally gone to intervene with Soldat, convincing the corrupt officer to turn-over the passport with a series of baseless but legal-sounding threats against the Czech police department. Handing Turner the passport, she suggested that he pack quickly and get to the airport as soon as possible. While she had little doubt of his innocence, it was only a matter time before Soldat's bruised ego at being bested by a woman would result in more questions for the doctor. So now Turner sat, after a long-flight to New York and a much needed night of rest in his Times Square hotel, in the home of his past rival.

Dr. Sheldon Greyson stepped from a small elevator, a luxury that seemed a little much even for Greyson. Once scrawny, Greyson had added a hundred pounds to his frame since the med school days. His mop of curly hair had thinned to a minimal wisp – an unsightly comb-over serving as the solution.

"Well, well. Luc Turner! I nearly fell off my chair when I read your email the other day. Didn't imagine we'd cross paths again. It's been what? Ten years?" Greyson's cringe-inducing nasally voice had not improved over the years.

"At least that. But I've been following your work. You've had some impressive breakthroughs in your flavivirus infection research." Turner nearly choked on the compliment. He was, after all, asking the man for a favor.

"It's all a work in progress. None of it matters until there's a more effective cure."

Anxious to get to the point, Turner moved on. "So you received my package?"

"Yes, both packages. I only received the antibiotic from your colleague in Somalia this morning, so I've yet to look at that. But I have fully analyzed the aerosol vitamins. Let's go down to my lab and take a look."

"You have a lab here?"

"Yes, a modest one in the basement. It allows me to work on some side-projects in the comfort of my own home."

Must be nice, Turner thought, reflecting on his own working conditions over the past decade.

They stepped into the elevator and made the two-floor descent into the deep townhouse basement. It was an awkward few moments as the men stood within inches of one another, Greyson's stale breath souring the air.

The lab was impressive, filled with state-of-the-art scopes, testing equipment, and a variety of other gadgets that Turner wasn't familiar with. Greyson barely concealed his conceited smile as Turner eyed the impressive set-up.

"Here we are." Greyson pulled a Petri dish from its temperature controlled storage and placed it beneath the lens of a high-powered microscope. "This is a sampling of the contents in the Geno-Vyt bottle. Without a doubt there is contamination. What's curious is that it appears to be a mutated form of tuberculosis. Your friend in Prague, Ms. Kubova, took it upon herself to include high-res photographs of a sputum sample from Somalia. Her note didn't disclose details but she mentioned you'd know the source of the photograph."

"Yes, that's a specimen from a patient infected in the Somalia outbreak that I mentioned."

"Well, it seems the contaminated Geno-Vyt is infected with the same disease as your patients in Africa."

"Would you be able to test both the standard TB treatment on the disease as well as the one my colleague shipped here?"

Jean-Pierre had sent the antibiotics used to treat the outbreak only three days before. The fact it had made its way from the third-world in so little time was proof that the parcel service was capable of miraculous feats, not just losing Christmas presents.

"Not a problem. I'll place an order with the pharmacy for the TB cocktail. They are quite quick and are usually willing to deliver here. Meanwhile, we can start with the treatment you used. What was it?"

"Same antibiotics, but for curiosity's sake, I want to compare the results against those from your pharmacy."

"Fair enough. Wait'll you see my new toy. It puts the MGIT to shame. Small little contraption and we can expect results within four hours."

"Can't wait." Turner loathed the thought of four more hours in Greyson's presence.

67

FBI Headquarters
Midtown Manhattan

Capelli and Ford had returned to New York forty-eight hours earlier. The rescue had been a flurry of chaos. Ford immediately found Capelli and took her to the chopper for a medical evaluation, leaving the Interpol team to secure Richter and gather what little evidence was in the house. Babineaux had been beside himself as a superior explained the FBI would be taking Richter into custody rather than Interpol. The diminutive man blamed Ford for the power play and again hurled a slew of expletives at the agent who was not at all offended given that he couldn't understand a lick of French.

The scene was carefully evaluated by Interpol CSI and, while an official report was still pending, they hadn't found much in the way of useful evidence. The snakes were confirmed to be Inland Taipan and were currently locked in an animal-friendly evidence room in the bureau's basement. Those who had seen the long slithery creatures were eager to have them relocated to a zoo ASAP.

With Richter keeping mum, the agents were now hoping the computer data would provide some information. Capelli's testimony alone could put Richter away, but they still lacked solid evidence on the murders and suspected an accomplice.

"Sing to me, Star Trek." Ford entered the basement at headquarters, home of Jimmy's technology lair. Since receiving the Richter computers forty-eight hours before, the young tech genius had not seen daylight. A complex set of security systems had been created to protect the computers, making the hack job a challenge even for the best in the business.

"Eventually you're gonna have to stop with the nicknames, Agent Ford."

"Maybe we'll settle on one. Criminal? Convict? Lucky shit?" Ford chided.

Jimmy had been picked up by the government and incarcerated three times before Masterson approached him with a job offer and the greatest carrot of all – freedom. He committed the exact same computer crimes as before – hacking into systems, monitoring communications, and deciphering codes – but now the three letters F-B-I after his name justified it all. It was hypocrisy at its finest, but for

Jimmy – a slight kid of 5'5 – he'd rather be a part of said hypocrisy than some jailbird's bitch.

"Hey, Jimmy." Capelli entered the room after Ford, shocking the young genius.

"Agent Capelli. I thought you'd be on leave. You okay?"

"Aside from a marathon session with Dr. Xavier and a fractured hand, yes, I'm doing okay. Coulda been worse."

Capelli had taken twenty-four hours off at Masterson's strict instruction. He'd ordered two weeks off but she came in anyway. The day Capelli let this case get closed without her was the day the Mets won the World Series. Masterson grudgingly let her stay, with the stipulation she pass a session with the shrink. Xavier declared her mentally fit for duty and she was back in the mix, avoiding the awkward looks from agents who viewed kidnap victims with the same look as a leper. In truth, she wasn't okay – not yet. But working served as a suitable distraction to thoughts of fighting off an attempted rape and sawing off the thumb of her captor.

"Well, I'm glad you're back."

"Thanks, it's better than the alternative. What have you got?"

"I've printed out the contents of all the files from both computers. The boxes are being taken up to your office as we speak. You'll find printouts of emails from an account this guy was using as well. Email tends to be the best way to dig-up evidence and accomplices in these types of cases."

Capelli rubbed Jimmy's scruffy hair – she had a soft spot for the kid – thanked him, and retreated to her office with Ford shuffling behind.

"This guy must be the luckiest bastard ever. Not one of these emails is spam. I mean, that's a true genius to rig up a filter like that. Not even a Viagra offer." Ford sipped his coffee, the muddy brown liquid dripping onto his shirt. They'd been pouring over the hacked emails for the better part of three hours now.

"Jesus, Danny. Your dry cleaning bill must be off the charts. And my guess is Jimmy didn't bother printing the junk mail."

"Nope, I checked. He gave us everything – in chronological order no less."

"Well, I'm almost up to this April and I haven't found anything suspicious yet."

"Me either. I'm going to jump ahead to September, just before the murders started. Keep plugging away in April over there."

Ford's first hit was an email dated September 19, just a few weeks before the murder of Edward Thorpe. It was a vague email, providing no actual hard evidence. But one thing stood out like a hooker in church – the sender was Vance Thorpe. Nearly dropping a bag of Doritos, Ford called to Capelli.

"Hey, get over here. You won't believe this."

"What do you want? I'm on a roll, made it to June."

"Read this."

Capelli grabbed the paper and read, not yet noticing the sender's email address.

The plan is a go. First phase to begin on date discussed.

-V.T.

"Okay... What's it mean."

"Wake up Capelli! V.T.! Vance Thorpe. The email address is vthorpe@polaris.com. That skeevy exec had been in contact with our man."

"But what's the email *mean*? It's pretty vague. Granted the connection between the men is appalling but nobody is spending their golden years on Rikers over this."

"I'm not sure. There are some other emails, equally cryptic, over the next few weeks."

"Well, then, let's do a little more leg-work on this and get a warrant to search Vance's home and office. And an arrest warrant just in case. He'd look pretty in my cuffs."

68

Greyson's Lab
New York, New York

The doctors rigged a microscope to a large computer screen, watching as their experiment came to life. The first slide contained a smear of the mutated TB strain. The antibiotic provided by Greyson's pharmacy was then introduced, its effectiveness against the bacteria tested. There was no contest. Not only did the bacteria fail to die, but it continued reproducing.

On a separate slide was the same mutated TB smear. This time Greyson introduced the medication Turner had used to treat the Jowhar camp. The drug was labeled same as Greyson's, but it was evidently another product altogether. Almost instantly the medication killed off the bacteria.

"This is no accident, is it?" Turner asked Greyson, knowing the answer.

"No, it's not. If this was simply a matter of mutated tuberculosis you could argue that a natural form of evolution had occurred, the disease manufacturing its own means of survival. But this is a genetically manipulated tuberculosis strain and its perfect antidote. Somebody has taken their experiment too far, would be my guess." Greyson rubbed his chin, disturbed by the discovery.

"Why would someone engineer a super-strain of TB? I don't see any possible upside."

"That's naive, Luc. There's an upside for somebody. Hell, look at Tuskegee. Our own government injected men with syphilis and not only was no one told, nothing was done to treat the disease. Every single man died from the experiment all so a few health officials could see its progression. Heck, a few years ago Hillary Clinton apologized to the Guatemalan people for the American government's part in conspiring with big pharma to infect Guatemalan citizens with STDs back in the forties so they could experiment with inoculations."

"Apart from terrorism, why create a disease worse than the ones we already have? I'm not defending the Tuskegee and Guatemala fiascos, but there at least some warped logic behind testing antibiotics for known diseases."

"I don't know what to tell you, Luc. I'll work on these samples and see if I can find what exactly was done to manipulate the bacteria. Beyond that I wouldn't know where to start."

"There's only one place I can think of. Thanks Sheldon. I owe you a lifetime of single-malt for this."

69

Polaris Pharmaceuticals
New York, New York

It was October 30th and a hum of energy intermingled with a brisk fall breeze as people prepared for their Halloween parties. Festive New Yorkers made last minute stops at costume shops for ill-fitting lycra get-ups that did no one any favors. The rest – the wise ones – stocked up on red wine and planned a nice night in, away from the inevitable mêlée of October 31st in Manhattan.

Turner took in the crisp air, its freshness tainted by the smell of burning street pretzels and wafts of sewer stench. The walk to Bryant Park wasn't long, but it just as well could have been an eternity given his nervousness. Had he been manipulated somehow? Or was this all a big misunderstanding?

During his stroll, Renata had called from Prague in hysterics. Between bouts of unbridled sobbing she'd managed to relay that Skala had been killed by an injection of snake venom. She'd also mentioned a small needle mark was visible in the vein of Skala's neck. The case was officially classified as a murder with no viable leads.

After careful consideration, Turner decided a visit to Polaris Pharmaceuticals was in order. The company created and distributed the drugs used in his camp. Besides that, two of their top execs had been killed – not to mention Skala. There were too many connections with the powerhouse company to ignore. Still, if his hunch was wrong, then not only was he about to insult to president of the second-largest pharmaceutical company in the world, but he'd also lose his job. Despite the paltry stipend and unpleasant working conditions, Turner adored his work.

After clearing security and a good long wait in the glass-ceilinged lobby, Vance Thorpe's secretary cheerfully announced that her boss was ready to see him. Turner followed her to the office, as requested, and watched as she comically attempted to speed-walk in a cling-on pencil skirt with sky-high heels. He guessed Thorpe didn't even look over the blonde's resume before offering the job.

"Dr. Turner, what a pleasure to meet you! I've always admired Doctors Without Borders. It's quite a sacrifice you make." Thorpe smiled, exposing his too-white teeth.

"We wouldn't be able to do it without the help of companies like yours." Turner participated grudgingly in the obligatory ass-kissing.

"So what brings you in today, Dr. Turner?" Thorpe motioned to a leather sofa and Turner sat, Thorpe opting for the matching chair just opposite.

"Actually, I'm afraid to tell you we've had a problem with one of the products. Geno-Vyt, it's the…"

Before Turner could finish a commotion in the hallway stole his attention. He heard the blonde bimbo scream, insisting whoever was in the hall couldn't see Mr. Thorpe at this time. Just moments later a man and woman burst into the room, badges in hand.

Vance immediately leapt to his feet, confused and embarrassed by the intrusion.

"Agents Capelli and Ford. It's always such a pleasure when you visit," Vance sarcastically muttered through clenched teeth, "but I'm in the middle of a chat with Doctor Turner. Can this wait a bit?"

Turner sat back in awe, amused by the scene. He couldn't help but be impressed by the stunning female agent; there was something alluring about a woman wielding a badge.

"No, Vance, you can't. Dr. Turner, I apologize for the intrusion but Mr. Thorpe needs to come with us."

"For what? Have you found my father's killer?"

"I believe so."

"Well, who is it!"

"You."

70

FBI Headquarters
Midtown, Manhattan

"**A**ny luck?" Capelli asked as Ford returned from his third visit to Vance Thorpe's interrogation room.

"Vance swears up and down he's both innocent and clueless. As much as I don't like the guy, he's got a good poker face. Seems genuinely dismayed to be considered a suspect and went so far as to request a lie detector test."

"Well, even if he passes, he's shit out of luck. Jimmy just recovered his deleted outgoing emails. There are multiple messages sent to a Mr. Hans Bruun, aka Eric Richter, that are a match to those found in Bruun-Richter's inbox. Guy's up shit's creek without a paddle."

"Maybe. I just wish one of those emails said 'I'll pay you twenty grand to murder my father' rather than a cryptic diddy like 'Plans a go. Start date confirmed.' It's all so damn vague."

"Well, we have proof he's been in communication with a kidnapper and suspected murderer. That's enough to hold him for awhile until we get something solid. What about Richter? Has he said anything?" Capelli hadn't been to see Richter since Switzerland. The fear of breaking down into a blubbering mess – or alternately shooting him on the spot – had kept her from going face-to-face until the roller-coaster emotions were in check.

"Nah. Guys like him don't crack. I suggest we ship him to a black site and let some sadistic freak torture the information from him."

"Our badges have the wrong three letters for that one, Danny."

"Yeah, yeah. Oh, that doc is still waiting in the lobby. Can you deal with him? My blood sugar is low. Need a Snickers."

"What you need is fat camp. Yeah, I'll deal with the doc."

"Hi, Dr. Turner. I'm Agent Kate Capelli," Capelli cheerfully greeted the doctor, extended her right hand. "Sorry about the interruption at Polaris. Probably one of your more exciting meetings, I can imagine."

"No question about that." Turner smiled. He did his best to hold eye contact, but boy did his eyes want to wander.

"What brings you by?"

"I know this is unorthodox, but is there any chance I could speak with Vance Thorpe? It's regarding some tainted products I received."

"I'm sorry but that's not possible. Come to my office for a minute and you can relay the information to me. If it's not a conflict to our investigation, I may be able pass your questions on later."

Turner relayed the events in Jowhar and Prague, Capelli dutifully scribbling notes on her yellow pad. She did her best to keep up with the medical lingo but couldn't help feeling she was wasting her time.

71

Ford Residence
Brooklyn, New York

"Caroline, I don't know what the world did before your penne pesto." Capelli ran garlic bread over her plate, soaking the last bit of pesto and parmesan cheese.

"They ate Chef Boyardee. Now hand me your plate and get to work before my husband starts banging the broom on the basement ceiling."

"He actually does that?"

"All the time."

"And thanks again for letting me spend a few nights here. It's good to be around friends."

"Hey, you're more family that my own sister. Besides, Danny would have heart failure if you were at your apartment alone after everything that happened."

"Well, it's appreciated."

"By the way, Allen called to see how you're doing. He wanted to give you space after the last week. Said he'll wait a few weeks to hound you for a second date."

"He's gonna have to wait until this case is wrapped up. I can hardly remember to brush my hair I've been so distracted." Not to mention being scared of my own shadow, Capelli thought, keeping up her brave face.

Capelli made it to the man-cave just as Ford had retrieved the broom.

"What are you? Ten? Your wife and I were having a heart-to-heart."

"My wife doesn't have heart-to-hearts. She's a dictator around this place."

"I'm sure. What's on your mind, broom-boy?"

"Well," Ford returned the broom to its closet, "I've being thinking about that doctor's statement – the *super-*

disease or whatever he calls it. And I've been wondering if that may have something to do with our case."

"How so?" Capelli grabbed a football and they began tossing it back and forth as they often did when mulling over theories.

"Well, what if Vance Thorpe decided he could benefit from a new disease strain. I mean, think about it, they're a pharmaceutical company. They make major bucks when the masses get sick. From what we know of Edward Thorpe he was a solid, upstanding citizen with a heart of gold. Not the type to bring more disease into the world, more the kind of man who would try and eradicate it."

"That seems to be the case."

"Well, what if his over-eager son took on a side project without Edward's knowledge? In a company that size it would be impossible for Edward to keep track of what absolutely every scientist, researcher, doctor, was working on."

Capelli picked up on the theory, continuing the thread. "And then he found out what Vance was doing, got angry, and, who knows, maybe even threatened to fire him. Vance, who had every intention of running Polaris, got worried about his future and so instead of putting a stop to his illegal activity, hired someone to off his pops."

"Exactly. It seems a little out there but so does this whole warped case. A killer uses snake venom as a murder weapon, and flies an FBI agent overseas on a private jet. It's not beyond the realm that Vance Thorpe bent the rules to make some profit." Ford replaced the football on his desk. "Let's get that doctor in again; I'd like us both to speak with him. If nothing else, he can give us the proper medical jargon to throw at Vance when we talk to him."

Fine with me, Capelli thought, not distraught by the notion of seeing the handsome doctor.

72

FBI Headquarters
Midtown Manhattan

"**S**on of a bitch! I'm going to kill whoever leaked this," Ford muttered as he steered his black town-car around the FBI building, a task made exceptionally more difficult given the large press pool that had gathered. The news of a possible arrest in the case of Edward Thorpe had leaked early in the morning on CNN.

"Jimmy probably tweeted something about the case. That kid just can't help himself when he's in front of a keyboard."

"Vegas money is on Caruso. That yuppie SOB is always spouting off confidential information," Ford griped as he slammed on the brakes, nearly taking out a cyclist.

"Jesus, Danny. Take it easy. Every news camera in town will catch you taking out a pedestrian." Capelli's phone chirped, distracting her. "Hey, Marcy. I've been meaning to get in touch, how are you?" Capelli listened and gave Ford a punch, getting his attention.

"Ouch! What?"

Capelli whispered under her breath so the phone wouldn't pick up her words. "Did Marcy Travers send something to you?"

Ford grimaced, acknowledging his guilt. The large folder had arrived just as the tip from PremierJets had come in. He'd stashed the envelope in his desk and completely forgotten about it in the ensuing chaos.

"Yeah, we've got the package, Marcy. Barney Fife here temporarily misplaced it. I'll check it out when I get to my desk."

At the bureau, Capelli made a bee-line for Ford's desk as he skulked behind like a scolded child. In his office, she began pulling open desk-drawers, finally stopping when she'd located a large manila envelope with the adoption agency's seal.

"Refresh my memory – what was Marcy helping us with?" Ford asked, his mind drawing a blank.

"The Warren adoption, remember? Eric Warren mentioned his father had a child way back in the day and put him up for closed adoption. Marcy un-closed it for us."

"How nice of her to break the law for you. Do you really think the file is relevant?"

"Not really, but Marcy's good to help us out and the least I can do is take a peek at the records."

"So I didn't totally screw up by not opening that. Nice."

"Yeah, pat yourself on the back, Colombo."

He did just that and retreated from the office in search of coffee.

Ford returned with two piping-hot Styrofoam coffee cups to find an ashen-faced Capelli.

"See a ghost?"

"Not exactly. Does the name Janet Williams ring a bell?" Capelli felt she was on to something, but hadn't fully arranged the puzzle of facts strewn across her mind.

"Should it?" Ford thought a moment, passing Capelli her coffee. "Oh yeah, Edward Thorpe's secretary. Why?"

"Look at this." Capelli placed an official adoption agency record in front of Ford, the page listing names and social security information for the birth parents.

"Well, shit. Janet Williams and Martin Warren had a son together?"

"Sure did. She never brought up an affair with Warren while we interviewed her."

"Why would she? Most people don't sit in front of law-enforcement and say 'Hey! Let me tell you about the stupid stuff I did in my youth.' "

"They list a name for him? We could run him in the system, just for giggles."

"It says here Nathaniel Wilde was adopted by Mimi and Roger Wilde. They're British expats who returned to London soon after the adoption, according to a change of address in the file."

Ford entered 'Nathaniel Wilde' into DIVS – the Data Integration and Visualization System. The relatively new program culled together all relevant information from the many other databases and provided a comprehensive file on the individual for which an agent was searching.

"Well, at least he has a file," Ford chirped, scrolling through the documents.

"Everyone has a file. I'm sure if the public knew how many non-criminals had all their records stashed in an FBI database there'd be a serious civil rights case in the Supreme Court right now."

"Don't get me started, Capelli. It's in the name of national security. If Osama II decided to blow-up Disneyworld and records such as these would have stopped him –"

"Okay, Rush. Let's not get into this now. See what we've got on Wilde."

Ford clicked the page which essentially pulled together the vital statistics and summary of the individual in question.

"Okay... Nathaniel Wilde, forty years of age, resides in London and New York. He's Senior Vice President at Babylon Capital, based in London but with offices in New York and Sydney. Educated at Oxford, received a masters at Columbia University in New York. Speaks multiple languages, sits on many charitable boards, and sounds like about forty percent of the boring crooks that work on Wall Street."

"Any mention of Warren or Williams in the file?"

"Hang on, that'll take some digging." Ford clicked and searched on various tabs, squinting in an effort to see the small print on the computer screen. He desperately needed a new contact lens prescription but admitting deterioration in his sight was admitting he was getting to upper-middle age.

"Don't see anything mentioning his birth parents. Adopted parents were killed in an automobile accident five years ago. When did the Warren kid say his dad told him about the son he'd adopted out?"

"I can't remember exactly, but I think he said around three or four years ago. Maybe the death of his parents sparked his interest in finding Warren."

"Perhaps. Let's see what this guy's worth." Ford clicked on the financial records and let out low whistle. "Eighty-million. I'd say that's not bad for a guy that just turned forty. Confirms that I chose the wrong profession."

"How'd he make all that?"

"Working hard at stealing people's money and calling it 'investment banking.' "

"How you've gotten through life with that chip on your shoulder I'll never know." Capelli leaned in and peered at the screen, curious. "Click on his investments."

Ford did so and after a few seconds let out another low whistle. "Looks like our friend Wilde saw great hope in the future of Polaris Pharmaceuticals. He's been purchasing additional stock every month for the last year, almost twenty-million dollars worth."

"You're kidding. Why would he do that? I thought these guys diversified."

"Not if you have the inside track on a company. Like say if a guilty birth father divulges company secrets to a long-lost son."

"You think Warren was feeding him information?"

"I don't know, maybe. Or Wilde just thinks it's a great company. According to this he made the biggest stock buy last month for seven million dollars. Just a drop in the bucket for a guy with his wealth, I guess."

"He didn't get that wealthy by being careless with his money. There had to be some reason for a series of such large stock buys. I remember just before Lipitor hit the market Pfizer's stock hit the roof. Do we know if Polaris has any drugs on trial with breakthrough potential?" Capelli leaned over Ford and opened an internet window.

"Look at Miss CNBC. You in the market? 'Cause I know for damn sure on my salary I'm not investing in anything other than Nerf balls and diapers for Lucy."

"The costly perils of reproduction. But to answer your question, yes, I have a little in the market." After a moment the results of her Google search flashed on the screen and she began reading the latest news on Polaris. "I don't see any news here that would justify a large uptick in stock price. If anything, this guy could have lost his shirt when Edward Thorpe was killed. Stock took a 48 hour dive but has since recovered to its pre-murder numbers."

"We could always ask Vance, seeing as how he's conveniently located downstairs in the tombs."

"I think we should do that. I also think we should talk to Janet Williams. She could well be the one spilling company secrets to her long-lost son."

"We're investigating a murder, not corporate scandals, Capelli."

"Well, what can I say, I don't like feeling duped. Let's re-schedule Dr.Turner and pay a visit to Vance and Ms. Williams."

73

Residence of Janet Williams
New York, New York

Ford and Capelli pulled up outside the home of Janet Williams. Her apartment was on 81st between Park and Madison Avenues in a classic brownstone with large bay windows. The tree-lined streets and beautifully appointed pre-war buildings gave the feel of old New York wealth.

"Guess being a secretary pays pretty well," Ford commented, taking in the scenery.

"Guess so."

As the agents neared the brownstone's front door, a resident of the building was exiting. Rather than ring the secretary's buzzer, Ford and Capelli walked into the building and up a flight to the second floor and approached Janet William's apartment.

Capelli held her index finger to her lips, motioning for Ford to be quiet and she attempted to decipher the words from the other side of the door. The sound of voices, one male, one female, came from inside the apartment. They spoke angrily, the unmistakable tension of stress and frustration evident in their hurried, raised voices.

"Is it the secretary?" Ford whispered, asking the obvious.

"Yes, but I can't tell who else." Capelli replied, still unable to make out the words.

"We'll find out soon enough."

Capelli knocked on the door with three loud raps of her fist. The voices immediately silenced, as if their sudden lack of noise would convince their visitors nobody was home. She knocked loudly again, this time declaring herself as an agent with a non-threatening voice. Still, no matter how pleasant she sounded, a visit from the FBI was never considered a welcome surprise.

The voices became hurried whispers, as if deciding what to do with the situation on the other side of the door. Ford gave Capelli a raised eyebrow, a pleading look which begged her to approve his shooting the door down.

"Hold your horses," she whispered to Ford, and then in a louder voice yelled into the door, "Mrs. Williams please let us in, we've just got a few quick questions."

Finally the door opened. Janet Williams stood innocently in an off-white cashmere sweater and grey slacks, her once perfectly-styled French-twist now showing loose strands, as if she'd been nervously pulling at them. Capelli gave a quick scan of the room, not seeing anyone.

"I'm sorry, I must have dozed off. I thought your voices were coming from the television."

"Oh, it's not a problem. Can we come in for a second? Just a few quick questions."

"Sure. Of course, come in." Ms. Williams answered with welcoming words and a tentative tone. "Would you like anything to drink? Perhaps a snack?" she asked as they entered the living room, which appeared to have been purchased directly from Ralph Lauren Home's showroom.

"No, no, we're fine. Just have a seat." Capelli gestured for Ms. Williams to sit on the cream-colored sofa, herself sitting on a chair directly facing the older woman. Capelli watched as the secretary nervously eyed Ford in her peripheral vision while he perused the apartment for her other guest.

"Again, Ms. Williams, we're sorry to come on such short notice. We've actually got some questions regarding a rather sensitive matter. As you surely know, since we last spoke Martin Warren was murdered in Prague. It's come to light that you have a child with the late Mr. Warren. I'm wondering why you didn't mention this when we last interviewed you."

"Well," the secretary nervously adjusted a loose strand of hair, "there didn't seem to be any need. It was a closed adoption and is a part of my past I rather prefer not to reflect upon."

"I certainly understand. Were you aware that your son, Nathaniel Wilde, reached out to Mr. Warren a few years back?"

Ms. William's face paled considerably, twisting into a nervous expression. Her reaction served as a wordless confession that she was well aware of her adopted son's efforts to re-connect. Just before Capelli called her out on this fact, the loud slamming of the bedroom window startled both women. Moments later Ford entered, his hand firmly gripping the right forearm of Nathaniel Wilde.

Capelli looked back to Janet Williams, "So it's safe to say you're aware of Nathaniel Wilde?"

Janet Williams simply stared ahead, shutting down as the situation spiraled from her control.

Ford interjected, "Looks like Mr. Wilde was just having a smoke break on the balcony. I too crawl out windows onto unsteady platforms and press myself tightly against a building wall when I want to indulge in a little nicotine fix."

"You exaggerate, Agent Ford. I was just being polite. It's not good manners to smoke in a woman's home. Not that I'd presume you have any manners."

"Look at you, trying to piss of the FBI. Keep goin' buddy. I got a big ole' gang banger awaiting arraignment and you're just his type."

Wilde kept his mouth shut, realizing his pompous talk was unlikely to get him anywhere in this crowd.

"Have a seat next to mama." Ford gestured to the sofa, the reference to Wilde's parentage drawing a painful grimace from Janet. The man sat and Ford continued. "So when did you two reconnect? It must have been quite a surprise for you, Ms. Williams, when this grown man knocked on your door claiming to be your son."

The older woman looked around nervously, internally debating whether she was better served remaining silent or divulging information. Wilde's posture grew increasingly tense as the woman continued to send signals of culpability.

"It was a wonderful surprise to have Nathaniel come back into my life. As you can imagine, I've had decades of regret over my decision not to raise him." A tear welled in the woman's eye, but she didn't bother to wipe it away.

Capelli gave her a moment to regain composure and started in on Wilde.

"Mr. Wilde, what sparked the sudden interest in finding your birth parents?"

"I think all adopted people have an interest in knowing their birth parents. After my adoptive parents passed away

I decided it would be a good time to reach out," Wilde smugly retorted.

"It must have been exciting to learn that your father was a wealthy executive. Did you ask for a handout? Suggest that maybe a little cash would go a long way in easing the guilt of ditching his firstborn?"

"Nothing of the sort. You should know – since you've clearly run background on me – that I've done rather well. I'd never degrade myself by asking for a handout."

"How about information as payment? Since meeting your parents you've obtained a rather large percentage of Polaris Pharmaceuticals stock. Did Martin ever pass along information of a drug breakthrough, or other finding that would bump the stock price?" Capelli turned towards Janet. "Or maybe you, Ms. Williams? You were the right hand of Edward Thorpe, you said so yourself. Surely you've obtained a few valuable company secrets over the years."

"Oh no, nothing like that." Williams answered, flustered. "A bit of puffery on my part, making my job sound more glamorous than it really is."

"Fair enough. Mr. Wilde, why the sudden interest in Polaris then?"

"It sounds silly but the purchase was more for sentimental reasons than anything. It felt nice to own a share of something my father had helped build. Don't get me wrong, I did my due diligence and knew the company would perform strongly in my portfolio."

"A share is sentimental. Twenty million dollars worth of shares is something altogether different."

"Well, maybe for you, Agent Capelli. But not for someone like me."

If it weren't for the cumbersome air cast calling attention to her fractured right hand, Capelli would have happily slapped the smug look off Wilde's handsome face.

"Yes, well, before you go making offensive statements consider who wears the badge in here. Which leads me to another question for you, Ms. Williams. Does Vance Thorpe ever visit you here, either for work or social reasons?"

"No, Vance has never been here. I'd occasionally go to Edward's residence for social functions but that was the extent of my out-of-office relationship with Vance."

"That's interesting, Ms. Williams. Is that your computer over there?" Capelli pointed to an older model IBM that sat atop a mahogany corner desk.

"Yes, it is."

"You only use it here?"

"It's not a portable laptop, so yes it stays here."

"Ms. Williams, does Vance Thorpe ever request you send emails from his Polaris account?"

Redness rose into the woman's cheeks, her sons' tall frame visibly tensing at the question.

"No, I only send emails from my account. Why do you ask?" The confidence had fully evaporated from the woman's face, a look of dread replacing it.

"Because you're lying to me, Ms. Williams. We had an interesting call from our tech department during our drive here. We'd flagged a few emails from Vance and it turns out the majority of them were sent from an IP address relating to this specific computer. So either Vance has been sneaking in at night to use your prehistoric computer, or you've been hacking into your boss's email and sending rather suspicious messages. Which, mind you, is illegal without his permission."

"This is clearly some kind of misunderst…"

Nathaniel cut his mother off with a booming voice of authority, his inner CEO taking over.

"Janet, mom, don't say anything. I'm not sure what these agents are getting at but I'd like retain a lawyer for you before any further questioning occurs."

With wide, frightened eyes, she looked to her son. It was a loaded look and Capelli sensed there was a lot more to their relationship than a reacquainted mother and son.

"I understand, Mr. Wilde. I'd suggest you retain one for yourself as well. You're both being declared persons of interest in the murders of Edward Thorpe and Martin Warren."

74

FBI Headquarters
Midtown Manhattan

Ford took a long pull of Pepto-Bismol and replaced the cap.

"This case isn't helping my acid reflux any, that's for damn sure."

"I doubt the case is your only problem." Capelli kicked her feet onto Ford's desk. It was after five and when on OT she had no qualms disregarding office etiquette. "So, let's try to work out this little puzzle. It feels like we're in the middle of a ten-thousand piece jigsaw of a sandy desert and I'm getting damn sick of it."

"Well, we're losing our grip on Vance Thorpe. If we can't locate evidence against him aside from the emails, which apparently weren't his doing, he's going to walk.

And frankly, the more I talk to him, I think he may be innocent. I'm not sure he'd have the brains or balls to pull a string of murders together and get away with it."

"Maybe, but there's no way Janet Williams pulled this off alone. I doubt she's plugged-in to the criminal underground to find a for-hire assassin. And why would she kill these guys? The emails are a glaring red flag but I don't see how she does this alone, or what her motive would be."

"My pick-of-the-litter is Mr. Wilde. He's an asshole, smart enough, and spite at Warren for adopting him out could be enough for motive."

"Two holes in that theory. One, where does he come across an assassin of Richter/Bruun's caliber? Two, why would he invest so much in a company if he planned to off the leading execs? That's a surefire way to lose money – not exactly a time to double down the bet." Capelli twirled her hair in thought. "Still, I like him for it. Jimmy's doing a deep background on him?"

"The deepest. We'll soon have all his skeletons." Ford sat up, pulling a rumpled trench on over his suit.

"Something tells me it's going to be a whole damn graveyard." Capelli grabbed her own jacket, preparing to leave the office.

"You're okay at home tonight?"

"Yep. Got my Glock and new deadbolts."

The agents had no way of knowing that seven thousand miles away a plan had been set in motion to start the greatest disease outbreak since the bubonic plague.

75

**Capelli's Apartment
New York, New York**

The landline startled Capelli. She'd been nodding off watching an over-coiffed, over-bleached news anchor cheerfully report a nighttime traffic accident on the Tappan Zee bridge. If not for the call jolting her awake, her precariously tipped coffee mug would have spilled its contents over her white couch. According to the news station it was 7:30 a.m. and a chilly thirty-two degrees.

"Hello," Capelli grunted.

"Hey, you aren't answering your cell. I thought you'd be working out." It was Ford, sounding uncharacteristically like a morning person.

"Well, I had a bit of insomnia since last time I was in this apartment I ended up drugged on an airplane. Why are you calling me so early?" She coughed, finally clearing the morning throat.

"Interesting development. Janet Williams met with her lawyer last night. I received an email at 7:00 a.m. sharp that she'd like to speak with us alone. Lawyer present of course, but she's requested we not inform Wilde of her cooperation."

"Huh, that is interesting. What time are we meeting?"

"8:30 at the office. And don't be late, sleepyhead, I feel good things happening today."

Capelli arrived to hot breakfast sandwiches and a fresh brew in Ford's office. Photos, clippings, spreadsheets, and every document under the sun pertaining to Nathaniel Wilde was scattered about the office. Those that seemed most relevant had already been pinned to the white board, awaiting analysis.

"I'm scared to ask what's gotten into you. When did you get in?" Capelli said, grabbing a coffee and watching as he excitedly looked through the papers.

"Bright and early. Caroline's at her mother's with the kids. Watched the Thursday night game without interruption and followed it up with the best four hours of sleep in my life. Then the case got me thinking so I came in at five to get started."

"Somebody wants a raise. Okay, Super Ford. What have you got here?"

"Jimmy came through with the background on Wilde so I've spent the morning comparing his past with our other players. Interestingly, he worked for a defense firm based out of Zurich up until about ten years ago. His position was in sales; a nice way of saying he'd sell deadly weapons to the highest paying terrorist. This sent him to the Middle East, Russia, and Israel on a frequent basis. Now, according to Babineaux's somewhat spotty recollection, our pasty assassin reportedly spent time in all those places, especially Israel and Russia. I don't have specific dates for Wilde or obviously Richter's travels but there's a circumstantial connection there."

"Why didn't we know about the weapons sales work from our earlier search? That should have been front and center in the DIVS database."

"Not sure. They buried the information pretty deep, according to Jimmy. Most of these defense firms do, and he used an alias on sales missions."

"At least now it seems plausible the two have crossed paths. Could be something."

"It gets better. Jimmy did some hacking into Babylon's financials and apparently the company has been padding its numbers significantly. Like, by the hundreds of millions significantly. Wilde's own wealth is questionable too: a lot of what he shows as earnings looks to have been siphoned off from the company. About five years ago, Babylon had some investments tank, which put them in quite a lurch. They never disclosed these losses; Jimmy managed to find the information through the company's internal communications. Despite the financial hit, all the CEO's salaries still managed to increase by the millions."

"So we've got a guy with no moral scruples whose wealth is in jeopardy. And he's got a past in weapons sales, which, inherently has him dealing with a shady cast of characters. His birth father happens to be in the upper echelons at a successful pharmaceutical company and he sees an opportunity. But what's the opportunity? It still doesn't make sense that this guy would kill the two people who started Polaris in the first place if his bet was to buy up stocks and watch them skyrocket."

"I'm telling you, it's in the research. Somebody at Polaris must have the inside track on a new drug and have tipped off Wilde. It could have been Warren, Janet Williams, or a colleague of theirs who'd met Wilde." Ford checked his watch; the face read 8:32. "We've got to get downstairs and see what Ms. Williams has to say.

The agents entered Interview Room B, a drab space with avocado-green linoleum floors and a stainless steel table in the center, bolted into the floor after one-too-many frustrated suspects had flung it across the room. On each side of the table sat two bolted-down stainless steel chairs. Janet Williams and her attorney were already seated. The latter thrust out his hand and introduced himself before the agents were fully through the door.

"David Harowitz, it's a pleasure to meet you." He smiled warmly, his sweaty hand remained extended until Capelli finally caved and shook it.

"It's a pleasure to meet you, Mr. Harowitz, your reputation precedes you. Please, have a seat." Ford grunted.

Harowitz returned to his chair and began reviewing a ream of paper bulging from a manila file folder. His focus on the documents was as intense as if he'd just received the nuclear codes. The lawyer was in his mid-forties and had successfully represented a long line of criminals. He was a super-star of his field, the kind of guy FBI agents loathed.

Janet Williams' demeanor couldn't have been further from that of her lawyer's. The once well-put-together secretary now looked in shambles. Her hair was unwashed and pulled into a haphazard bun. The creases in her face looked far deeper without the careful application of make-up, the stress evident in the squint of her eyes and pinch of her mouth.

"My client has information pertinent to your investigation. It is her request that she be granted full immunity against any actions you would find unsavory or conspiratorial on her part."

"I can't make any guarantees, I'm sure you know that. But all cooperation will be considered if we were to bring charges against Ms. Williams."

As Ford spoke, Janet Williams layered one hand over another, attempting to calm their shaking. Her eyes stared at the table top as if ashamed, a small quiver of sadness in her upper lip. The agents continued their back and forth with Harowitz until she finally broke in.

"I'd just like to get this over with. May I please say what I have to say?"

"Go ahead, Ms. Williams." Capelli said with a sympathetic voice.

"First off, you have to understand that I don't fully know what's gone on in the last few months. The details of the plan were never made clear to me; I was just a naïve pawn in the whole thing." She paused a moment, debating for the last time whether she was making the right move. After a deep, shaky breath she continued. "You could say this whole disaster began over forty years ago, at the Polaris Christmas party. The company was in its infancy, and still struggling for cash, but Edward always made a point to celebrate the holidays with his staff. I'd been working at Polaris a year by then and each day my desire for Edward grew stronger and stronger. He and Audrey were not yet married, so I reckoned there was still a chance for me, and that party was my chance to make him notice me. Not to toot my own horn but I looked good that night in a red velvet dress and pumps.

"Of course, it turns out he really only had eyes for Audrey and politely avoided my flirtations throughout the night. I sat alone, drowning my sorrows in champagne, until Martin Warren approached me, eighth glass of scotch in his hand, and suggest we rendezvous in his office. Like a fool, I agreed and we had relations on his desk for all of about thirty seconds. That was all it took to conceive.

"Martin and I agreed the pregnancy should be kept quiet, both realizing the night had been a horrible mistake. So, I took a six month leave from Polaris before my belly began showing. My mother lived in Connecticut where I went to stay until the baby was born. Edward believed my story that she'd taken ill and needed me by her side. Once the baby was born, I had little regret at giving him up, which I know sounds awful. In a matter of weeks I'd lost the gained weight and returned to work, never knowing what happened to my baby boy.

"After ten years of living alone, never having found a husband or bearing another child, I'd begun deeply regretting my decision not to raise the boy. That feeling grew intensely with each passing year. I'd considered trying to locate him, but how do you approach the person you grew in your belly only to give away him away like garbage? Then, three years ago, a man rings claiming to be my son. I met him at a café off Central Park and immediately knew it was him. He had my eyes but otherwise looked the spitting image of a young Martin.

"Never once did he ask me why I'd given him up, or accuse me of being a bad person. He showered me with expensive gifts around the holidays, took me to four star restaurants when he was in town from London, and we'd talk for hours as he'd catch me up on his life. Finally, I had a family." She paused for a sip of water, taking a moment.

"Did you discuss any of this with Martin Warren?" Capelli asked.

"No, Nathaniel requested I not. He said they'd spoken, and occasionally if they found themselves in the same city would briefly meet, but I don't think Martin was keen on a relationship. He probably didn't want his home life disturbed, seeing as he'd married and had a son.

"Anyway, I'm rambling. About a year ago now, Nathaniel began telling me I was owed more – that for all my dedication to Polaris, Edward, and Martin, I'd not been given enough. Over time I began to agree. His words had me convinced I'd been burned, that I'd sacrificed myself and received nothing in return. That Edward used my love for him – and it was love – and loyalty for all those years. I can't believe it myself now, but I began hating everyone I'd worked so hard for – and I wanted payback.

"I voiced these feelings to Nathaniel and he claimed to have a plan. He wouldn't give me all the details, but guaranteed large profits."

"Did he disclose any details of the plan at all?" Capelli asked, growing excited at the idea of a witness against Nathaniel Wilde.

"It was vague initially, and still is to be honest. But I'd managed to piece together some of it. All he told me in the beginning was that he had a researcher friend at Polaris who had the inside track on a new product. Apparently this scientist kept the breakthrough to himself and approached Nathaniel, inquiring how best to profit from his discovery. I think the idea was that Nathaniel would purchase a great amount of stock before the discovery was announced, take the profits, and pay the researcher his share and cut me in as well.

"All I was asked to do was send emails from Vance's account. Nathaniel would call me with the email address and message and then I would access Vance's email, send the information, and then delete the email from the sent folder. I had no idea to whom or what I was communicating but for a long while I didn't care. I trusted Nathaniel and felt scorned by Polaris. The whole thing seemed harmless enough. I figured at worst it was something along the lines of insider trading and no one would get physically hurt."

"Did something happen to change your mind?" Capelli encouraged.

"Yes. A few months ago Nathaniel was in New York with his girlfriend, a doctor. They stopped by for coffee and cake one afternoon when she got a call. After she was finished I went to the kitchen to clean the plates and overheard their conversation. You know how New York apartments are, you can hear everything. I heard the woman, Eva, say King had called. She then said something about children having died but they thought the kink had been worked out and they'd do another trial. Initially, I thought surely I'd misunderstood, but when I returned to the living room they immediately changed topics and had sheepish expressions. There was no question whatever had been discussed was meant to remain secret."

"Any idea what they were referring to?" Ford interjected, adjusting his too-tight Barney Miller tie.

"My best guess is a drug. The scam we were running depended on a breakthrough with a medicine. To know the product's effectiveness it has to be tested on human subjects and, though I hope it's not the case, I believe they had unintentionally killed children during one of the test-runs. And the way the woman said it, she was so cold. I liked Eva the few times Nathaniel brought her by, but she had a hardness that day."

"Who is this "King" they refer to? Anyone you know?" Ford had by now fully loosened his tie and unbuttoned his collar, the source of his near asphyxiation.

"No idea. I didn't really inquire, to be honest. They weren't offering up information and at that point I figured the less I knew the better. But my guess is he was the researcher who'd reached out to Nathaniel. As secretive as the whole thing was I can't imagine they'd have too many additional people in the loop."

"What happened then?"

"That conversation brought me face-to-face with reality. Whatever spell had come over me suddenly evaporated and I realized what a huge mistake I'd made. I was afraid to ask Nathaniel what the whole plot entailed. There was a reason he was keeping secrets and I'd begun to fear him. My actions shamed me greatly and I couldn't bear to come forward with the information directly to Edward so I set up an anonymous email account and wrote to him and Martin. It was vague, because I too had no idea what's actually going on, but said there was secret research taking place and steps being taken by outside individuals to greatly profit from it."

"Did they respond to the email?"

"Not wanting a back and forth I immediately closed the account. But over the next few weeks Edward became withdrawn and worried, as had Martin who'd visited New York during that time. Maybe they discovered what was going on, I'll really never know. If they did conduct any type of investigation it's likely they'd have suspected Vance of wrongdoing, since the cryptic emails had been sent from his account."

"You were Edward's right-hand. Don't you think he'd have discussed the situation with you?"

"Not if he suspected me of something, though I don't think he did. My guess is he felt Vance was a guilty party and wanted to find a way to remedy the situation without exposing his own son. But I'll never know since just days after Martin Warren returned to Prague, Edward was killed."

At this, tears welled in Janet's eyes. Capelli suspected the woman was aware that one of her emails had possibly signaled the go-ahead to take out Thorpe.

Horowitz leaned across the table, passing a 4x6 photograph of a smiling couple seated on Janet William's couch. "My client took this photo just before overhearing conversation between these two. The woman's name is Eva. I just received this earlier in the morning so can't provide a last name but it should be easy enough to find."

"They were very social, always at nice functions when she was in town. I'm sure her full name is listed somewhere online." Janet wiped her nose with a Kleenex and leaned back, signaling she had nothing more to say.

Capelli and Ford exited the interview room on a mission. Once they uncovered Wilde's plot, they could use the evidence against him. If he felt cornered there was a chance he'd give up Richter who'd not yet spoken a word since his arrest, bolstering the murder charges that were brought against him.

"Alright, let's track down this Eva and King. They may be a link to uncovering this whole mess," Ford said as he struggled to keep pace with Capelli.

"I already sent a text to Jimmy. He's on top of it."

76

FBI Headquarters
Midtown Manhattan

Lisa Stiles ushered Dr. Luc Turner through the winding rows of cubicles toward Capelli's office. The secretary's repeat backward glances did little to hide her instant infatuation with the handsome doctor. She kicked herself for wearing her baggy suit and flats today – her 'always be prepared to meet the man of your dreams' motto having not been heeded, today of all days.

The door was cracked slightly, so in typical Lisa fashion she barged through without a knock. The intrusion startled Capelli and both agents instantly jumped up.

"Doc's here to see you," she announced, shooting Capelli a 'why didn't you tell me he was so hot' look.

"Hi, Dr. Turner, thanks for coming in so late in the day. I'm sure you have better places to be on a Friday night," Capelli said, pushing past Lisa as Ford watched in amusement.

"Sadly no," Turner smiled, shaking both the agents' hands.

Lisa strutted off, no longer needed and feeling left out of the conversation.

Ford now stepped in, offering Turner a seat. "Dr. Turner, we've had some recent developments in our case pertaining to Polaris Pharmaceuticals and it turns out you may have some valuable information for us."

Ford displayed a series of photographs on the desk. One was a group picture taken a few years before of the doctors based in Kenya. Both Turner and Eva Abrams were in the photograph. Next to it was a photograph of Nathaniel Wilde and Eva both dressed to the nines at a charity fundraiser just a month before. The final face was that of a bloated-looking red-headed man. "What can you tell us about these three individuals?"

"The woman is Eva Abrams, a colleague of mine in Doctors Without Borders. She's an extremely gifted surgeon, and a somewhat less-than-desirable girlfriend." A slight grimace distorted Turner's lips at the sight of her, still put-off by their Somalia encounter.

"And the men?"

"I've never met the one in the gala photograph. The other looks similar to a man I met at Polaris' Lab in Prague but I couldn't be for sure."

"Name Leo King ring a bell?"

"That sounds right."

"King was a University colleague of the man pictured with Eva, Nathaniel Wilde. He worked for a private medical company in London until an abrupt transfer to Polaris Pharmaceuticals in Prague last year. He's quite under the radar but apparently very talented in microbiology – more specifically, bacteriology."

"Interesting. He seemed like more of a lackey when I was in Prague. But I could be wrong; my time there was limited." Turner had yet to see the relevance in this information.

Ford spent the next twenty minutes relaying Janet William's story from earlier in the day, adding the information Jimmy had produced on the connection between Wilde, Eva, and Leo King. Turner listened intently, connecting the dots as he went.

"So," Ford concluded, "When we saw the connection between Wilde and Abrams, your story about manipulated bacteria and sick kids, the whole far-fetched conspiracy seemed a little closer to earth. And I'll be honest, you'd be a person of interest in this as well had you not already come forward with the information you had."

A few moments passed as Turner absorbed and processed the whole conspiracy, his expression turning angry as things clicked into place.

"When I called in to place an order for the TB antibiotics, my colleague said one had already been placed. With the chaos of the situation I didn't think much of it; I figured there was some sort of mix-up. More than anything I was grateful the medicine would be arriving sooner rather than later. But Eva had paid a visit a few days before and she must have been the one to place the order, knowing King would send the drug they were testing rather than the standard meds. She was probably in Shatoy, too. The doctor there said an attractive woman who'd never made drop-offs before had made the delivery, the records having been cleared from computer logs."

Capelli leaned her elbows on the desk, looking intently at the doctor. "The whole purpose behind this is money – a means for Wilde to make huge profits and keep himself from financial ruin. How can he do that with this drug?"

"Well, if they can infect a population with their genetically modified disease, Polaris would be the only company to have the antidote. They'd make a killing on selling the drug and the stock prices would soar through the roof."

"Wouldn't it seem suspicious that they magically had the cure?"

"Not if they held off a few weeks. If King has a reputation in bacteriology it would be logical to feign work on a cure for a suitable amount of time and then put the drug on the market."

"Would that be too late for some?" Capelli asked.

"Yes, but I don't think a little more blood on their hands would concern them too much." Turner felt sick at the thought of all the graves he'd dug in Somalia, a feeling made even worse by the fact he'd been duped by a former lover and become an unwilling participant in the plan.

77

FBI Interrogation Room A
Midtown Manhattan

"See, you son of a bitch, you're finished." Ford slammed his hand on the table, Wilde jumping back in reaction. "The only way you don't face the death penalty on all this is if you give up your friend, Mr. Richter/Bruun or whatever he calls himself today. A very detailed summary of your crimes would also be much appreciated." Ford could see in Wilde's physical response that the man was guilty. Still, he sat with a smug look on his face, unwilling to confess to anything.

"You're really doing yourself a disservice buddy. We've got people tracking down King and Dr. Abrams at this very moment. Odds are pretty good one of them will rat you out for a deal, in which case you'll be royally screwed."

"Oh, please, you have nothing on me. This is all circumstantial nonsense."

"Not anymore buddy. Every hour we're getting more solid dirt on you. Remember Juan Perez, the kid you hired to kill Thorpe's housekeeper? He's in the clink now but we showed him your photo and he said you fit the bill. Apparently your mask wasn't the greatest."

"Oh, and we got your former boss over at Sterling Defense to open up. Said you were canned for selling ultra-secret test weapons while on a trip to Russia. And guess what? One of those guns was used a few months later in the killing of a British parliament member. I don't need to tell you who's suspected of that one – your neighbor down there in the cell block! Guess you kept his number all those years in case you needed a little killing done without dirtying your own hands. Not to mention your financial records, stock buy up, and your own mother's testimony that will help put you away." Ford watched closely for a reaction but the man didn't flinch, speaking calmly, like someone who never had to answer for his crimes.

"Now you're feeding me lies. It's Sterling policy to keep all records confidential. Even if such a thing were true, you'd never learn of it."

"Turns out we have some dirt on your former boss. It was either cooperate with us or answer for his own lesser crimes. You see, the smart ones cave when they're against the wall."

Capelli, who'd been watching from behind one way glass alongside Masterson and Dr. Luc Turner, interrupted Ford's bad cop routine and buzzed the intercom to the interrogation room.

"Wrap it up, Ford. They've picked up King and we've got a lead on our lady doc." Capelli chirped in speaker.

Ford nodded to the glass and then looked back to Wilde.

"You'd better hope your partners in crime are equally mute. But I wouldn't count on it."

"I don't know what you're referring to, Agent Ford. This is all a misunderstanding."

As Ford exited, he heard Wilde mutter under his breath. It sounded like "you're too late anyway" but he couldn't be sure.

"What's the update?" Ford asked, entering the viewing room.

"Tesar and his team picked up Leo King – mid-escape – from his Prague apartment. He must've gotten word we were onto Wilde because when they arrived he was dumping computer files and destroying evidence. The crime scene team is doing a thorough run through of home and office and they'll send the computers and files to us ASAP."

"And the woman?" Ford asked, grabbing a bottle of water. Interrogations always parched him.

"That's a little trickier. I was able to reach a colleague of hers at her home base in Dadaab. Abrams left for a small rural village yesterday to launch a new charity. I've tried to track her known cell phone numbers but haven't been able to locate her anywhere. We know the name of the town she's headed to but don't have any nearby teams to pick her up."

"Did they name the charity?" Turner interjected.

Ford shot him a "none of your business" look but waited for Capelli to answer.

"Ah, hang on… " Capelli flipped through her notes. "Angels of Africa. I don't know anything more than that, though."

"It's a scholarship program that's just been launched for youngsters to live abroad and study." Turner's mind was spinning, trying to piece together Eva's involvement with the charity, Polaris, and the drug-testing.

"Maybe she's trying to ease the guilt of killing so many people." Ford glumly added.

"Don't count on it. It's actually the perfect way to spread the disease. I've been wondering how they plan on infecting major population centers. It wouldn't make sense to keep it restricted to the African continent where most people don't have the funds to purchase the antidote. It would have to spread elsewhere."

"My colleague in Somalia, Jean-Pierre, has been raving about this charity since learning of it. This year they're sending twenty children to twenty different major cities around the globe where they'll live with a host family and have their education, food, books, and all other needs supplied. Before flying, these kids will go through a rigorous health check, inoculation process, and of course, receive vitamins in the process. Now knowing what Eva and Wilde have been up to, it seems like the perfect opportunity. They infect the children with the bacteria via the Geno-Vyt, scatter them across the globe, and with each sneeze and cough they are spreading an extremely contagious drug-resistant illness."

Turner, Capelli, and Ford looked around the table at another, each considering whether the idea was a far-fetched guess or dead-on reality. A few moments of thought ensued before Capelli broke the silence.

"We can't afford not to check it out. Dr. Turner, is there any way to find out whether the Geno-Vyt was sent with Dr. Abrams?"

"We can contact Katrine Johansson in Dadaab. She keeps the place running and should know whether Eva went out empty handed or with supplies."

"Okay, Dr. Turner, you can call this Johansson woman from my office. If Abrams left with so much as a shoe-box full of Rolaids I want to know about it. Let's get an exact location and time for where this flight is taking off and scramble a team to be there. I'd rather have Masterson down my throat for firing the trigger on another long-shot than a bunch of innocent kids being sent around the world as disease incubators." Ford stormed from the room, Capelli and Turner in pursuit.

78

Somalia

Jean-Pierre pressed the gas pedal with such force he feared his foot would go through the floorboards of the rusted old truck. The vehicle strained under the weight of four men as it bumped along the pothole-ridden roads at maximum speed.

Just hours before, Turner had phoned Jean-Pierre and provided a summary version of the situation with Eva, Wilde, and the possible disease outbreak. Since Jean-Pierre had shown great interest in the charity scholarship program, Eva, on her previous visit, had suggested he attend the send-off party at a private airstrip in Beledweyne, a small town located near the Somalia-Kenya border. She'd disclosed both the location and time of the event, apparently feeling confident that he was clueless to her wicked plan. He'd declined the invitation, having responsibilities in Jowhar, but had now changed his mind.

With only hours to go before the scheduled departure time, Capelli and Ford feared it would be impossible to scramble a team to such a remote location. The agents had hesitantly agreed to let Jean-Pierre – located only three hours away in Jowhar – along with young men from a local gang, attempt to stop Dr. Abrams. They now sat with Masterson and Dr. Turner next to a satellite phone, nervously awaiting contact from 7,000 miles away.

Getting violently bounced around in the flatbed of Jean-Pierre's truck were Gaani, his brother Johro, and Qani. They'd been affiliated with one of the many pirate gangs until Johro had been injured by a gun-shot last year. The boys had come to Jowhar where Jean-Pierre and Dr. Turner had managed to remove the bullet from Johro's stomach and save his life.

It took several weeks for the wound to heal, during which time Gaani and Qani stayed with Johro in the camp. Jean-Pierre developed a trust with the trio, eventually counseling them to end their affiliation with the violent gang. The boys still stole, but now they worked pilfering from their former gang colleagues, bringing spoils back to the residents of their village.

Looking in the rear-view mirror, Jean-Pierre managed to grin as the young men tied bandanas over their bald heads, applied black ink to their faces, and readied their weapons. He doubted this would be a violent encounter. Eva was assumed to be working alone, but nonetheless he was grateful the trio of hoodlums had agreed to accompany him.

A half-hour later the airstrip came into view. A small gathering of people mingled around an old Antonov A-24 that would fly the future students to Cape Town International. From there, the kids would go on their separate journeys.

Jean-Pierre waved at his sidekicks, signaling them to lay low and hidden. If things went his way, he planned to peacefully approach Eva and put a stop to the situation without violence. Three young men with guns and bandanas would not help in that process.

Eva was busy talking with another doctor as the children ran around, saying goodbye to their friends who'd come to see them off. Fifty feet from where Eva stood, Jean-Pierre looked over a table lined with beverages and candy bars, a send-off treat Jean-Pierre guessed. The giant man bent down with creaking knees and opened one of two medical transport crates that sat beneath the table. The first was filled with generic aspirin, bandages, and medical basics. In the next crate, Jean-Pierre discovered the Geno-Vyt. He shook the bottles and realized they'd already been administered.

"Jean-Pierre, I'm so glad you could make it!" Eva's spoke with false-excitement. "It's a big day. Maybe the biggest in these kids lives."

Jean-Pierre lifted his gaze from her brown work boots and stood, his knees straining. "Certainly will be if you have your way. I see you administered some vitamins."

"You know how flights are. That recycled air does a number on the immune system." She gave a winning smile through gritted teeth, a knot in the pit of her stomach forming as she sensed Jean-Pierre was onto her.

"Eva, I know what you're planning here. Luc called from New York and explained everything that you've been up to. You have to come with me." He took a step toward her, ready to grab an arm if she made a break for it.

"What are you talking about? What I've been up to? I'm just helping some kids to a better life, that's all." While speaking she reached an arm behind her back, grabbing from her waistband a Smith and Wesson handgun. She slowly walked closer to Jean-Pierre, pressing her body close to his. The move disarmed him somewhat: he'd expected her to run, and only after he felt the pistol's muzzle in his stomach did the situation register.

"Come on Eva, this won't help you at all."

"Just walk with me, nice and slow. Right to that airplane hangar."

"What are you going to do, kill me?"

"I've worked too hard for this. Sorry, Jean-Pierre."

Seemingly out of nowhere Johro leapt from behind the table, tackling Eva and knocking the gun from her hand. In moments Johro had her wrists tied with ropes and began hauling her off toward the truck, while Qani made violent threats against Eva, pressing his gun to her temple for added effect. She had no way of knowing that Jean-Pierre had insisted all guns be emptied of ammunition before they left Jowhar. Within minutes, Eva divulged the location of the antidote.

Jean-Pierre rounded up all the infected children and those who had come to see them off, including the charity sponsors and pilot. He explained the situation, quelling the momentary panic that rippled through the crowd, and insisted they were not allowed to leave until receiving treatment, since by now they'd all been exposed.

Once order was restored, Jean-Pierre placed the call. A nervous Turner answered the phone on speaker, as Capelli and Ford leaned in to hear each word.

"Luc, we've got her. The kids will be okay."

79

**Hudson River
New York, New York**

Three Weeks Later

Capelli tugged her black pea coat across her chest against the cool river air. The case having nearly wrapped – conspirators awaiting trial – she finally scheduled a second date with Allen. When he suggested sailing – in November no less – she'd hesitated, but was now a bottle of cabernet into the trip and thoroughly enjoying herself.

"Let me know what you think of this one." Allen said, emerging from the gallery with another bottle of wine. "It's from Paso Robles, one of my favorite regions."

Capelli sipped the earthy red, her insides warming as the liquid worked its way down.

"Mmm. Even better than the first, thanks," she said just before the rocking motion of Allen's sailboat sent her grasping for the railing.

"I guess I don't have my sea legs yet," Capelli laughed while walking shakily back to the table where Allen sat. "Should we discuss the elephant in the room?"

"I'm curious, of course, but I think you deserve a break after the last month and a half."

Capelli laughed, "You'd be the only one. Reporters have given my Blackberry email overload."

"Well, it is quite a scandal. Is Thorpe junior really off the hook?"

"Yup. All the evidence against him was the doing of his father's secretary. Prosecutors are throwing the book against Nathaniel Wilde. He ordered the deaths of Warren and a scientist in Prague. Worse, he personally killed Thorpe using snake venom – also his killer-for-hire's weapon of choice. He'll never see the sun again."

"And the asaassin?" Allen asked tentatively, not sure how Capelli would react at the reference to her kidnapper.

"Oh, that asshole will never see daylight either. You don't kill two people and kidnap a federal agent only to get offered a deal. The only person who may get a reduced sentence is the woman, Eva Abrams. She caved and ratted out both King and Wilde. But she'll call jail home for a nice, long stretch."

"Well, I'm glad it's over for you now."

"Months of courtroom testimony isn't exactly over."

"Occupational hazard, I suppose."

Capelli's phone buzzed, she rolled her eyes and checked the number. Ford.

"Please don't tell me Masterson wants us in." Capelli answered, not wanting her perfect day ruined.

"Nope. Can you come over today? I want to run some plays with Brian, it may spark his interest in the game." He continued rambling until Capelli finally cut him off.

"Sorry, partner. Not today."

Acknowledgements

I'd like to thank my family for their constant support and advice.

Wilfy, your detailed feedback on the early draft is greatly appreciated.

Most of all, thanks to my husband. Without your belief in me – and tireless editing – this book would still be an outline on a diner placemat.